Murder in the Hamptons

Murder in the Hamptons

Amy Garvey

KENSINGTON PUBLISHING CORP.
http://www.kensingtonbooks.com

For Stephen, who always knows when
chocolate needs to be administered
(and who says his favorite mystery is my brain)

Chapter One

Maggie Harding was on edge even before she walked into Paige Redmond's Hamptons estate to find her worst nightmare staring at her. Lucy had insisted on picking her up at seven-thirty this morning for the drive out to Long Island, specifically to avoid the infamous Friday afternoon traffic, and they'd arrived in Southampton at ten.

"So it worked," Lucy argued, checking her hair in the rearview mirror for the dozenth time. "No traffic, no stress. You should be thanking me."

"Somehow sitting in this car for the last five hours doesn't inspire gratitude," Maggie grumbled, peeling the bodice of her black linen dress away from her chest in an attempt to get some air moving. Her bra was soaked. June 10th and it was already over eighty, without a cloud in the sky. She would have been grateful for the weather if she hadn't been parked in a convertible Thunderbird on the quaint main street of Southampton with the top down. The last of her sunscreen had melted away by noon.

"We got out for lunch," Lucy argued, digging in her bag for a lipstick. She angled the rearview mirror down while she smoothed on another coat of deep, sparkly pink gloss. "Stop snarking at me. This weekend is a big deal, and I don't want to screw it up."

Since she was covered in multicolored sticky notes, and

therefore looked like a bizarre, last-minute Christmas tree, her definition of not screwing up was a little bit suspect.

At least in Maggie's book. She sighed and reached out to pluck a neon pink scrap of paper from Lucy's right arm. It read: "Shrimp? Call. Six X 12. And Variety!" What shrimp had to do with *Variety*, unless Lucy meant a variety of shrimp, was beyond Maggie. That was the problem anymore—organization had become too complicated. All the day planners and Blackberries and cell phones in the world couldn't make up for the fact that no one appreciated the beauty of a good old-fashioned to-do list.

"You're not going to screw it up," Maggie told her, picking a deep violet Post-it off the dashboard. "It's a party, not a rocket launch. Relax."

"A party." Lucy rolled her eyes and sighed dramatically. "You're so charmingly naïve, it's almost touching." She took the purple note out of Maggie's hand and scrunched her brow, muttering, "Champagne. I can't forget the champagne."

"It's not a party?" Maggie found her issue of *Metropolitan Home* on the floor and fanned herself with it. "What is it, then?"

"It is a party, of course," Lucy said in her you're-being-dim-witted voice. "But it's not *just* a party. It's PR, it's encouragement, it's buzz making, it's schmoozing. And Drew needs all four if Hollywood is going to take his comeback seriously. Tonight's dinner is just the prelude—you know, casual, relaxed, hanging around stuff. It's just to ease him in, really. Tomorrow night is the blowout. We're talking big-time celebrities, Mags, if everything goes the way it's supposed to. A-list. Page-Six types."

Wiping a bead of sweat from her forehead, Maggie stared down the street, trying to wish herself into the charming little antique shop with the rocking horse in the window, and fanned faster. Magazines made lousy fans. Too many pages.

Also, chaos made her itchy. And Lucy's plan sounded like

chaos, especially if her scattered Post-it note approach to organization was any indication.

When Maggie had agreed to come for the weekend, Lucy had made vague noises about an actor coming back from rehab and the party his society girlfriend wanted to throw. That was all—vague noises and an I-can't-be-bothered-with-details fluttering wave of her hand. Maggie had let herself imagine a day on a pristine beach, some antiquing in Southampton for her newest design client, and the chance to see inside one of the Hamptons' famously sprawling—and fabulously decorated—estates for herself.

This is what happens when you succumb to real estate porn, she told herself. *You get stuck in a convertible in the blazing sun hoping you don't pass out from heat stroke. All to spend two days surrounded by egos and Versace and bling bling. Oh, yay.*

"Look," Lucy whispered, grabbing Maggie's arm as she pointed across the street at Hildreth's Department Store. "I think that's Barbra Streisand!"

"I don't think so," Maggie said doubtfully, but she squinted in the direction Lucy had pointed anyway. All she could see was an expensive-looking pair of trousers and a head of blond hair through a drooping screen of maple leaves, but before she could make up her mind, Lucy tsked. "Nope, the nose is all wrong."

Maggie shook her head and picked up her magazine. Maybe if she held it spine out, she could get a decent breeze going. She knew all too well that Lucy was not going to start the car and head to the Redmonds' before she was good and ready, even if they were both soaked to the skin with sweat when they knocked on the front door. Lucy wasn't organized, but she had willpower to spare.

They'd met when they were in college—Maggie at Parsons and Lucy at Hunter. Maggie was looking for a roommate, since hers was moving uptown to her prelaw boyfriend's apartment near Columbia, and Lucy was looking for a room. *Her* roommate had fallen in love with a guy she'd met at a blues bar on lower Second Avenue and had decided to head off to a kibbutz with him after a week of spiritual discussion in between listening to old John Lee Hooker albums. Since Maggie's love life was checkered with impulsive decisions she'd just as soon forget, she wasn't about to criticize.

Lucy's roommate's father held the lease on the tiny two bedroom on East 74th Street and was turning it over to his younger daughter, who was not interested in sharing, so while Lucy hadn't exactly gotten a "room" when she moved into Maggie's studio, at first glance Maggie hadn't gotten the roommate of her dreams, either. That year, Lucy's hair had been platinum blond with cotton candy pink streaks, and she'd arrived at Maggie's building with everything she owned stuffed into an amazing assortment of shopping bags, ancient suitcases, shoeboxes, and a stolen D'Agostino's cart.

The one thing that hadn't frightened Maggie was the hair. The muffled scratching from the depths of the torn Bloomingdale's bag was another story.

Especially when it turned out not to be a kitten, but a ferret that had the hiccups several times a day.

It was the way of the world, Maggie knew even then. Lots of people—well, most people, to be honest—didn't understand the need to alphabetize spices, or print out neat labels for school notebooks. Or hang clothes according to color *and* fabric. Or make to-do lists for the coming week. And month. (And, okay, year.)

So she'd welcomed Lucy—and Chester, the ferret—into her apartment, and her life, and they'd been friends ever since. Lucy never remembered to store the margarita mix in the section of the cabinet very clearly labeled "drink mixes," but she knew how to salt a glass perfectly, and every time Maggie came home from a bad date or a rough class, Lucy drew her a hot bath with her own weirdly soothing mix of oils. It made up for the fact that she never remembered to wash Maggie's white towels and her purple ones separately. Maggie had caved in and painted the bathroom lavender after a while.

Anyway, she figured their friendship was a little bit like allergy shots. Exposure to the cheerful confusion of Lucy's life, in slow, steady doses, would up her tolerance for messiness. Stop the restless itch that started right between her shoulder blades when a friend forgot which night they'd planned to meet for drinks, or couldn't find her keys, or shelved the Pilates DVDs in with the complete collection of Julia Roberts movies.

Today's chaos was a bucket of cold, wet reality, though, instead of a slow drip. She and Lucy had found their own apartments three years ago, and sudden large doses of Lucyesque disorder made Maggie nervous.

Especially when they were possibly tabloid-worthy. She could see why Lucy had insisted on the Thunderbird—a rented Ford Taurus never would have cut it in this town, which looked a little bit like David Hockney channeling Norman Rockwell, all surreal blue sky and homespun charm, with a generous helping of money, money, and more money.

"Stop fanning—I'm losing the guest list for Saturday," Lucy said, reaching for a pale blue sticky note that was fluttering across the dashboard.

Maggie groaned. "That's your guest list? A Post-it?"

"Ooh, grab the orange one—that's the maybes."

"The Olsen twins are a maybe?" Maggie said, trying to make out Lucy's scribbles.

"Oh, yeah. They love Drew," Lucy said, scratching the tip of her nose with the eraser end of her pencil. "They watched *Hollywood High* religiously."

Reaching into Lucy's bulging tote, Maggie took out an 8x10 glossy of Drew Fisk, the actor whose comeback Lucy was currently helping to promote. It was an old photo, from the immediately post-*Hollywood High* days, and Drew looked the way Maggie remembered him from the show—young, clean-shaven, just sexy enough to make teenage hearts throb all over the Internet message boards, but not enough of a bad boy to make their mothers nervous. With his light brown hair swept back off his forehead and his big dark eyes glistening earnestly for the camera, he looked like a sweet-natured older brother, the harmless boy next door who shoveled old ladies' snow for free. They were usually the most dangerous types, in Maggie's opinion, but thousands of teenage girls nationwide didn't care which type he was, as long as his character was duking it out for the love of virginal Summer Blake every week on their TV screens.

Maggie secretly believed that if he and Summer had achieved "happily ever after" before the show ended, Summer's virginity would have been a thing of the past pretty quick. Maybe that was the reason Drew's character was so popular in the first place.

"Paris Hilton, too," Lucy said, shuffling the stack of Post-its into a loose pile and tucking them into her bag. She blew a stray blond curl off her forehead and regarded Maggie with eyes that were the rich violet of pansies, courtesy of a new pair of contact lenses. "Big fan. But I think she's in L.A. this weekend. Her publicist didn't get back to me."

"Doesn't anyone return their own phone calls anymore?" Maggie wondered out loud, sliding Drew's photo back into Lucy's tote. "My mother had my father call me back last week."

Lucy smirked and grabbed her sunglasses off the dashboard. "Okay, are you ready to go?"

"Ready?" Maggie echoed in disbelief. "I've been ready for the last three hours. Everyone in Southampton probably thinks we're here on the most public stakeout in recorded history." But she put on her own sunglasses and smoothed the wrinkled lap of her skirt.

The engine started up with an elegant growl, and Lucy waved cheerfully at the old man who braked his Mercedes to let her back out of the parking spot. She headed south on Main Street, and Maggie rested her head on the seatback, grateful for the faint stirring of breeze on her flushed cheeks.

"Now, Paige might seem a little shy at first," Lucy said as she slowed down, waiting for someone else to back out of a parking spot. "But she's incredibly sweet, and she's so in love with Drew, it's almost sickening." She shrugged. "In fact, she's probably not cut out for this Hollywood stuff at all."

"How did they meet?" Maggie asked, grabbing a stray Post-it Lucy had missed. Paige Redmond came from money so old, it had once been counted in gold coins, and she wasn't one of the young heiresses who had been making the columns on Page Six so often in the past few years. Maggie had never heard of her until Lucy mentioned her name.

"At a pediatric cancer benefit," Lucy explained. "She started a foundation two years ago, and Drew was there."

"Does he volunteer?"

Lucy snorted. "Uh, no. He was there for the PR."

Maggie restrained a disgusted sigh with effort, but she couldn't help rolling her eyes.

Lucy caught her at it. "Oh, come on. Everyone does it. He donated, at least."

"And now they're engaged?" Maggie said dubiously. If she were the betting type, which she wasn't, she wouldn't place odds on a Redmond-Fisk fiftieth anniversary celebration.

"Almost." Lucy flipped on her turn signal and pulled onto Gin Lane. "The truth is, Drew really is a decent guy, and Paige has been very understanding about his time in rehab, and what he wants to do with his career now. *The Truth About Simon* is a huge step for him, because it's got that indie-flick cachet, and promoting it this weekend at the Redmonds' house is huge. They haven't entertained in years, since Paige's father passed away." She glanced sidelong at Maggie, who felt a lecture coming on and sighed. "And it's huge for *me*. Paige is trusting me to do this right, at least tonight, and even with Regina's help tomorrow, I'm the reason Paige hired us. It means a lot that you came, you know. I'm going to need some—"

Maggie held up a hand and smiled at her friend. Lucy's job at Fountain Publicity was a big step up from her last position, and screwing it up would probably mean getting fired. "I got it. Moral support, ego wrangling, Post-it patrol—whatever you need. Promise."

"You won't regret it," Lucy said, flipping her hair over one shoulder as she turned into a driveway and stopped at the gate. An elegant brass plaque fastened to the brick gatehouse wall read, Spindrift. "Lucy Petrillo and Maggie Harding," she said into the intercom. With an electronic buzz, the heavy wrought-iron gate swung open, and Lucy steered the convertible down a narrow driveway shaded by tulip trees that looked almost as old as Maggie knew the estate was.

The house crouched at the end of the curving lane, a sprawling white limestone mansion that would have looked at home next door to the Breakers, the Vanderbilts' infamous Newport summer place. Maggie sat forward, gripping the dashboard, vaguely aware that her mouth was hanging open. As if the crenellations and lancet windows and sheer size weren't enough, the house had actual wings. People didn't live in houses with wings anymore, at least not nineteenth century ones. Most of those houses had been torn down, or turned into museums and college administration buildings, and, in one notable case, a spa.

"Wow," Lucy breathed, slowing the car until it stopped at the front entrance. "Now that's an old-money house if I ever saw one. And I haven't seen nearly as many new-money houses as I'd like."

"Oh, yeah," Maggie answered, trying to count the number of windows on the second floor. "Even in nineteen hundred, this place would have cost a small fortune to build, much less to furnish." An honest-to-god thrill of anticipation raced through her when she imagined the rooms she would be able to wander through, without a velvet rope or "Do Not Touch" sign in sight. The weekend was definitely looking up. In a house this size, maybe no one would notice if she lurked around, drooling incoherently on the antiques, and skipped the party entirely. "How did the Redmonds make their money?"

"Railroads, I think," Lucy said, shutting off the engine and grabbing her tote. "And oil. Or something. Come on."

Maggie grabbed her bag and climbed out, feeling like a damp, crumpled T-shirt someone had left on the floor for two days. Lucy started up the steps, and Maggie was brushing helplessly at her wrinkled skirt when the door opened and a slim young woman with caramel blond hair stepped onto the porch.

"Lucy!" Her smile revealed an endearing combination of excitement and relief.

"Everybody here?" Lucy said with a one-armed hug.

"Almost. And this is . . . ?"

"Maggie," Maggie told her, offering her free hand.

"Paige," the other woman said with a warm, wide smile. "Paige Redmond. I'm so happy you could come."

The thing was, despite the fact that they had never met, and she really had no idea who Maggie was, she seemed to mean it. And what was more, she didn't look like an heiress. She was wearing spotless chinos and a red sleeveless blouse, with what seemed to be regular old white Keds on her feet, and they matched her friendly smile. Maggie hadn't been expecting a tiara, but Paige's down-home ordinariness was sweet, and so was she, just like Lucy had promised. Maggie suddenly felt overdressed in her black linen sundress.

"You must be dying for something to drink," Paige said, taking Maggie's weekend bag before she could protest, and opening the door. "Come on in and I'll get you settled, and then I can show you the house."

Maggie shot Lucy a suspicious glance, but she just shrugged, eyes wide and innocent. "I didn't say anything."

Paige laughed. "I know you're a designer. I've actually seen some of your work for the Atlantis Group, and if there's time, I wouldn't mind asking your advice about a project of mine. I figured you'd get a kick out of looking around this old mausoleum."

Bright, generous, and all-around nice. She was almost too good to be true. "Honestly, I'd love to see it," Maggie told her. "I promise not to break anything."

Paige turned wry hazel eyes on her. "Well, yes, we do prosecute anyone who chips the Limoges."

"Words to live by." Maggie laughed, but the sound died in her throat when she stepped through the door and the sheer scope of the house hit her. She stopped short, staring up at the foyer's ceiling, a full two stories above. This wasn't a house; it was a castle.

"It's impressive, I know." Resigned embarrassment flushed Paige's cheeks. "My great-great-grandfather was very proud of his money, and this place was his dream, his one true love. He talked about this place like it was a person, or so I've been told. Spindrift needs this, Spindrift would love that. It's kind of creepy if you ask me."

"Love can be like that," Maggie said feebly. She didn't care if the guy had been a certified loon; she was itching to poke around. The woodwork on the banister alone was worth a little rapture of joy.

"Can you point me in the direction of the ladies' room?" Lucy said to Paige with a sheepish smile.

While Paige took Lucy down the hall, Maggie admired the marble floor and the round ebony table. If this was just the foyer, she couldn't imagine what the rest of the house looked like.

"Leave your bags and I'll show you around," Paige called from the other end of the hall, where she opened the door to the library. Maggie sighed over the deep red Persian carpet and a group of sofas and chairs in buttery, saddle-colored leather and red and gold stripes. She was on design overload already.

"There's a ballroom, you know," Paige said, smiling as she leaned against the doorjamb.

"A ballroom." Maggie sighed. "A ballroom. Excuse me, I just like saying the words out loud. It's not every day a girl from New Jersey gets to stand in a ballroom that isn't a feature of the local Sheraton."

Paige laughed, tucking a stray hair behind one ear. "Let's go, then. But don't ask me to waltz."

Maggie took one last look at the library as Paige led the way. The room was perfect—the colors, the proportions, the fabrics. It wasn't really Maggie's style, not personally, but it was agelessly beautiful.

Just like the ballroom. She drew in a quick breath as Paige pushed open the double doors, taking in the soaring ceiling gilded with rosettes and the lacquered brilliance of the parquet floor. Her entire apartment would fit into the space, with room to spare.

Someone else was already admiring it, and as Paige crossed the room to greet him, Maggie mused that he was pretty much a dictionary definition of perfect design, as well—this time flesh and blood male, gazing up at the dentil molding that surrounded a pair of French doors leading onto a terrace. He was tall, leanly muscled, all strong, clean lines, even from behind. Dark hair, not too long, but just enough to run her fingers through, broad shoulders, and, as he turned toward Paige, evidence of a firm, chiseled jaw. Even from behind, he was the kind of man God made specifically every once in a while, as if to say, "Look. Learn. Drool a little bit if you have to."

Exactly the kind of man who set off her internal radar in a three-alarm way.

That was bad. This weekend was going to be complicated enough with the Celeb-o-Rama planned for Saturday, and she was here to back Lucy up—and, okay, rhapsodize over the house—not flirt.

Then Paige gestured toward her, and the stranger did a

double-take, turning around completely, realization dawning on his face.

Oh, God. A matching jolt of recognition hit Maggie square in the gut. No, she wasn't going to be bored this weekend. Not when evidence of the one part of her life that she'd never been able to wrestle into submission was staring at her.

Her weak spot was men. The right men—no, wait, make that the wrong men—flipped some switch inside her, and sensible, practical, organized Maggie Harding became someone else entirely. And *that* Maggie was prone to all kinds of impractical, spontaneous things, like maxing out her credit card for two tickets to Paris, and streaking her hair, and piercing things not meant to be pierced. There was an unfortunate karaoke incident she preferred to forget, and she'd learned that it was never a good idea to buy a man an exotic pet if you weren't sure he wanted one, especially when it was a boa constrictor and adamantly not returnable.

Then there was holing up in a Florida hotel room for three days with a mouth-wateringly delicious, funny as hell, complete stranger who did things to her no man had ever come close to doing since.

A stranger named Tyler . . . Oh, God, Tyler what? She stared at him, watching in humiliation as one of his dark eyebrows arched in her direction. After five years, she could still picture the defined muscles of his abdomen, but she couldn't even remember his last name.

Wait—had she ever known his last name?

It's official. I'm a slut, she thought, her heart suddenly slam dancing despite the polite strains of Bach coming from some hidden speaker. *Hello, my name is Maggie, and I'm addicted to men who bring out my inner Girl Gone Wild.*

"Maggie, this is Tyler," Paige said, waving her over, and somehow she made her feet move across the polished parquet to join them.

"Hi, Tyler," she managed, her voice strangled into something very much like an embarrassed squeak.

"Brody," he said, offering his hand, one corner of his mouth quirked in amusement. "Tyler Brody."

"Right. Maggie Harding." She slid her hand into his, waiting for lightning to strike or the floor to open up beneath her. Or both.

One-night stands—okay, three-night stands—were supposed to be just that! They were supposed to . . . well, stand. Stop. Be over, for good and for all. If she'd known she was going to run into him later on, she never would have spent the weekend with him in the first place. Or she would have at least left a note when she snuck out of the hotel room that last morning.

You're such a liar. And not even a good one.

And Tyler was holding her hand as though he intended never to let go, the amusement in his eyes sharpening into something very much like indignation. Apparently his damned eyebrow wasn't done with her yet, either; it had quirked into a very determined question mark.

"Do you two know each other?" Paige said, frowning.

"No," she said, just as Tyler barked, "Yes," which made Paige's eyes widen in confusion.

"You know, I should probably check on Lucy," she said quickly, backing up. Away from the crazy people, clearly. "Feel free to look around wherever you want, Maggie. Tyler, you can show her . . . well, you can . . . show her."

And then she was gone, disappearing onto the terrace and leaving Maggie alone with her worst nightmare.

Not the one who got away. The one she got away from, just in time. Before she could fall in love and ruin everything.

Chapter Two

*U*p close, her eyes were actually as dark as chocolate, Tyler thought, brushing a strand of hair off her forehead. She gave him a drowsy smile, dragging one foot up his calf lazily.

"Don't close them," he murmured as her eyelids drooped. "I'm enjoying the view."

"Of my eyes? You've been in this room too long."

"Not possible," he whispered, sliding one hand across her stomach and up to her breasts, which were still warm and flushed from making love. He couldn't get enough of them.

Or of her, to be truthful. They'd been in this room since Friday night, and it was now—he lifted his head to glance at the clock on the night table—three o'clock Sunday afternoon. And at the moment, he was content to stay put for a good long while.

"That feels incredible," she sighed as he stroked her breast, stopping just long enough to leave a light trail of kisses along her collarbone.

"That's good," he murmured. "Since that's what I was going for."

"Don't stop, then," she whispered, arching her neck as his tongue licked a hot path over the pulse there.

His mouth curved into a smile against her skin. "Don't worry."

* * *

Staring at her now, Tyler could hardly believe five years had passed since he'd seen her. Kissed her. Touched her—everywhere. She looked just as he remembered, although the severe, dark slash of dress was new. When he'd met her, she'd been windswept and mussed, with sand in her hair and little more than a flimsy scrap of a skirt accompanying her purple bikini top. A sarong, she'd called it, laughing as he untied it and let it flutter to the dingy hotel carpet.

He'd called it sexy and left it at that. And now he could call her Maggie Harding, instead of simply Maggie. Knowing that little detail would have made finding her a lot easier five years ago, when he'd awakened after three days of constant, naked togetherness to find her, and every last trace of her, gone.

The flush of shock in her cheeks was new, though. Or maybe it was pain. He realized he had a death grip on her hand, but damned if he was going to let her pull another disappearing act. Not until he got some answers.

She stared up at him, her eyes as huge and brown as he remembered, framed with those incredibly long lashes, and punctuated with a fascinating pencil-point mole high on her right cheekbone. Her hair was a little bit longer, but still had that dark, glossy swing of silk against her neck. He'd never been a big brunette guy, but that had changed. A lot of things had changed when he met Maggie.

Until—he gritted his teeth, feeling the rush of surprise and frustration all over again—she ran away.

"I'm losing the feeling in my fingers," she said, tugging at his hand, and he let go reluctantly.

"Yeah, well, I'm never sure when you're going to evaporate into thin air."

She winced, and he didn't feel even a little bit sorry about it.

"So you're still mad, huh?" she said, attempting a smile.

He folded his arms across his chest. Good try.

"Look," she went on, nervously shifting her weight from one strappy black sandal to another. God, her ankles were cute. And her toenails were painted a rich, dark, flat-out sexy red. "I don't think this is really the time or place to get into it. You're staying the weekend, too, so why don't we talk . . . later?"

Oh, right. He heaved a patient sigh. Obviously she had no clue that the idea of escape had flashed in her eyes like a neon sign.

"There's not a lot to talk about," he said, biting off each word with crisp precision. "You left. I want to know why. Simple."

Her forehead wrinkled into an anxious frown, and he resisted the impulse to smooth it away. Damn it, he wasn't going to feel guilty for making her uncomfortable. How the hell did she think he felt after three days of the best sex he'd ever had—not to mention the most laughter—only to wake up to a cold pillow and the vague imprint of her body on the sheets beside him?

"Tyler . . ." Her voice trailed off, and she stared at him with something very much like panic in her eyes.

What the hell was this? *Who* was this? The woman he'd met in Key West had never been tongue-tied, and the only time he could remember her frowning was when he'd eaten the last of their third delivered pizza while she was in the bathroom. The woman felt pretty strongly about her extra cheese and green pepper.

But then, that Maggie hadn't been so . . . sharp. So severe. The image he'd been carrying around for the last five years was of loose, soft hair, a wrinkled white oxford, and sandals that had been broken in long before he met her. Soft was the key word. When he let himself remember the way her body felt—warm, silky skin, the give of her breasts in his hands, her mouth yielding to his—there was nothing hard about her. The woman standing in front of him was businesslike, stylish . . . *polished*. A little scary, to be truthful. If she'd walked into his hotel looking like this, he would have straightened his tie and thought, *Tough customer.*

Still, this Maggie was just as sexy as the one he'd spent that weekend with so long ago. But something—hell, a lot of things—didn't add up. Why was this Maggie so nervous she was twisting the heavy silver cuff on her wrist hard enough to leave a mark?

The sound of footsteps in the hall carried across the polished parquet, and he took her elbow to steer her toward the French doors leading out to the terrace. She didn't protest, although the hopeful look in her eyes was a clear indication she thought rescue was on the way.

"Okay, how about a different question?" he said, keeping his voice low but no less demanding. "Do you run out on every guy you spend the weekend with?"

Her head snapped up, her eyes crackling with outrage. "Of course not," she said in a furious whisper, glancing behind her when the footsteps in the hall got louder. "And I did not run out on you." She sighed when he arched his eyebrow at her again. "Well, okay, I did, but it was just a . . . a fling. I didn't think—"

Then Lake Healy walked into the ballroom, gazing up at the ornate ceiling, and Maggie shut her mouth, relief flooding her face.

"Hi," Lake said absently, glancing at them. "This place is amazing, huh? I feel like I accidentally wandered onto a Merchant-Ivory set."

Maggie cleared her throat and offered Lake a polite smile. If Maggie recognized her, Tyler mused, she wasn't showing it, but with Lake's face plastered all over magazines and movie posters lately, there weren't a lot of people left who didn't know who she was. Paige had told him a lot of "industry types" would be invited this weekend, but when he'd walked in to find Lake drinking iced tea in the kitchen with the hostess, he'd still been momentarily speechless.

He tilted his head toward the actress. "Maggie, this is Lake Healy. Lake, this is Maggie Harding."

"Nice to meet you," Lake said, striding toward them to shake Maggie's hand, her hot pink flip-flops slapping the floor. "Are you a friend of Paige? Or Drew?"

"No, I'm here with Lucy Petrillo," Maggie said. If she thought he didn't notice her edging closer to the French doors, she wasn't as smart as he'd given her credit for. They weren't finished talking, and if now wasn't the time, later would do. They had all weekend, after all.

"I don't think I've met Lucy," Lake said, scrunching her brow thoughtfully. Her eyebrows were as white blond as her short cap of hair. She was tall and model-thin, but the hair still made her look like an unusually sexy pixie. "I'm a friend of Drew's. And Paige, of course."

"I saw *Water's Edge*," Maggie offered. "It was great. *You* were great. Of course, I didn't take a bath for a few weeks afterward, but it was well worth it."

Lake laughed, her cheeks flushed with Maggie's praise. "It was a fun movie to make, believe it or not. I'm starting a romantic comedy next month, though, so unless dating scares you, I wouldn't worry about seeing it."

Tyler stifled a snort and gave Maggie a pointed look, but she wouldn't meet his eyes.

"I should really finish unpacking," she said quickly, with another backward step toward the door. "It was nice to meet you, Lake. Tyler," she added awkwardly with a little bob of her head.

Lake wandered toward the row of gilded chairs lined up against one wall, and Tyler followed Maggie onto the terrace. She heaved another sigh when he grabbed her elbow, turning around to face him in resignation.

"What now?"

"Are you sleeping on the lawn? The guest rooms are through there," he said, cocking his head back at the ballroom.

"I'm going the long way."

"Would that involve the Long Island Expressway and a detour through Manhattan?"

"No," she said, all offended dignity, tilting her chin at him.

In the sun, her hair gleamed like dark silk, and her arms were already faintly stained bronze. "We're not finished talking, you know," he said, wishing he could just pull her against him for a kiss and forget the argument he was apparently determined they were going to have.

She crossed her arms over her chest in defeat, the beginning of a smile curving her lips. "I'm beginning to get that idea."

"I always thought you were pretty smart," he added, grinning at her.

"You'd be surprised." She tucked a stray hair behind her ear and shaded her eyes as she squinted up at him. "We'll . . . talk. Later. I promise."

He nodded, watching as she crossed the terrace, heading toward the doors into the large main living room. He was going to hold her to that promise, whether she liked it or not. He wanted answers.

To the basic issues, at least. Like where she'd gone when she took off. Why she hadn't left a note.

If she'd been involved with someone else.

The idea stung even now, he realized, perching on the brick wall and tilting his face up to the sky to let the afternoon sun heat his skin.

Not because he was . . . in love or anything. That didn't happen in three days—love at first sight, or in this case first weekend, was for Hallmark cards and the movies. And possibly dogs.

No, this was purely an issue of ego. His, to be precise, bruised and still a little resentful. Women liked him, usually. He was good-looking, he knew that, and he was successful. He didn't drink to excess, he didn't have an ex-wife, and he paid the check with a generous tip. Hell, he had a picture of his mother on the mantel at home.

And—damn it—he'd never had a complaint when it came to sex. When he pictured the two of them tangled in that hotel bed, and on the floor, and in the shower, he couldn't make himself believe Maggie had been disappointed.

Which made it all the more frustrating when he woke up to find her gone. If she'd been seeing someone else, though, that would explain it.

And while that explanation left his ego intact, the idea of her with another man made something way down deep tighten in jealousy.

He glanced up at the smooth stone façade of the house, searching the second-floor windows. Something about her made him nuts. She could have slept with a dozen other guys since that weekend. She could be engaged right now, for all he knew. Married, even.

She could have been married then, you ass.

Either way, he was going to find out.

Chapter Three

Maggie sighed and twisted in the circle of Tyler's arms, stretching languidly against him. "I think I know what 'replete' means now. It's lovely. Everyone should be replete once a day, at least."

With her head resting on his chest, his laugh was a low rumble in her ear. "Just once?"

"Well, to start. Too much . . . repletion? Is that a word? It may be overwhelming for some people."

"Not for you, though, huh?"

"Not at all." She angled up on one elbow and reached over him to grope around the night table. "Although it does make me thirsty. Becoming replete clearly requires proper hydration."

He twisted and grabbed a bottle of water off the floor. "Here. I think it's your only choice other than wine."

She glanced at the disaster they'd made of the hotel room and promptly shuddered. A half-full bottle of red wine sat on the bureau beside two pizza boxes. A beer bottle slanted out of the top of the ice bucket, and two empty bags of microwave popcorn rested on the carpet like greasy deflated balloons. Tyler's clothes had been flung over one chair, and her sarong was draped over the lamp on the bureau. Her bikini top was nowhere in sight.

*"We're going to have to tip the maid," she said before rais-
ing the plastic bottle to her mouth.*

*"Not yet, though," he murmured, taking the water from
her and rolling her beneath him. "Stay a little longer?"*

*She swallowed hard, then nodded, tucking her face against
his chest again and breathing him in. Even the scent of him
was addictive.*

*A man who could make her heart flutter in her chest the
way it was right now was dangerous. Not just dangerous, explosive. Apocalyptic. Because the impulsive part of her
would follow him to Nepal, if he asked. Because the irra-
tional part of her had already sort of forgotten what her
apartment looked like and that she was expected back at
work on Tuesday. And because every part of her wanted to
stay forever.*

Maggie found Lucy upstairs, coming out of her bedroom
with handfuls of Post-its, a legal pad, and her cell phone wedged
precariously between her shoulder and her chin. Maggie's
bags sat on the floor outside the room next door, beneath a
portrait of silky, sad-faced spaniels. Maggie stared at them
while she waited through a chorus of uh-huhs until Lucy clicked
the phone off. *Right there with you, boys,* she thought.

"What's wrong?" Lucy asked as Maggie grabbed her bags
and went into her room. "You have bad-news face."

"It's worse than bad," Maggie said, leaving her bags on
the floor and sagging onto the enormous four-poster bed. She
kicked off her sandals. "It's catastrophic. You remember that
trip to the Keys a few years ago?"

"How could I forget?" Lucy dropped her things with a
clatter on the secretary by the door and joined Maggie on the
bed, leaving her own purple leather mules in a heap on the
carpet. "That was when Terrible Tom decided to break off
your engagement by voice mail, wasn't it? And you got that
weird client who wanted everything done in green toile? And

you met that guy . . ." Her voice trailed off as Maggie nodded gravely. "What happened?"

"He's here."

"Here? In the Hamptons?"

"Here in this house." Maggie groaned and flopped backward on the lilac-sprigged coverlet. "I knew it. I knew this
weekend was going to be disastrous."

"Oh, you did not," Lucy scoffed. "And what do you
mean, he's here in this house? Really?"

When Maggie opened her eyes and saw the look of
amused disbelief on her friend's face, she glared. "Really. I
saw him myself. Talked to him, in fact."

"God, he was gorgeous, Mags." Lucy stared off into
space, apparently liking whatever image she'd conjured from
memory. "I wasn't sure you were going to make our flight
home that week."

"Yeah, well," Maggie grumbled. "I did. But now he's
here."

"Am I missing something?" Lucy asked, shrugging in confusion. "Hot guy, you know what he's like, free weekend in a
gorgeous house . . . What's the problem?"

For a moment, Maggie tried to make her mouth work,
without any luck. The problem? The problem was that her past
had shown up unexpectedly, demanding answers to questions
she didn't even want him to ask—and looking just as mouth-
wateringly, meltingly delicious as he had five years ago. Seeing
Tyler again was not part of the plan.

Of course, Lucy wouldn't understand why it was awkward, because Lucy was all about spontaneity. Once, she'd
asked out a cute waiter when her date had gone to the men's
room.

Lucy thought running into Tyler again was a *good* thing.

"Close your mouth," Lucy said, wrinkling her nose in distaste. "You look like a goldfish."

"I can't . . . I mean, I don't want . . ." She groaned again, staring at the ceiling as if an answer was going to show up written on its delicately painted surface. "It's too awkward. When the weekend ended, I kind of . . . took off unexpectedly."

Lucy narrowed her eyes. "What do you mean, unexpectedly?"

"I don't think I actually mentioned that the weekend was over," she said, staring at what looked like hand-tinted wallpaper to avoid Lucy's eyes. Friends were a wonderful thing until they started lecturing.

Lucy nudged her thigh with a bare, hot-pink-painted toe. "What did you do?"

"I left," Maggie said, sitting up. "I just . . . left. Without a note. Or a . . . good-bye."

"Oh, Mags," Lucy said, shaking her head. Then she shrugged. "Of course, that's exactly what lots of men do. So apologize. Make it up to him. You should be flattered he's still interested after five years. That he cares." Her eyes widened when Maggie stared at her. "But he doesn't care too much, right? I mean, he's not, like, Obsessed Stalker Guy, is he?"

If only, Maggie thought. Then she could call the police and be done with the whole mess. "Yeah, he cares. I think I wounded his male pride."

"Well, if he's like most men, it could probably stand coming down a notch or two." Lucy stood up and slid her feet back into her shoes. "We should write a book—*The Ego Diet for Men: How to Lose the Bloat.*"

Except Tyler's ego wasn't really the point, Maggie thought, staring absently at the striped slipper chair tucked up to the mahogany vanity. Was that a Hepplewhite piece? A real one? Maybe she really could hide in this room all weekend, appraising the antiques. The house was big enough. Maybe Tyler wouldn't be able to find her.

And a pig just flew over the pool outside. No, the only way to avoid Tyler was not to be here.

"Lucy . . ."

Lucy turned around and shook her head the minute she saw Maggie's face. "Oh, no. You promised, Maggie! You are not taking off because some guy is here who might make you uncomfortable for a few minutes."

"What about *really* uncomfortable?" she tried, cringing when Lucy shook a finger at her.

"No way. Do you know what I have to do between tonight and tomorrow?" Lucy ticked off each item on her fingers. "Check with the caterer and the decorator. Make sure the lawn is cleaned up in the morning and the tent is ready to go. Go over the guest list with Paige and Drew, and make sure the press knows exactly who's coming. Deal with the parking issues, and the valets . . ."

She grabbed Lucy's finger. "Okay, I get it. And I did promise. I'm sorry."

"Don't be sorry," Lucy said, sitting down next to her again and winding an arm around her shoulder. "Be helpful. You can keep tabs on everybody, run interference for me."

"Run interference?" Maggie said doubtfully.

Lucy gestured vaguely, and Maggie felt a stab of panic in her stomach. Whenever Lucy got nonspecific, trouble followed. "You know, make conversation. Let me know if anyone's unhappy, or anyone needs anything. Keep egos in check, in case anyone gets . . . testy."

"Testy?" So far, Tyler was already pretty testy, and that was enough to deal with.

"Don't worry, you'll be fine. You're good with people." Lucy squeezed her shoulders and stood up again, calling over her shoulder as she left, "Wander around and introduce yourself. I have to check in with Paige."

Maggie got up and shut the door, resisting the impulse to lock it and crawl under the bed until Sunday night. She was a grown woman. She could handle this. She handled worse every day.

Okay, that's another really lame lie. She could deal with

unexpected client temper tantrums, and last-minute dead-lines, and the occasional surprise party, but in none of those situations did her lack of preparation lead to real disaster. Disaster being, of course, chucking it all for some guy who would likely break her heart, ruin her life, and leave her penniless and starving in some alley.

She shook herself and glanced in the mirror, frowning at her reflection. Maybe she should have been a soap opera writer. Melodrama obviously ran in her veins.

Seeing Tyler again was . . . strange. Inconvenient. Tempting. *No, not tempting. A world of no to that.* But it didn't mean her life was about to fall apart.

Especially not if she could hold out till tomorrow at noon, when Lucy's boss Regina was scheduled to arrive. She could waylay Tyler and his eyebrows until then, certainly, and she'd keep her promise to Lucy at the same time. Regina would be the one asking Lucy to run interference at that point.

Squaring her shoulders, she took a deep breath and reached around to unzip her dress. If she was going to do battle, at least she could do it more comfortably.

Outside a half hour later, Maggie followed the sound of a tennis ball thwacking against a court. Beyond the stone terrace, the lawn curved downhill toward the beach, a lush green swath of grass bordered with crowded beds of hot pink peonies, the purple bells of foxglove, and yellow primroses, past the guesthouse where Lucy told her Paige and Drew stayed. If it was Tyler practicing his serve, at least she'd changed into shorts and a T-shirt. Ten to one, she could out-run him.

But when she rounded the hedge separating the court from the lawn, she found a sandy-haired man about her age slamming each tossed ball over the net. He stopped midserve when he noticed her, letting the bright yellow ball bounce away.

"Hello," she called, pausing at the white sideline. "Don't let me interrupt—I'd love to watch."

"Do you play?" he asked, tucking his racquet under one arm and striding toward her. "I could use a partner."

"Oh, no." She gave him her best apologetic smile. "I took lessons once as a kid, and it turned out badly. I've been told I'm better off sticking to solitary sports. Like . . . solitaire."

He flashed a smile that she was sure used up all the charm wattage in the tristate area. "You can't be that bad. And I'll go easy on you."

She shook her head. He pulled a face, and the dimple indented in his left cheek winked at her. She knew that dimple. "You're . . ."

"Connor Wheaton, that's me." He stuck out his hand, then changed his mind, wiping it on the back of his shorts. "Star of screen. And smaller screen. And the occasional really bad movie of the week."

For some reason, he sounded savagely bitter about this. *Yeah, tough break being on the cover of* People *all the time,* she thought, remembering to nod politely. Then it clicked— Lucy had told her about Drew's new movie and Connor was his costar.

Apparently, he wasn't happy about it.

He'd given up on the idea of shaking hands, too, and had pulled the tennis ball out of his shorts pocket to bounce it idly. Waiting, it seemed, for her to introduce herself. Or maybe ask for his autograph.

"I'm Maggie Harding, a friend of Lucy Petrillo's." When this produced no reaction, she added, "She's handling the party."

Bounce. "Ah yes, the party. The great comeback party." *Bounce.* "Never hurts to go for more than your fifteen minutes in this business."

His sandy hair was spiked up in fashionable little tufts, and his eyes looked too blue to be natural, but he was good-looking in a very Hollywood way. Tall, athletic, tan. A little too perfect for her taste, but she knew plenty of women who would have paid good money to be standing where she was right now. Pity he seemed like a big jerk.

She searched for something to say as he walked back to the base line and whacked a ball over the net. "Lucy said we'll get to see final edit of the movie tonight."

"Yeah?" *Thwack.*

Maybe she would have been better off to find Tyler out here. At least she knew what he was pissed off about.

"What's your role like?" she tried, itching to grab one of the tennis balls and throw it at his head.

"Supporting," he said, casting her a sardonic glance as he stretched his arm up in another serve. "I play Simon's cousin. The poor relation." *Thwack.*

"What is the truth about Simon?" she asked, desperate for some neutral topic. Even if giving away the movie's end wasn't exactly neutral, she figured he'd probably enjoy the chance to spoil it for her. Not that she'd mind. It was easier to relax and enjoy anything from a movie to a book if she knew how things turned out in the end.

"Wait till you see it," he said, stopping to lightly hit a ball in her direction. Suddenly his grin was back, complete with flashing dimple. "I'll sit next to you when they screen it so I can tell you all the behind-the-scenes gossip."

Uh-oh. She forced a polite smile and threw back the tennis ball she'd managed to snag before it bounced down the lawn and onto the beach. "Great. I'll let you get back to your practice for now, then."

She took off before he could protest, silently muttering to herself. He wasn't her type, he was a spoiled ass with a capital A, and attention from him was another big unknown she had no intention of encouraging. There were too many balls in the air already, between Tyler and her new duty on ego patrol.

She headed back up the lawn toward the miniature

Spindrift that was the guesthouse and then past it, looking for the pool. Sitting on the edge and dangling her feet in the cool water sounded like a safe idea. Rounding the side of the main house, she caught the sharp chemical tang of chlorine in the air.

The pool was just as lovely as the rest of the estate. Huge and classically rectangular, its skirt was plain white, but the inside of the pool had been laid with azure tiles. They weren't real azure, of course, just that intense shade of blue—or at least she thought so, squinting at them curiously.

A redhead floating on a raft in the water glanced up at her, shading her eyes with one hand, but didn't introduce herself. She squinted at Maggie curiously until Maggie lifted her hand in a halfhearted wave. "Hi, I'm Maggie Harding."

"Shelby Byrne," the girl said, as if Maggie should have known. She dropped her hand and shut her eyes again, clearly disinterested. Her white bikini top was stretched so taut across her breasts, Maggie wondered if it would pop when she sat up.

"Charming, isn't she?" someone said in a low voice to Maggie's right. She found another woman reclining in a lounge chair, flipping through an issue of *Vanity Fair,* an enormous straw hat protecting her face from the sun. "Nell Brooks-Winship. You're the . . . publicist's friend?"

She managed to make the word "publicist" sound like something that got dragged into the house on the bottom of a shoe, but Maggie nodded anyway.

"Are you a friend of Drew's?" Maggie asked her, pulling another chaise into the shade of a linden tree. It was still too hot. She thought briefly about the air-conditioned peace of her room upstairs—and even more longingly about the silent peace of her apartment in the city—with a sigh. The next time Lucy asked her to go away for the weekend, she was getting all the details first, via signed affidavit.

"I'm a friend of Paige's," Nell said, idly flipping another page of the magazine and pausing to study a Manolo-Blahnik ad. "We've known each other since we were children. Went to school together, all that."

"And Shelby?"

"She's an actress." This was clearly something else that deserved scraping off on a doormat, if her tone was any indication. "I think she has a part in this movie, or maybe the next one Drew is scheduled to do."

Well, she beat Connor when it came to bored indifference—he was all sarcasm and discontent, Maggie thought. New topic.

"You must be excited for Paige since she's such an old friend," she suggested, watching Nell's face.

"Excited?" Nell glanced up for the first time, her face shadowed by the brim of her hat. She was beautiful in that pinched, upper-crust way that must have worked its way into the old-money gene pool long ago. Her hair was a severe dark brunette bob, and her eyes were a startling, cold blue. "About what?"

Please get me out of here. "Um . . . about Paige's engagement to Drew?"

"Oh. Yes." She delivered the words without even a hint of a smile and turned back to her magazine.

"Drew is an absolute doll," Shelby said. She'd climbed out of the pool, and her white suit clung to her scant, damp curves like tissue paper. Without bothering to wrap a towel around herself, she sank into a chaise positioned directly in the sun, turning her face up to its heat. "He's been through so much, but he's a fighter, you know? He's really one of my biggest role models."

Maggie nodded politely. Again. It was obviously the best bet for nonverbal communication so far this weekend. She wasn't sure how a male former drug addict made the right idol for a twenty-something starlet, but she wasn't about to argue the point.

"And he's been so helpful, you know?" Shelby continued, stretching like a cat in the sun. "When we were filming

Simon, he gave me such good advice about my role, and he ran lines with me all the time in my trailer."

Alone in her trailer, Maggie bet. Which could have been completely innocent or completely . . . not. She wondered if Paige knew that one of her houseguests, not to mention Drew's costar, had a major crush on him she apparently wasn't even trying to hide. She was nearly gushing with lust already, although it was hard to tell with the tanning oil that had beaded all over her skin.

"Yes, Drew is a terrific guy, isn't he?" Nell said suddenly, turning her gaze up at Shelby with a telling smile. If Shelby was the playful kitten in this picture, Nell was definitely the experienced cat. "It sounds like you two got pretty close while you were making the movie."

"Oh, we did," Shelby agreed without even a trace of irony, lifting one leg to peer at her pedicure.

"That's nice," Nell replied, looking exactly as if she'd just eaten something wonderfully sweet. Any minute the woman was going to lick her lips.

Leaning back and closing her eyes, Maggie sighed to herself. Yup, this weekend was going to be far from boring.

Chapter Four

"Maggie, there you are!" Paige called from the top of the lawn ten minutes later. "Come on up. I want you to meet Drew."

Excusing herself from the pair at the pool, Maggie ran up the grass, grateful for the interruption. Another minute of Shelby's drooling praise of Drew and Nell's none-too-subtle encouragement for her to continue, and Maggie would have started—very politely, of course—banging her head against the cement pool surround.

Besides, she was curious to meet the famous Drew. His days on *Hollywood High* aside, anyone who inspired such bad behavior among people who actually knew him had to be worth a peek.

He was standing beside Paige on the terrace, hands jammed deep in the pockets of a pair of ancient chinos, his hair as casually rumpled as his dark T-shirt. His smile was a whole-body thing, with a shrug of his shoulders and a lopsided twist of his mouth.

"Hi, Maggie," he said. "Nice to meet you." His tone was low and soft, nothing like the smoothly precise voice she remembered from the show. Put together, the whole package reminded her of a friendly, aging dog, the kind who liked lying on the porch in the sun better than chasing sticks.

"Nice to meet you," she said, offering her hand. When he

took it, his grip was as loose and comfortable as the rest of him.

"You finding everything okay?" he said. "I still get lost around here, which is why Paige and I sleep in the guest-house. It's a little more manageable."

"I haven't seen everything yet," she admitted, warming to him immediately. "I think there's a whole wing I missed."

"Oh, let me take you!" Paige insisted, leaning into Drew's arm when he wound it around her waist. "Go relax," she told him, elbowing him lightly in the ribs. "I'll be up in a little while."

"Any more relaxed and I'll lapse into a coma," he said, but his tone was fond. He smacked her ass lightly before he ambled away, and she called teasingly over her shoulder, "You could always hang out down at the pool."

He shuddered visibly without turning around, obviously for effect. That was a relief, Maggie thought when Paige laughed. At least Shelby's crush seemed to be one-sided.

She followed her hostess across the aged stones of the terrace into the hallway off the kitchen. She'd already seen the kitchen and the breakfast room, as well as the huge family room. The last was clearly a mid-century addition to the house, but whichever Redmond had wanted it had also made sure it looked original to the house, right down to the ornate crown molding and the fireplace several small children could stand in. Paige had called it the "den."

"This is the conservatory," Paige said, leading her into a bright, clean room with a curved wall of floor-to-ceiling windows—a kind of industrial-sized bay that poured late-afternoon sunlight over the oak floor. A cascade of potted ivies and ferns hung from wrought-iron hooks above a plush Victorian love-seat and settee, and on the shadier side of the room a baby grand piano faced a quartet of Sheraton chairs upholstered in pale green brocade.

"This is . . . there are hardly words, Paige," Maggie said softly. "It's like something out of a vintage photograph."

"Yes, very little change here, thanks to family tradition," Paige said wryly. "But it is pretty."

"The sheer size of the rooms alone," Maggie explained, venturing across the polished floor. "And they weren't even wearing hoop skirts anymore at the turn of the century."

"No, thank God." Paige laughed and sat down at the piano bench, flipping the lid to trail her fingers across the keys.

"I probably sound like Woman Who Loves Design Too Much," Maggie admitted, running her hand gently along the lush walnut curve of the piano's top. "But this house is just so exquisitely beautiful. It's like a secret paradise. Nothing bad could happen in a place this lovely."

Paige didn't reply to that, but her smile suddenly seemed frozen in place.

"Wait till you see the billiard room," she said lightly, standing up, and Maggie could have kicked herself. Bad things happened to everyone, everywhere, and Paige was no exception just because she lived in an enchanted mansion and was about to marry a movie star. It was a good thing Lucy was the one in PR instead of her.

She followed Paige out another set of doors into the hallway that ran across the front of the house and realized her bad-things philosophy applied to her, too.

Because the original Bad Thing himself was strolling out of the dining room and heading her way.

"Another tour?" he asked Paige with a grin. "You must have collected a lot of quarters by now."

"Are you kidding?" She rolled her eyes. "I charge a dollar. Pay up, Maggie."

They laughed together, and Maggie forced a smile. Oh, good. Chummy togetherness. Actually, it might work to her advantage if she sank silently to the carpet and crawled out of their line of sight. . . .

"Tyler's here giving me some ideas," Paige said to Maggie, and she straightened up. "When we were at Moonstone in

February, I fell in love with it, and I'd already been talking to Drew about opening a boutique hotel in San Francisco."

Maggie nodded, not really following, trying to figure out why the name Moonstone sounded familiar.

It wasn't easy with Tyler staring at her, arms folded over his chest, that amused eyebrow hard at work again, and his hair pushed up far enough on his forehead to expose the faded scar above his right eyebrow.

"What Tyler's done with that place is incredible," Paige went on, leaning against the chair rail and staring at some far distant point over Maggie's shoulder. "He showed me pictures of what it looked like when he bought it." She shuddered. "The carpet was the worst, don't you think, Ty? All that lime green shag?"

Lime green shag. Maggie froze, her eyes widening in disbelief as she pictured the clothing-strewn floor of the hotel room she and Tyler had shared. The Moonstone Inn had been the name of the Keys hotel where she'd met him. And now it was *his* hotel?

"Maggie, are you okay?" Paige said, narrowing her eyes and resting a hand on Maggie's arm.

"Oh. Um, yeah. I just . . . well, you know, interior designer here." She gave them a shaky laugh. "The idea of lime green shag just made me slightly nauseous for a second."

"It was pretty awful," Tyler said easily, but his eyes never left her face. "The carpet, I mean."

"Sounds like it." She nodded like a fool, wishing her brain hadn't told her legs to run minutes ago. Resisting the impulse was harder every second.

She didn't need any more revelations about Tyler Brody, his hotel, or their weekend together. Escaping him once had been difficult enough. He was all wrong for her. He was too reckless, too carefree. He was the antiplan.

"I'll let you two talk, then," she said, edging toward the foyer. The stairs were there, and she wanted to go up them and into the peace and quiet of her room. Now.

"Oh, we've got plenty of time," Paige said, waving her

hand with a rueful smile. "We have the premiere to get through, and wedding stuff . . ." She sighed happily. "And I should probably find Lucy again and check on dinner. We're doing drinks beforehand, around seven. Tyler, why don't you show her the billiard room?"

"Glad to," he said, placing his hand lightly on the small of her back as Paige started off toward the kitchen.

"That's okay," Maggie said grimly. His hand was much too hot through her shirt. Much too strong. "I'm rotten at pool. I think I'll just go up to my room for a while."

"I'll walk you."

"I don't think any dangerous types are lurking between here and there," she said. *Don't clench your teeth. It's a dead giveaway.* She didn't want him anywhere near her bedroom, simply for her own sanity.

"Well, you never know." He gave her a cool smile. "I'd never forgive myself if you just disappeared."

She rolled her eyes, snapping, "I'm *not* going to disappear," even while she was trying to figure out just when she could leave in the morning. That wouldn't be disappearing. This time she'd leave him a note.

He ignored her retort and steered her toward the stairs, hand still firmly planted against her back. She resisted the impulse to wriggle away like a cranky toddler. She wouldn't give him the satisfaction.

Plus, his hand felt kind of nice. Familiar. She knew what else it was capable of.

No, you don't! Forget that. Forget him. Concentrate on that possibly authentic Monet on the wall.

But Tyler hurried her past it too quickly for her to come to a conclusion and stopped at the door to her bedroom.

Well, that was a bad sign. She had no idea where he was sleeping, but then again she hadn't exactly been looking. She'd been wishing he would magically disappear.

"Aren't you going to invite me in?" he asked blandly, leaning against the doorjamb.

"If you arch that eyebrow at me again, I may be forced to do it violence," she told him, sighing. "Come in. We'll talk. I'm getting the feeling I'm going to have a new shadow otherwise."

"Hey, it's just friendly conversation," he said, following her inside and shutting the door behind him. He sank into the slipper chair by the window, looking around with interest. "Very floral. I have stripes and nautical stuff."

She stared at him, finally perching on the end of the bed. "That's nice. Are we done?"

"Maggie, come on," he said, leaning forward and letting out a rough laugh. "Five years ago we spent more than forty-eight straight hours together, most of it naked. I just want to know what happened, why you left." He pinned her with those dark blue eyes, and she tensed, waiting for the caveat she knew was coming.

He didn't disappoint her.

"And I want to figure out how to make sure it doesn't happen again."

She closed her eyes briefly, as if he'd voiced her worst-case scenario, and frustration boiled in his gut. What the hell had happened to the woman he'd spent that weekend with? The one who was up for anything, including very pleasant things, among them a convenience-store can of whipped cream and a new use for the showerhead in the tub.

The woman who'd let him stroke her back until she was nearly dizzy with the pleasure of it, purring like a cat under his hands.

The woman who'd played twenty questions with him in the middle of the night and giggled helplessly at the dubbed karate movie they'd found on cable.

This woman didn't seem like she'd be up for any of those things, and he had no fucking clue why.

"I'm not giving up, Maggie," he said quietly. "I never thought I'd see you again. It's not like I've been some monk in a tower all this time since, but now that we're here, I thought we could at least talk about it. I had a great time with you. I wanted to keep having a great time with you. If you felt differently, you could at least tell me why."

She swallowed hard, and he watched the muscle in her throat working. When she lifted her gaze to his, she looked almost sad.

"You're right. I'm . . . being ridiculous. I did have a good time. A great time." She tilted her head, her mouth twisted in a rueful smile. "I just . . . well, I didn't—*don't* live in the Keys. I had a job to go back to. I didn't think what happened between us was going to go anywhere."

She was lying. He knew it, just as well as he knew his own name. Not about it being great—he believed her there—but about why she left. She was staring at the carpet again, so pointedly *not* looking at him.

Before he could argue, she said, "The hotel is yours? When did you buy it?"

At least she wasn't considering the conversation over. "About two months before we met," he said, leaning back in the chair. "It was a spur-of-the-moment thing."

"A hotel is a spur-of-the-moment thing?" She'd actually paled at the thought. "That's a pretty enormous impulse buy, don't you think?"

He thought about that for a minute. "Not if it pays off, which it has."

"But . . . but . . ." It was fascinating. She was actually sputtering. "It's a business. Don't you need a plan, and investors, and a . . . a *plan?*"

"I had investors, and I had an idea of what I could do with the place. Remember that crappy patio off the back? You should see it now."

"An idea?" She shook her head in disbelief. "That's . . . crazy. What if it was a disaster? And where did you come up with investors for a spur-of-the-moment buy like that?" She paused, screwing up her forehead in thought. "And what patio? I don't remember a back patio."

"Which question do you want me to answer first?" he said. "I didn't bring my notebook."

"This one," she said, suddenly serious. "Why didn't you tell me it was your hotel?"

"Would it have mattered?"

She shrugged, then leaned back on the bed as she started to toe off her sneakers. "Not at all. It's just a little weird that I didn't know about it. And who was running the place while we were, um, otherwise occupied?"

"The staff." He pushed up out of the chair when her right sneaker wouldn't come off, kneeling down to untie it for her. She tensed when his fingers circled her ankle, but she didn't protest.

Well then, he'd take a mile. He sat down beside her, close enough to feel her body heat and catch the scent of her hair. Strawberries. Five years ago it had been oranges.

"Why do you care so much about the hotel?" he said, glad that she hadn't scurried off to the other side of the room.

"I don't, really." She shook her head, frowning again, and he wanted to reach over and smooth her mouth into a smile. No, scratch that. He wanted to kiss her. "I'm just not a fly-by-the-seat-of-my-pants type, so it's a little hard for me to understand."

He raised an eyebrow. "The seat of your pants seemed pretty carefree five years ago."

"Hey!"

"That didn't come out right," he said, biting back a grin. "But you know what I mean. A three-day fling with a strange guy isn't something you plan." Now it was his turn to frown. He searched her face for a minute, reading confusion in her eyes. "Is it?"

"No!"

"Well, you can't have it both ways, Maggie," he said. "You've lost me."

She got up and paced the length of the room, her bare feet silent on the plush carpet, and her face creased with frustration. "I didn't plan to spend the weekend with you," she said finally, turning around. "I'd had a crappy week at work, my sister was in one of her famous join-the-circus moods, and the reason Lucy and I went away in the first place was because my fiancé had broken off our engagement. With a voice mail message."

Ouch. So he'd been rebound guy. Somehow, that stung. But he didn't say anything, because he was still stuck on the whole join-the-circus remark.

Maggie went on, pacing away and then back, this time furiously twisting a ring around one slender finger. "Everything about my life, to put it bluntly, was crappy." She sank into the chair he'd vacated, her dark eyes wry but a bit defensive, too. "And then I met you."

"And I wasn't crappy, huh?" He smiled at her, grateful for her relieved laugh.

"Exactly. Far from it, in fact. But I wasn't thinking 'marriage proposal,' and I was pretty sure you weren't either." She shrugged apologetically, and he forced himself to ignore the gentle rise of her breasts beneath her T-shirt. *Pay attention, buddy. She's saying sorry.* "I know it was wrong to just up and leave, but I thought you knew as well as I did that it was going to be over at some point."

It sounded right, and it wasn't far from the truth, but when he looked into her eyes, he knew she was still lying. They were too neutral, too blandly dark brown. Maybe she was just carefully omitting some of the truth, but either way, her little confession wasn't the whole story.

He had known it would end, sooner or later; he just hadn't counted on how much sooner. Even back then, he'd been used to doing what he wanted, when he wanted, and he'd wanted more of Maggie. Maybe it was simply the fact that she'd put a stop to the fun so completely by disappearing like that, but there was more to it than that. Had to be—a woman had never gotten to him before the way she had.

He'd felt something with her he'd never felt with another

woman. Something that crackled like a dangerous loose wire. No, wait. It was more like something as comfortable and familiar as a favorite shirt. Shit. Maybe it was both.

And it was stupid to ignore it, especially now, when they were both here for the weekend, with nice private guest rooms to take advantage of, and each other to get to know, all over again.

Even if it was only for the weekend.

It was time to get serious.

"I get it," he said then, standing up and crossing over to her, taking her wrist to pull her to her feet. "It was convenient. Blowing off steam, sowing wild oats, whatever cliché you want to call it. That's fine. But we're agreeing it was good, right?" He tucked a finger under her chin, tilting her face up to his, and her cheeks heated with a pretty pink blush, remembering it. "And now we're both here. So I say, why not have some of that goodness again? Just for the weekend. If you ask me, you're wound pretty tight at the moment, and blowing off some steam might be just what you need."

"I don't think—" she started, panic in her eyes, but he interrupted her by lowering his head to kiss her, hard and long, no room for argument.

God, she tasted good. It took a second to adjust, for her body to soften against his, all giving curves and the warm, rich scents of heated skin and ripe strawberries, but once they were pressed together, her arms wound around him, and her mouth opened under his.

She was as hot and dark and hungry as he was, letting go with a shudder as he explored the taste of her, the feel of her, with an urgency that snapped to attention the moment he felt her tongue against his. He'd wanted to kiss her, to feel her, solid and real, in his hands, but he wanted more than that, too, right now. The plan, such as it was, had been to tempt her, to plant the idea of reacquainting themselves later, after dinner, when they had the whole night to spend, but as always, his plans sucked.

She wriggled when he slid his hands under her T-shirt, smoothing his palms against the silky expanse of her back, and dug her fingers into the small of his back. Holding on? Or about to yank him away? He couldn't tell and didn't much care while she was still kissing him back.

Because right now, he felt it again—that sizzle he'd never felt before that was somehow more than "hot woman, good sex." And if she tried to tell him she didn't feel it, he'd never believe her.

She shuddered again, a whole-body ripple of sensation that reverberated against him, and then groaned into his mouth. He twisted to steer her toward the bed and lay her down, lowering himself over her.

That was when she planted her hands squarely on his chest and breathed, "Wait."

"Why?" He went in for another kiss, but she pushed harder.

"Because," she grumbled. "Because I have to think about this, this time. Because it's almost time for dinner. Because you can't just waltz in here and get me all hot and trembly without warning."

"I'll hold up a red flag next time," he said, heaving a sigh as he rolled away to lie on his back.

Before she could retort, a brisk knock on the door preceded it opening wide. Maggie scrambled into a sitting position as a blonde with a head of wild curls walked in, stopping midstride when she caught sight of the two of them. The famous Lucy, he figured, angling up on one elbow.

"Oh," she said with an embarrassed grin. "Sorry. I didn't think you'd be, uh, busy."

"We're not," Maggie told her, yanking her T-shirt into place and blushing furiously.

"Oh. Okay, then." Backing up, Lucy said, "Tyler, right? Nice to see you again. Maggie told me—"

"Did you want something, Lucy?" Maggie asked. If he wasn't mistaken, she'd actually clenched her teeth.

"Just to tell you we're having drinks in the drawing room in about half an hour." Her eyes were bright with curiosity under a generous helping of makeup. He squinted at her. Were they purple?

"We'll be there," Maggie said, standing up and all but pushing her friend out of the room, shutting the door behind her.

"That's Lucy, huh? She looks different," he said.

"I think she was a redhead when we were in the Keys. It's hard to keep track."

She wouldn't meet his eyes, so he got up and slid an arm around her waist, pulling her so close she had to look up to avoid pressing her nose into his chest.

"To be continued," he said meaningfully.

"The talking? Or the kissing?"

He crushed his mouth to hers to forestall any more questions, but as he left, he silently scored a point for the look of dazed heat on her face and said, "Both."

Chapter Five

There was nothing like a little predinner lust to increase a girl's appetite, Maggie thought, eyeing the hors d'oeuvres on the console table when she walked into the drawing room a half hour later. Passing over the bruchetta and the paté, she realized she was subconsciously searching for chocolate. It would probably take a five-pound box to sublimate her hormones at the moment. If seeing Tyler hadn't been in the plan, kissing him definitely wasn't.

One touch, and that internal switch had flipped on. Even before he touched her, if she was going to be truthful about it. Way back when she'd realized it was him across the ballroom, actually.

Damn it. She had to figure out how to disable the stupid thing.

And letting him kiss her—oh, all right, kissing him—had not only *not* turned off her impulsive side, it had revved it up into a whole new gear.

Her body still hadn't recovered, and she'd spent fifteen minutes in the bathroom splashing cold water everywhere she could think of.

It didn't help that he was only ten feet away now, sitting in a broad window seat that overlooked the terrace. He looked up from whatever Connor was sniping about and pinned her with a smoky, dark blue gaze.

She felt a flush creep up her neck and looked away. The drawing room was big enough to land a helicopter in, but it still felt too crowded. She wasn't looking forward to dinner. With her luck, Paige would seat her right next to him.

She was spearing a cocktail shrimp with a toothpick and pretending to ignore Tyler when Paige waved at her from across the room. Squaring her shoulders, she took her wineglass and made her way past Drew and Lake, who looked up and smiled at her, across the enormous room toward the fireplace, where Paige was standing with an older couple. Beneath the enormous seascape over the mantel, the three of them looked like they were posing for a portrait.

"Maggie, this is Marty and Sybil Margolis," Paige said from the protective circle of Marty's arm. "Marty is Drew's agent, and they've known each other forever."

"You're the interior designer Lucy mentioned?" Sybil asked, squinting at her from beneath frizzy red bangs that matched the wire frames of her glasses. "Let me ask you about some china I picked up in East Hampton this morning."

"She's not an antiques appraiser, Sybil," her husband said with a gruff chuckle. "Nice to meet you, hon. Glad you're here."

Maggie shook his hand, trying to ignore the cracker crumbs stuck in his shaggy brown beard. The backs of his fingers were covered in wiry hair, too, which was harder to ignore with her hand all but lost inside what was pretty much a paw. "I'm glad I could come," she said, gently pulling her hand free.

"So you don't know anything about antique Wedgewood, then?" Sybil said. She was still squinting as she raised a glass of white wine to her mouth, and she was clearly disappointed.

"Not really," Maggie said, grateful when Paige put an arm around her shoulders.

"Excuse us, Sybil, I should introduce Maggie to everyone

else," Paige said with a gentle smile and steered her away
from the fireplace. "Sybil's sweet, really," she added in a
lower tone, "but she's a little bit single-minded."

"Got it," Maggie said, and let Paige lead her around the
room on hostess duty.

She'd never been in an official drawing room before, unless it was part of a museum, but this one qualified. It was the
size of two large rooms, and a graceful arch in the middle de-
lineated each seating area. Floor-to-ceiling windows overlooking the terrace along the south side of the room were
dressed simply with creamy sheers and blue and white toile
valances. The walls were a soft, inoffensive yellow, and the
sofas were covered either in sea-glass green raw silk or blue
and white stripes, with throw cushions that echoed the walls
in modest floral prints or muted geometrics. Everywhere she
looked, something pricey and antique stared back at her,
from a brass ship's clock in a walnut case to a crystal vase
and delicate china candlesticks. The designer in her wanted
time to inspect every detail, but the rest of her was a little in-
timidated, especially when she noticed the way everyone else
was lounging around, perched carelessly on a chair's arm or
dropping a cell phone with a clunk on the mahogany coffee
table. Personally, she was afraid her shoes were making too
many marks in the carpet.

But it was clear that this house wasn't a museum. People
lived here. There was even a water mark on one of the
Chippendale side tables.

And everyone else seemed comfortable enough, whether it
was because they knew each other well or they were simply
used to houses that deserved their zip codes. As Paige led her
around the room, they found Nell in an armchair with yet
another magazine and a huge snifter of what looked like
brandy, her bare feet tucked under her and her sandals on the
carpet, and a lanky, dark-haired man sprawled on one sofa
with a bottle of beer, an expensive-looking Nikon on the
cushion beside him.

The magazine was the latest issue of *Town and Country*, and the man was Bobby Gleason, a photographer. Maggie remembered his name from a series of celebrity portraits she'd seen in the spring—stark, gorgeous, black-and-white close-ups. He and Drew had arrived in L.A. around the same time and, according to Bobby, had shared a lot of ramen noodles and cheap beer before Drew had scored his first guest spots on a couple of sitcoms and Bobby had moved from the ranks of the paparazzi to assignments with some of the L.A. magazines.

He was friendly and easygoing, Maggie thought, all long skinny limbs, swinging his tousled mane of dark hair each time he laughed, but as she followed Paige toward the other side of the room, she realized he was jiggling one black-booted foot across the opposite knee and three empty bottles of beer sat on the floor against the sofa. Apparently, happy hour had started early.

Everyone was drinking, except for Drew, and even though there were only thirteen people in the room, the buzz of conversation and music made it seem like a much bigger party. Marty and Sybil were back to antiques and the shops she hadn't had time to poke through today, and Drew and Lake were discussing horror movies, from the few snatches Maggie caught as she walked by—either that or they were a little more interested in axes than was probably healthy. Shelby had joined Bobby on the couch, a huge pink cosmopolitan in one hand. She was giggling about something someone named Eden had told her, but Bobby was mostly watching the way her shirt, which was a kind of peasant blouse/halter combination, kept slipping off one shoulder, where there wasn't even a hint of bra strap in sight.

Paige introduced her to producer Tony Angelino, who had spread a sheaf of 8x10 photos across the top of an antique trunk doubling as a coffee table at the other end of the room. He grunted something vaguely resembling a greeting at her before holding up two shots of olive-skinned brunettes and asking her which one was sexier. Beneath the bushy shelf of his eyebrows, his eyes were a watery light brown, and completely serious, as far as Maggie could tell.

She was saved from answering when a woman in black leather pants and a crisp white blouse walked into the room, a gray parrot on her shoulder.

"Is this day over yet?" She heaved a sigh and sank onto the nearest sofa, the bird still clinging to its perch, and called over her shoulder to Tony, "Bring me a drink, would you? Something strong."

For emphasis, the bird squawked, "Something strong. Something strong."

Paige caught Maggie's eye and gave her a grim smile. "Whitney, this is Maggie Harding, a friend of Lucy's. Maggie, this is Whitney Craig, Tony's wife and business partner. And this is . . ." She hesitated, amusement and despair battling it out. "Bogart."

"Call me Bogart," the parrot sang, craning its head at Maggie.

"Hi . . . Bogart," she said, coughing to cover a giggle. "Nice to meet you, Whitney."

"Who's Lucy?" the other woman asked, reaching around her to accept what looked like straight scotch from her husband, who ignored the parrot ruffling its feathers at him and went back to his glossies.

"The woman from the PR firm," Paige explained. Maggie watched as her fingers tightened into a fist behind her back, out of Whitney's line of sight. "You met her earlier."

"Oh, right." She looked Maggie up and down over the rim of her glass. "And what do you do?"

"I'm a designer," she said, stepping back when the parrot leaned forward to peer at her, both beady little eyes narrowing. "I'm just . . . here for the party."

"Oh. Stop that, Bogart," Whitney said, stroking the bird's tail feather. "Where's Drew?"

"He was right over there," Paige said, her gaze traveling

the room. Lake had joined Connor and Tyler, but Drew was nowhere in sight. "I'll find him."

"Oh, let him be," Whitney said, gulping down another swig of her drink. "He's just nervous. It's a lot of attention all at once, after everything he's been through."

Maggie realized the other woman was staring at her as she spoke, and she wanted to protest that the party hadn't been her idea, but just then a man walked up and put an arm around Paige's shoulders.

"Need help with anything?" he murmured. "Everything set to go for dinner?"

"You're a guest, not the staff, remember?" Paige laughed, twisting out from under his arm to face Maggie. "Maggie, this is Ethan Winship, Nell's husband and my very good friend. Ethan, this is Maggie Harding."

"Lovely to meet you," he said softly, but behind a pair of round wire-framed glasses, his eyes never left Paige's face. He slouched, either to make up for his height or simply to be closer to Paige, and pushed his glasses up on the hooked bridge of his nose with one finger.

"You, too," she said. She put out her hand, but he wasn't paying attention.

She noticed that Nell was, though. Her magazine lay open on her lap, and her dark, perfectly plucked brows had drawn into a frown.

Ethan was nudging Paige toward the bar, offering to refill her glass, so Maggie cast around for someone else to talk to. Whitney was examining a scratch on her sunglasses as Bogart gently poked at her knot of bleached blond hair with his beak. It was oddly intimate, and Maggie flushed when the bird looked up at her.

Shelby was leaning back on the sofa, giving Bobby a stream-of-consciousness account of a dream, and Marty and Sybil had moved to the couch opposite them, where Marty was falling asleep over his gin and tonic and Sybil was squinting at a small carved elephant on the coffee table.

Where was Lucy when she needed her?

She glanced around again, and this time her gaze landed on Tyler, who hadn't moved from the window seat. Lake was gone, but Connor had pushed in beside him and was gesturing broadly as he spoke; Tyler's eyes were on Maggie, though, and she swallowed hard as a familiar ripple of awareness pulsed through her.

No safe harbor there, that was for sure.

The door to the hallway was only a few feet away, and she turned around to wander through it, hoping she looked casual and curious, instead of desperate and distressed. If she could just get through dinner, she could lock herself in her room afterward and pretend that Tyler wasn't just somewhere down the hall, tempting her every time he as much as breathed.

Which was, of course, every minute. Her internal radar was bad enough, but the urge to escape the other guests and their assorted quirks, egos, and bad manners made grabbing Tyler and escaping upstairs even more appealing.

And that was a very bad idea.

Or at least one she had to put off until after dinner.

She heard piano music somewhere down the hall, turned into the foyer and then down the hall past the dining room, following it. The only piano she'd seen had been in the conservatory, and when she stopped at the open door, someone was playing the baby grand. An old standard, melancholy and pitched low.

She stood in the doorway, but it was impossible to see inside—the lights were off, and the front of the house was shaded by the tulip trees along the drive. Counting in her head, she tried to figure out who was still back in the drawing room when she heard, "Come on in. I don't mind an audience."

Drew. Trying to get away from the crowd, probably, and she'd followed him like a groupie.

"I'm sorry," she said, making her way over to the piano. "I was following the music. But if you want to be alone . . ."

"There's not much chance of that this weekend." His laugh was gruff and not very believable. She couldn't see him well in the dim light—he was just an indefinite shape with a voice. "Plus, you're much better company than half the people in the other room."

She settled in one of the chairs grouped at the foot of the instrument. "You don't even know me."

"That's a point in your favor." He punctuated the words with the tune to "shave and a haircut," and Maggie laughed.

"I'm looking forward to seeing the movie," she said after he'd noodled his way through part of "Strangers in the Night."

"It's not bad, actually. Of course, since rehab, making *Police Academy 17* would have seemed like a stellar career choice, so I could be slightly biased."

There didn't seem to be anything to say to that, so she sat and listened while he segued into another old tune that conjured images of World War II and dance halls full of uniformed soldiers and girls in swishy skirts and pearls.

He didn't seem to be in any hurry to leave, and sitting in here with him was much nicer than trying to make conversation with Whitney or Sybil—or ignoring Tyler, for that matter—but she felt guilty for sneaking out when Lucy was probably trying to round everyone up for dinner. If someone didn't come looking for them soon, she would have to come up with a polite way to interrupt him.

She was about to say something when Shelby walked in and flipped on a light without warning. Drew blinked in surprise.

"They're ready for us in the dining room," Shelby said, peering at the sheet music on the stand. "They were looking for you."

It sounded strangely like something you'd hear on a movie set, Maggie thought, getting up to follow them when Shelby ignored her and linked a bare arm through Drew's.

"Do you know what we're having?" she heard Shelby say. "I'm totally in the mood for Thai, but you probably can't get that out here, huh? Not many Chinese people in the Hamptons, I guess."

Please let her spill cocktail sauce all over that shirt. And then she restrained a snort when Drew looked over his shoulder at her and rolled his eyes.

He didn't remove Shelby's arm, though, and when Paige walked into the hall a moment later, the disappointment in her eyes asked why.

In the dining room, Maggie sighed as she found her seat, closing her eyes briefly when Tyler patted the chair beside his with a pleased grin. It was going to be a long meal.

Chapter Six

"You're not eating that," Tyler said. The caterer had brought out a glossy fruit tart layered with vanilla mousse and was pouring coffee and tea.

"I reached maximum capacity somewhere during the fourth course," Maggie said. His leg was too close to hers under the table. His everything was too close. How was she supposed to eat when the scent of him kept making her libido whisper, *Yum*.

It didn't help that the atmosphere in the room had clouded over like a storm front. Bobby had knocked back two more beers during dinner, as well as knocking over his water glass, and Nell had only picked at her food, refilling her glass with Armagnac twice instead, stony-faced and silent. Shelby was still chattering to Drew, oblivious to his boredom and Paige's discomfort, and Whitney had finally taken Bogart up to his cage after he had flapped around the table, stealing part of Lake's garlic brioche. Connor was on Maggie's other side, and she'd finally turned toward Tyler in self-defense when he wouldn't stop flirting. Shrugging his hand off her thigh should have been a clear signal, but he was on his way to being drunk, too.

Lucy had given up trying to make innocuous small talk sometime during the lobster ravioli, but she was glancing desperately at Maggie every few seconds. The meal had been a disaster from the beginning, and even Paige seemed to have lost her enthusiasm for the party.

"You mind?" Tyler said, pointing at Maggie's plate. He'd eaten his own dessert in five big bites.

"Go right ahead." She shook her head when he broke off an enormous piece with his fork, watching him swallow it with pleasure. Men could eat during a train wreck.

"We're going to screen the movie in a little bit," Lucy announced, standing up and waving her wineglass to get everyone's attention. She looked wilted, Maggie thought; her curls had drooped by the time she rounded up the group for dinner, and her flirty pink dress was a map of wrinkles. "Until then, why doesn't everyone relax in the other room or on the terrace?"

Nell couldn't leave fast enough, Maggie noticed as she got up with Tyler following close behind her. For once, she sympathized—Ethan had directed nine out of ten comments to Paige during dinner. It made Nell's catty encouragement of Shelby's crush on Drew a little more understandable.

Not that Paige seemed to view Ethan as anything more than a friend. If she'd patted him on the head like a much-loved pet or a younger brother, Maggie wouldn't have been surprised.

The caterers came in to start clearing away dinner, and she realized she'd let herself be caught up in Tyler's wake as they all wandered back to the drawing room—he was like a human magnet. A big, hot, hard magnet, in fact, close enough to reach out and touch. So close he was about to drape an arm around her, too, but she ducked out of reach at the last moment. No way was she snuggling up to him on the sofa, or anywhere else. Not right now.

Later was a different story.

He arched that dark, smooth eyebrow again as she dropped into an armchair a good twenty feet away from him, and she looked away to avoid the amusement in his eyes.

Shelby kicked off her stiletto-heeled sandals and flopped onto the sofa next to Drew, who stiffened and moved as far away as Connor, who was seated beside him, would allow. She was, as usual, oblivious.

"So tell me about the engagement, Drew! Or maybe Paige should—did he propose romantically? I can see Drew being kind of mushy about something like that." She flipped her hair over her shoulder, which seemed like another thinly veiled excuse to stick her chest out, and then leaned closer to Drew, poking him in the shoulder with one finger. "Come on, fess up. Tell us. Did you do it on top of the Empire State Building? Or in a hot air balloon?"

"I don't know . . ." He looked about as uncomfortable as a human being could possibly be, and on the opposite couch Paige was blushing furiously.

"A hot air ballon?" Whitney snorted and set down her wineglass on the mantel. "Oh, God, that's funny. Didn't you know Drew is afraid of heights? I thought you saw that whole scene on the roof when we were filming. And he is— well, *was*—quite a player, but romantic is not the word I'd use, right, babe?" She turned to face him, arms folded across her chest, the look in her eyes unreadable, at least to Maggie.

The silence in the room pulsed like a timer ticking down to a bomb's explosion. Connor broke it with a bark of laughter and the heavy clink of the bottle of Glenfiddich against the table. Lake got up, a grim smile on her lips, and walked onto the terrace without even a backward glance. Tony looked up from his sheaf of photos but didn't comment, and Paige appeared to be struggling to hold back tears. Her huge eyes were glassy and distant, staring at some point far from Drew, who seemed to be struggling not to lunge over the coffee table and slug Whitney.

The producer of his latest film. His comeback movie. A woman who was supposed to be on his team, in a major way. What the hell was wrong with these people, Maggie wondered, frozen in her seat, watching as Lucy's lips quivered with the need to say something to break the tension and failing completely. She didn't look far from a minibreakdown herself.

Ethan broke the silence by settling onto the sofa next to Paige and asking, "So tell me more about this hotel you were thinking of opening. Do you have a location? Lucy said you were looking for some advice from . . . Maggie, is it? And Tyler?" Behind his thick glasses, his eyes were huge and concerned, blinking at Paige in sympathy.

"What hotel?" Shelby said blandly, picking at a scab on her bare, tanned knee.

"A boutique hotel, one of those pricey, five-star places I could never get into before Drew made it big." Marty's gruff voice was amused. He cleared his throat and crossed an ankle over one knee. Above his sock, springy dark hair covered his calf. "I think it's an excellent idea—seems like there aren't enough of them to go around anymore. Everyone in town wants to be holed up in the most exclusive place with the softest sheets and the best minibars."

By "town," Maggie assumed he meant L.A., or maybe the more rarified idea of Hollywood, since it seemed to her that most actors wouldn't be caught dead living in Hollywood proper. And somehow she didn't think catering to pampered stars was Paige's plan, but then again, who knew? She never would have guessed half the things she'd seen and heard since three o'clock this afternoon.

"It's not quite that simple," Paige said gently, "but yes, I'd like to . . . I mean, *we'd* like to open a hotel. I'm not sure where yet. I'm mean, we're not . . . Maybe San Francisco." She swallowed hard, staring at her lap.

Bobby grunted as he got up and ran a hand over her hair as he stumbled toward the patio. "Anywhere you put it, honey, I'll be there," he muttered, and disappeared through the French doors, another bottle of beer in hand.

Lucy stood up just as suddenly, announcing that she was

going to get the movie ready in the screening room. She grabbed her own wineglass as she left, and Maggie sighed. For her first important solo party, to say this one wasn't going well would be an understatement.

At least Drew had managed to shake off Shelby. He took Paige's hand and pulled her to her feet, murmuring something in her ear. She was stiff and silent in the circle of his arms, but she finally gave him a weak smile. It was a good thing she wasn't the actor in the family—it was hardly a convincing performance.

The whole scene was too weird. In between the antiques and the good upholstery, Paige's guests were acting like kids before a recess brawl, hinting and taunting and whispering. Spitballs would probably be next.

And they were kids she didn't know, and really didn't care to. Paige was sweet, and Drew seemed decent enough, if a little bit moody, but aside from Lake, and maybe Marty, everyone else was just plain unpleasant in one way or another. She was off ego patrol for good. If a real fistfight broke out, she'd give Lucy all the help she could, or at least call 911, but there was no way on earth she could defuse whatever this situation had become. There was too much history between some of these people, and obviously too much of it was not of the rainbows and puppies variety.

She was an interior designer, for God's sake, not a crisis counselor, unless the crisis was an abuse of chintz.

Whitney was watching Drew and Paige, arms still folded across her chest, her eyes bright and interested. God, she was creepy. She was as whipcord thin as Tony was heavy, and even though her voice was silky, every word that came out of her mouth seemed designed to sting. Suddenly she cut her glance to Maggie, who felt her cheeks burn and looked away.

Out. That was where she needed to be, just for a minute, before they were all crowded into the screening room in the dark for the movie.

Tyler had taken his drink to the doors overlooking the patio, and when she glanced at him, he gestured for her to join him, crooking one finger.

It was all the incentive she needed.

"Some party, huh?" he murmured, slipping an arm around her waist as they stepped outside. She didn't wriggle away this time. The night air was still warm, and the breeze tasted like salt and sea spray, but he felt good beside her, a solid, sane presence she could hold on to.

Even if the feel of him made parts of her insane with the urge to skip the movie entirely and drag him upstairs.

"Well, it's certainly not boring," she said, turning her face up to the night sky. It was dusted with stars above the ocean, which crashed and roared in the distance. Bobby and Lake, she realized, were nowhere in sight.

"True enough." He chuckled and set his glass down on the marble railing so he could rest his other hand on her hip, turning her to face him. "But then, nothing about this weekend has been boring so far."

Also true. She looked up at him—his eyes were little more than a faint gleam in the darkness, and they were too close. *He* was too close, as usual. Or, to be more specific, not to mention more truthful, too irresistible.

She could smell him, clean and crisp in the sultry evening air, and if she closed her eyes, she could call up the taste of him, five years ago or this afternoon. Her tongue had a long memory.

Resist, she told herself firmly. *For now, at least.*

It wasn't going to be possible without conversation. "How long have you lived in the Keys?" she asked him, stepping out of the circle of his arms.

"Back to small talk, huh?" He sighed and leaned against the railing, crossing his arms over his chest. "About five years."

Five years? "So . . . you'd only just moved there before you bought the hotel?"

"I didn't move there until I bought the hotel," he said. She could hear him smiling.

"Until? What do you mean?" she asked, even though she thought she knew.

"I was almost finished with my law degree, and I headed down there for a few weeks to study for the bar," he said, shrugging. "When I realized the Moonstone was for sale, I decided to buy it. And then I just stayed."

Oh, God. He really was her worst nightmare. The antiplan personified. Who scrapped years of studying for a law degree to buy a rundown hotel and move to Florida on a whim? Tyler Brody, that's who.

"You just . . . stayed." She stared at him, wishing for once she could read the expression in his eyes. "You bought a hotel on a whim and moved to the Keys. And gave up law." Saying it out loud didn't really make it any more understandable.

"I don't think I would have made a very good lawyer," he said, shaking his head. "But it turns out I run a very good hotel. So that worked out, huh?"

"But what if it hadn't?" The risk of it all terrified her, and it wasn't even her life. She found herself clutching the cool marble railing as if it were a life raft.

And trying very hard to ignore the fact that as much as what he'd done scared her, it was turning her on, too. Tyler Brody reached out and took what he wanted, when he wanted it, and tonight, this minute, he wanted her.

"But it did work out." He frowned—she could hear that, too, even though she couldn't see his face very well in the dark. "And I was tired of Chicago."

"Right." She couldn't quite wrap her mind around it. She thought hard before she switched dry cleaners.

"I'm freaking you out somehow, aren't I?" he said, sliding his hand over hers on the railing. It was huge and warm— hers seemed lost beneath it, instead of sheltered.

"A little bit," she admitted. "I was picturing a quiet weekend at the beach, which was obviously a mistake, what with the whole movie star thing, but still—a little surf and sand, a little antiquing, a nice big mansion to drool over—and instead I got a nosy parrot, Ego Battle of the Stars, and you."

"I'm not sure being lumped in that category is a compliment," he said, but he laughed anyway. It was such a delicious sound, low and rumbling and a little bit wicked.

She didn't have a chance to deny it, because Lucy stuck her head out to call, "We're screening the movie now. Come on in. Now."

"She sounds desperate," Tyler murmured as they walked across the terrace.

"Wouldn't you be?" Maggie whispered as they stepped back into the drawing room. "I wouldn't be surprised if it comes to blows in there before the night's over."

"Let's hope not," Tyler said with a grim smile, falling in behind Marty and Sybil as Lucy led the way to the screening room. It was dark and lush, like the inside of a piece of chocolate, and had been professionally fitted with a gently sloped floor to accommodate five rows of armchairs and oversized loveseats facing a huge screen that had been pulled down against one wall.

Lake hadn't reappeared, and Drew was murmuring to Paige that he was going to look for Bobby, who was still gone. She nodded, busy with the film equipment, which Ethan was helping her set up, not bothering to look up. Whitney frowned as Nell wandered out of the room behind Drew, but settled into a seat beside Tony. Marty and Sybil were already seated in the row behind them, Sybil twittering something unintelligible to her husband.

"Where's Connor?" Maggie whispered to Lucy, who was setting out bowls of popcorn and hard candy on the tables at the end of each row.

"I couldn't care less," Lucy whispered back fiercely. "He's been an ass all evening."

"Well, he's not the only one," Maggie answered.

Shelby walked past them, barefoot and pouting, and dropped into a chair in the back row. She reached into the bowl of popcorn absently, dropping half of the handful on the carpet.

Maggie stifled a sigh and went to the doorway, looking for the others, but no one was in sight. She heard Nell's brittle laugh out on the terrace, though, and the sound of men's voices—Drew's and Bobby's, probably. Or maybe Connor's? Maybe it didn't matter. Drew and Connor knew what the movie was like—they were in it. And Bobby was too drunk even to fake praise effectively.

"I think it's ready to go," she heard Ethan say, and then the lights dimmed. She walked back into the room and curled up next to Tyler, who had, of course, chosen one of the loveseats and stretched his arm along its back, waiting for her. That didn't matter, either. Denying that she wanted to sit with him, his long, firm body beside her, was idiotic.

Denying that she wanted more than that was the problem.

The Truth About Simon was a thriller, with Drew in the title role. The camerawork was edgy and handheld, for the most part, and the lighting was all shadows intercut with flashes of jarring brilliance. Even the color palette was spooky—dark greens and grays over a muddy blue. Maggie jumped in all the right places, even with Tony and Whitney picking apart issues that would need to be taken up with the director in the final cut. They didn't bother to whisper, even when Drew and Bobby returned.

Tyler kept his arm around her, every now and then massaging the back of her neck with his fingers, strong, firm points of pressure that circled her nape, alternately teasing and soothing. It was a reminder of what his hands could do, and she knew he intended it that way, but it was when he stroked his fingers through her hair that she had a hard time resisting the urge to grab his hand and race him upstairs.

Nell wandered in during the second half of the movie, another full snifter of brandy in her hand, and took a seat across the room from Ethan, who was sitting dangerously close to Paige. Lake and Connor never showed up, though, not that Maggie cared much. Between the movie, which was actually very good, and the Tyler-shaped temptation reminding her with every brush of his arm and low whisper in her ear that she had a decision to make, she couldn't be expected to keep track of the wayward guests. She felt sorry for Lucy, though, who was probably anticipating Regina's arrival tomorrow with relief.

When the credits rolled, someone got up and turned on the lights, and Tyler stretched.

"I didn't see that coming," he said over his shoulder to Drew. "Great ending."

Drew's thanks was subdued. He'd looped an arm around Paige's shoulders, but she didn't look any happier than she had before the film started. And Marty was trying to ask Drew something about the credits, but as Maggie got up from the sofa, she caught Drew waving him off with a scowl.

"Later, Marty, all right? Jesus."

She flinched when Paige wrested herself out from under his arm. Whatever was going on between them, it wasn't going to be smoothed over with a kiss and a quick hug. Marty took Sybil out of the room, right behind Whitney and Tony, who were still arguing.

"That scene in the bathroom gives away too much—you can see motive written all over Joe's face," Whitney hissed. "We're going to need to reshoot."

"Yeah, tell that to Nigel, honey," Tony scoffed, his voice fading as they disappeared down the hall.

"I'll help you clean up here," Ethan offered to Paige, picking up an untouched bowl of popcorn.

Lucy took it from him, sighing. "You go on," she said. "I'll do this. You, too, Paige. You look . . . well, it's a big day tomorrow."

Nell walked past them all silently, followed by Shelby, who was sucking on a piece of hard candy.

"Anyone feel like walking down to the beach?" she asked, stopping short, the last-minute light bulb practically visible over her head.

She pursed her lips when no one responded, an irritable kitten denied her ball of yarn, and Maggie swore she could feel Paige's blood pressure rising even from ten feet away.

She moved up the aisle, forcing Shelby toward the hall, and murmured to Lucy, "What about Bobby?" He was sprawled in an armchair in the back of the room, his boots kicked off, his shirt untucked, an empty bottle of beer between his thighs, snoring.

"Leave him. He's a big boy."

Maggie scooped up a bowl of candy, and Tyler followed suit, leaving Ethan and Paige fiddling with the film equipment and Drew scowling over his friend's unconscious form. They went into the kitchen with Lucy, who spun around and glanced behind them to make sure they were alone before she blurted, "This is it. I'm going to get fired, not one day, not soon, *tomorrow.* I mean, I know I'm not the manners police, but oh my God, I've never seen so many supposedly civilized adults behave so horribly. It was like a . . . a bar brawl, without the actual violence. And then there's Ethan lusting after Paige right in front of his wife, even if it was in the most chaste way anyone could possibly lust anyway, and Shelby practically drooling on Drew, and that stupid bird squawking all over the place, and—"

Maggie laid a hand on her arm. "Luce, honey, relax. Please. You're going to burst something."

"Yeah, it's not your fault," Tyler added, picking through the candy bowl in search of something good.

Maggie elbowed him, and he looked up, startled. "Really."

"It's not funny, you two," Lucy said, drooping onto a stool, a fat blond curl falling over one eye. "This is bad."

Maggie glanced into the hall when she heard footsteps. It was Drew, headed toward the drawing room, his cheeks flushed with anger.

Uh-oh.

Lucy hopped off the stool, edging toward the doorway into the hall, ear cocked. Maggie grabbed her arm, but she shrugged it off, then flattened herself against the full-length maple cabinets when Paige walked by. A moment later, they both heard her footsteps thudding up the stairs and a door shutting with a heavy click.

"Oh, God," Lucy whispered. "She's sleeping in the master bedroom. Without him. Damn it."

"It's not your problem," Maggie whispered back, grunting when Lucy pulled her out of sight. Ethan was passing by. His feet were quieter on the stairs, but they both heard an insistent knock somewhere upstairs a moment later.

"He doesn't give up, does he?" Tyler murmured, and Maggie cast him a withering glance.

You would know, she mouthed, and he shrugged shamelessly.

Lucy sagged against the cabinet. "Well, that's it," she said. "I am now officially raiding this kitchen for chocolate. An IV drip would probably do it."

"Luce, really, it's going to be okay," Maggie said, taking her friend's hand. She didn't believe it, of course, but she hated to see Lucy so dejected, and she hated even more to think that Regina would fire her for other people's obnoxious behavior.

Tyler laid a hand on Maggie's back as Lucy looked up at them both with a sad little laugh. "Well," she said, sighing, "I guess things can't get any worse."

Chapter Seven

The upstairs hall was dark and silent, especially down at Maggie's end. Bobby's was the room to her left, but he was still downstairs sleeping off his drunk, and Lucy was presumably still in the kitchen smothering her sorrows in pilfered chocolate.

Aside from the spaniels, who were staring at her mournfully, she and Tyler were completely alone.

"Isn't your room somewhere on the other side of the house?" she said, leaning against the door.

"Yeah," he answered. In the faint light, the outline of his body was reassuringly solid. "But you're here."

"In a minute, I'm going to be in there," she said, tilting her head toward the bedroom. Her heart was pounding, junior high, first-kiss style. Every inch of her was tingling in anticipation. *Will he kiss me? Should I kiss him?*

She knew what she wanted—either. No, both. It didn't matter, as long as it happened. Two minutes alone with him and every one of her good intentions curled up and died. It was probably hard not to, with her hormones staging a surprise attack, complete with battle cry: *Want him! Now!*

"I'd like to be in there with you," Tyler said, his voice lower now, this close to seductive. Boy, did he know how to make her shiver.

Playing coy was stupid. It wasn't as if they hadn't slept together before, and judging by the smile curving his lips, just visible in the soft glow of the hall light, he knew exactly how much she wanted him. She hadn't tried to hide it all those years ago, and there was no sense hiding it now.

It was what happened afterward that counted. Not letting her impulsive side get the better of her, that was the thing. One night together was probably just what she needed. She'd satisfy her curiosity, see if being with him was as good as she remembered, get him out of her system. For good. He lived in Florida; she lived in New York. There wasn't a future here, not that Tyler necessarily wanted one. He was a guy, after all. He was probably remembering all the naked things they'd done together last time and just wanted another turn.

He was staring at her, and she realized she'd left him hanging while she argued with herself. Straightening up, she put a hand on the doorknob.

"Come in, then," she said, surprised that her voice was husky with anticipation.

"I thought you'd never ask."

There was that hand again, firm and warm on the small of her back, not steering, just suggesting, moving her gently over the threshold and into the room, where she broke away to turn on the light.

It cast a puddle of soft gold light on the bed, which looked absurdly prim with its lilac-sprigged cover. She had the ridiculous feeling that the bedspread would be offended by what she knew they were probably about to do underneath it. Or possibly on top of it. It was a white nightgown kind of room if she'd ever seen one.

And she and Tyler were suddenly staring at each other as awkwardly as kids at a church picnic. After the electric shock of meeting again, and the way they'd steamed up this room and earlier the couch downstairs, they both seemed strangely shy.

In Maggie's case, it was because she was pretty sure if she made the first move, it would be nothing more than a running tackle and a storm of clothes flung all over the room. She wanted slow and drawn-out and all-night-long, but if Tyler touched her now, she was afraid she'd go up in flames.

He didn't seem ready to jump her bones any second, either. Sitting on the edge of the bed, he said, "It's hard to believe we're in the same room even after this afternoon—I've been thinking about you for five years."

She melted a little at that. She'd forgotten that he could be sweet. "I've thought about you, too."

"I've also thought about that thing you did in the shower." He grinned, and it was pure devil, wicked and not even a little bit ashamed of it.

So much for sweet. But she couldn't help grinning with him. She sat down next to him, kicking off her shoes. "Yeah, well, every once in a while I think about that thing you can do with your tongue."

"What thing?" He was teasing her now, but his eyes had gone dark blue again. A hot, deep, dark blue. "Maybe you should describe it. You know, so I can do it again."

She let herself lean closer to him, until her thigh brushed his. "Oh, I couldn't do it justice with words. You'll have to search your memory."

He nudged back, his leg flat against hers now, length to length. Then he leaned in, bumping his shoulder against hers. His voice was even lower now, a husky whisper. "If I do that, I'll wind up thinking about that cute noise you make near the end, when you're close."

Her breath caught in her throat as a thrill of arousal rippled through her. *Kiss me*, she thought. *Now.*

But she couldn't wait. Every nerve ending in her body was screaming for satisfaction, right now. When he slid his hand up her back, she twisted to face him, lunging so clumsily that they smacked noses.

Ty seemed to understand, though. He caught her around the waist, hauling her onto his lap, and she hiked up her skirt to straddle his legs so they were chest to chest, her thighs around his waist, and his firm and warm beneath her.

Then she was kissing him, or maybe he was kissing her. It didn't matter, because that hot, dark point of connection was what she wanted. She felt his hands on her back and then in her hair, and she was vaguely aware of her own hands sliding along the hard ridge of his shoulders, but all she really knew was the wet heat of his mouth against hers.

He tasted faintly of scotch and the sugary fruit of the dessert tart, but there was more, something that was Ty and nothing else, dusky and spicy and incredibly addictive. She could lose herself in the heat of his mouth, she thought, groaning when the gentle pressure of his lips changed, demanding more, and she fell into the kiss, giving everything he asked and demanding some things of her own.

His tongue swept against hers, and she answered with her own before pulling away just far enough to take his bottom lip between her teeth, gently. His growl of surprise raced through her, and she shuddered, suddenly aware of her breasts against the hot, solid expanse of his chest.

Nice. But her bra felt too tight, and her dress was suddenly made of too much fabric. Skin to skin was going to be so much nicer.

She wriggled away, breaking the kiss, and before she could say a word, his fingers were clutching the hem of his shirt. The man was psychic.

"Let me," she breathed, and he let go, leaning back so she could get a hold of the black cotton, and raising his arms so she could pull it over his head.

Maybe she had forgotten a few things. For all the nights she'd lain in bed, replaying that weekend in her head, aching and lonely and reliving every kiss, her memories had obviously dimmed a little bit with time. Because his upper body was even more beautiful than she remembered, and just the kind of male body that made her inner siren bump and grind.

He was lean and firm all over—she hated the steroidal guys whose muscles never got a workout on the weight bench. Tyler was perfect—long, attenuated muscles, his shoulders and pecs cleanly defined, fine dark hair tapering down from his chest into a line that led to his abs. She'd forgotten the jagged scar that cut across one side of his chest like a lightning bolt, silver now and just as mysterious as it had been five years ago.

She sighed, running her palms over his collarbones and lower. He dragged in a deep breath as she circled her fingertips around the dark brown discs of his nipples. She could explore his body for hours, but she didn't think he'd let her. Judging from the groan deep in his throat, he was ready for some exploration himself.

His hands slid under her ass, hiking her up higher, and she rubbed against him, letting the silk of her dress whisper against his skin. God, she loved that she could make him growl that way, that she could feel his arousal jack up, pulsing through him in the ripple of his muscles flexing, his breath hitching in his chest, his heart thundering against her breast.

And she was right there with him, hot and shivering at the same time, pure need tingling electric in every nerve ending even as she seemed to melt, her knees going soft and insubstantial, her spine nothing more than a gauzy ribbon, holding her together in only the loosest way.

But when she felt him pushing her backward, his fingers edging under the hem of her skirt, she snapped to attention. "Let me," she murmured again, climbing off him and reaching behind her to unzip the dress. He actually grunted.

The carpet was soft beneath her bare feet, and the dark gray silk slid cool and smooth over her back and her legs as she let it drop to the floor. Nothing but bra and panties were left, sheer, flesh-colored satin edged in lace, and she stood still as he watched her, his gaze roaming the length of her body in appreciation.

"Stop," he whispered when she finally reached between her breasts to unhook the bra. "My turn."

Standing up, he ran his hands over her shoulders lightly, then down her arms, and she trembled. It didn't seem possible that he could have such strong, huge hands and touch her so gently.

But then it didn't seem possible that any man could appear to want her more than he did right now. His eyes were hot with it, so dark they looked nearly black, and the pulse in his throat ticked wildly.

She remembered this, too, she thought as his palms skimmed over the sheer fabric and his fingers ran beneath the straps, lowering them inch by inch until they slid off her shoulders. Tyler Brody was nothing if not honest, and when it came to the two of them in bed, the stark intensity of the way he wanted her turned her on as much as his body did.

As much as *he* did, body and soul.

A shuddering breath escaped her as he eased the cups of the bra away, exposing her breasts to the cool air. Her nipples were already hard, straining forward, and when he stroked one with the tip of a finger, she felt the pull of sensation clear down to her belly.

She wanted him naked, too—suddenly she wanted everything right away, his mouth, his hands, his cock, all of him, above her and inside her. She was such a very deeply stupid person to think she had actually considered denying herself this. But when she grappled for his belt, he smacked her hands away lightly.

"My turn's not over," he growled. "Be good."

He slid his palms over the curves of her ass, teasing her through the fragile fabric, his fingers long and firm and obviously determined to make his turn last as long as he wanted it to. Without thinking, she pushed back against his hands, and he squeezed.

She was more than ready when he hooked his thumbs into the waistband, tugging it over her bottom. Holding on to his upper arms, she wriggled out of the panties, kicking them away. But Ty wasn't done yet—he hauled her against the faded warmth of his jeans, his belt buckle smooth and cold against her belly as he stroked down over the curves of her ass, tugging gently until she spread her legs, and the fingers of his right hand slid up into the crease.

Too much. Not enough. She was trembling all over, desperate to get his clothes off and get onto the bed—or down on the floor, for that matter—and take him inside her, where he would make that wet, wet heat even hotter, even slicker, until she was weak with the pleasure of it.

She made an incoherent noise as she stepped backward, just far enough to plant one hand on his chest, the other fumbling for his belt. He didn't argue this time, but he did say, "Let me help," untangling her fingers and opening the buckle.

She went for the button and the zipper herself, vaguely aware that her bottom lip was caught between her teeth and her hands were shaking.

He let her do it, and she pushed the jeans over his briefs before tugging them down, too. He stepped out of both and toed off his shoes before setting her away from him.

She glanced up at him, confused, expecting length-to-length contact, the heat of his skin burning into hers, but she understood what he was offering when it hit her that he was finally as naked as she was.

And then she looked, wondering somewhere in the back of her head if it was taking as long as it seemed—there was so much to admire: The firm line of his shoulders curving down to his arms, the solid expanse of his chest, and the hard, defined muscles of his abs above the nest of dark hair that sheltered his penis.

Which was long and hard, the plum of its head bobbing against his abdomen, the sacs beneath it round and taut.

And for now, he was all hers.

She reached out one hand wordlessly, and he pulled her to

him and onto the bed, rolling them over until she was beneath him and his mouth had found hers again.

"Are we still taking turns?" he murmured into her mouth, licking the curve of her bottom lip and then the line of her jaw. "Because I want to go again."

"Oh yeah?" But she couldn't finish the thought—couldn't really think, to be truthful—because he was already edging down the mattress, tasting the hollow of her throat, her collarbones, and finally her breasts.

Her fingers twined in his hair when he took one aching nipple into his mouth, rolling it on his tongue before suckling hard, drawing it deep into his mouth. That dizzying bolt of sensation arced through her again, breast to belly, and then lower, until she was squirming with it.

She hadn't forgotten how well he could make her squirm, either. She'd just never imagined that he'd have a chance to do it again.

His hands were everywhere then, stroking, exploring, teasing, and she gave herself up to it, boneless and liquid. He didn't just make her feel good—he made her incoherent.

Everything that held her together was loosening, sliding apart, until she was nothing but need and impulse. The sensation should have been scary, but it wasn't—what frightened her was how much she liked it. How good it felt to let go and ride out each new crest of pleasure without thinking about it, without planning when or where she would touch him, or how she would respond when he licked a hot, wet path from her breast to her hipbone.

And what was scariest was that with Ty, she didn't feel it only in bed. With Ty, the concept of coloring inside the lines and making tidy little lists went right out the window.

Ty made her want to scribble on the walls with every color possible and then stand back to see what she'd created. He made her forget there was such a thing as a list of any kind. He made the idea of a plan seem like something strange creatures on a distant planet did.

But right now—oh, God, yes, right now—with his finger gently thrusting into the slippery heat between her legs, all of that was unimportant. As far-off and vaguely perceived as the dark bulk of the furniture in the room and the expensive curtains hanging at the windows. As oddly amusing as the girl in the painting above the bed, chaste in her white ruffles and picturesque bonnet.

You shouldn't be watching this, she thought absently as she arched her neck, seeing the painting upside down. *This is already rated NC-17.*

She groaned as Ty slid another finger inside her, stroking down with them both.

"Oh, God," she managed, digging her heels into the mattress as he thrust deeper. She felt too full already, stretched in the best possible way, but she knew there was more.

"You mean, oh, good?" he asked, using his other hand to pull her thighs farther apart.

"Mmmm," she murmured. "Definitely . . . good."

Then he moved between her legs, pulling them over his shoulders and circling her thighs with his arms. "You know, I dreamed about you a couple times," he said, idly parting her, sliding a fingertip through the lush wet heat. She whimpered as he circled her clit, which was already swollen and aching. Slow and drawn-out and all-night-long didn't seem like such a good idea anymore—when he finally touched her there, she was going to explode. "And every time, I woke up swearing I could taste you."

"Ty . . ."

"But I have to find out if I was close," he murmured, leaning down to press gentle kisses to her pubic bone, her damp curls, and finally to slide his tongue along her cleft, parting the lips gently, even more gently nibbling each one, until she was squirming in earnest. It felt so good, each lazy swirl of his tongue dizzying, but she knew he was far from finished.

She remembered all-night-long from that weekend, too.

He lifted his head to look up at her, and his eyes were dark with pleasure. "Even better than I remembered."

She shivered—evidence of his pleasure, especially when he was focused on hers, was an amazing turn-on.

And then he bent to his work again, and she couldn't think clearly anymore. He was licking her slowly, his fingers moving in and out of her in rhythm at the same time, and she was so close now, there was no stopping it. She could feel the orgasm trembling through her, and she wanted to cry out for him to stop, to come inside her first, but it was too late, and it was too damn good anyway—it broke hard, humming along her legs and deep in her belly, bright and white hot, a starburst.

He stroked her down from it gently, his fingers nothing more than a whisper of contact, pressing his lips to her belly at the same time. She drew a shuddering breath as he finally crawled up the bed, lowering himself over her. She wrapped her arms around him, holding on, breathing in the scent of him—crisp and spicy at the same time, the musky smell of her arousal still on his lips.

"I wanted to do that together," she murmured when she found her voice.

"So you got a bonus," he said, burying his face in her hair. "I've been wanting to taste you again for so long, making you come is my bonus."

She reached between them for his cock. It was rigid and hot in her hand, the head pulsing in anticipation when she circled it with one fingertip, wet with a pearl of semen.

He groaned, thrusting into her hand, and then pulled away just as quickly. "Shit—I don't have a condom in here."

"I'm on the pill," she whispered, reaching for him again. The last waves of her orgasm were still vibrating between her legs, and she wanted him inside her now. "And you don't have anything . . . communicable, do you?"

"I swear," he said, taking a deep, steadying breath as she stroked his cock, tip to base.

"Me either," she told him. "Please . . ."

He positioned himself over her as she spread her legs, and leaned down to kiss her as he thrust inside. His tongue swept through her mouth as he plunged deeper, bracing himself above her, but she wanted him close. Wrapping her legs around his waist, she slid her arms around his neck, tugging him down to her, skin to skin, his chest hard against her breasts.

As good as it had been just minutes ago, this was so much better. She moved with him, taking him deeper, arching up to meet him, shuddering with the force of it as his heart pounded against hers. Everything was blurred but the heat where they were connected, dark and wet and endless.

His head reared back suddenly, and she found him staring at her, those dark, dark eyes smoky and intent. She couldn't look away. She held on to his shoulders, riding it out with him, only distantly aware of skin smacking skin as he ground into her, and one of the box springs complaining with a rusty whine.

He stroked deeper, and suddenly said, "Now, Maggie. Come for me now."

It always worked—the sound of his voice, gruff and strained as he held back, waiting for the first ripple of her orgasm deep inside, was enough to send her over the edge. With a strangled cry, she let go as it thundered through her, and shuddered as he spilled inside her, again and again, his chest heaving against her.

She hung on as he slowed down, resting his damp forehead on hers. And when he started to pull away, to pull out of her, she hooked her legs tighter around him, nuzzling his neck with her lips.

"Stay," she whispered. "Just a little longer."

He settled onto his side, pulling her with him, and stroked her thigh with one lazy hand, kissing her forehead at the same time.

But she hadn't missed the ironic twist of his brow when

she asked him to stay put. She was just glad he wasn't going to call her on it, out loud, at least, right away.

She ran her open palm over his chest in circles, enjoying the weight of him inside her, and wondering how long she could stay awake and make sure the one night she was going to allow herself with him would last.

The sun was streaming in the window when Maggie opened her eyes, batting wildly for the alarm clock. Where the hell was it? It was shrieking, which was weird, because she always set it to music.

Then she realized that the window across the room wasn't her own, and that the huge, warm weight at her side was Tyler, and that she wasn't home at all.

She was in a guest bed in the Hamptons, with Ty, who had definitely made good on her all-night-long wishes. She twisted her head to face him, repressing a smile when he suddenly snored, reaching for her unconsciously. She stroked his hand, which had come to rest on her hip, and was leaning down to kiss his shoulder when she realized the alarm clock was still screaming.

Except there was no alarm clock, she discovered when she turned toward the night table. What the hell was that noise?

Pushing back the sheet gingerly so she wouldn't wake Ty, she swung her legs out of bed and searched the floor for his shirt. She tugged it over her head, frozen in place when the shriek became intelligible.

"Help! Oh my God, somebody help!"

It was a female voice, and whoever it was, she was screaming. Outside on the back lawn, it sounded like, which was strange because it was barely eight o'clock.

Running to the window, Maggie threw the sash up and looked down at the terrace and the grass beyond.

It was Shelby, clad in a short nightie and a robe belted

so loosely at her waist, it was about to slide off one shoulder. She was barefoot, and still screaming to wake the dead.

But it wasn't working, because the body on the lawn beside her didn't move.

Chapter Eight

Lucy was just coming out of her room when Maggie opened her door. Her hair was standing on end, and she was only semidressed in a baby doll T-shirt over a pair of pajama pants with fuzzy yellow ducklings on them.

"What the hell . . . ?" she said. She looked confused and only partly awake—the eyeliner she hadn't removed last night had made dark gray smudges beneath her bottom lashes.

"I don't know, but come on," Maggie said, pulling her own T-shirt into place over her shorts. Tyler was right behind her, his hair spiked up in tufts, and wearing last night's clothes.

The three of them pounded down the stairs, with Connor right behind them and Whitney leading the way. Everyone but Whitney was barefoot—her little black mules tapped against the ballroom floor as they all headed toward the French doors, which had been flung open and left that way.

Paige was standing on the terrace facing the lawn, stock still, a sage silk robe wrapped around her. It was so thin, Maggie could see the pointed angles of her shoulder blades and the delicate bracket of her hip bones. She was barefoot, too, and her dark gold hair was scraped back in a ponytail. Marty had his arm around her shoulders, but he didn't seem too steady, either—as she watched, his knees trembled, and he curled his right hand into a fist that he put up to his mouth.

"Help me," Connor said to Tyler, gesturing at Shelby. She was still screaming, her voice nothing but a tortured rasp by now, and she had sunk to the grass beside the body, which Maggie could now see was Drew.

Oh, God.

Tyler followed Connor, and together they lifted Shelby up and dragged her onto the terrace, where they put her in a chair as far away from Paige as they could find. Lucy went to Paige, who had begun to shake, and took her hand, stroking the back of it by rote.

Which left Maggie, Whitney, and Lake, who had just appeared, to edge closer to the body as Nell and Ethan emerged from the ballroom. Nell sank into the first chair she came to, but Ethan rushed to Paige's side, pushing Marty out of the way to put his arms around her. She shrugged him off, sinking to her knees on the cool stones, tears running down her face. Ethan went down with her, but he kept his distance. Maggie could hear the low murmur of his voice, but not what he was saying.

"Is he . . . dead?" Lake asked. She was pale with shock, her eyes huge in her face and her slender arms wrapped around her torso. "I mean, has anyone . . . checked for a pulse? Should we call 911?"

"He's dead," Whitney said flatly. "Look at his head. And his neck. Jesus."

Maggie glanced up at her, but she simply seemed drained, not malicious, although it was hard to tell beneath her pointy little sunglasses. She looked like a new-wave Bette Davis with her frizz of bleached hair and the black silk robe. No one had worn slippers with heels since the 1940s.

Maggie shook off the thought and stared down at Drew. Someone had to take his pulse, just to be sure. She knelt in the grass beside him, her stomach clenching. She wasn't cut out for this. He was lying on his back, his neck twisted at an impossible angle and his arms and legs sprawled out in a loose X. Worse, his eyes were open, staring out at the beach, an expression of angry surprise on his face. She couldn't blame him for that.

She swallowed hard as she touched two fingers to his neck, hoping she was in the right place for a pulse. Nothing. She inched to the left and then the right, trying to ignore how cool his skin was even in the early sunshine, and how sickly pale he was already, nearly translucent.

It was harder not to notice that he was as stiff as the proverbial board. Dead? No question.

She stood up, suddenly dizzy and petrified that last night's dinner was going to make an appearance right there on the grass. *The crime scene,* she thought wildly. *If there's a dead body, it's a crime scene.*

She glanced at Tyler, who caught her gaze and frowned. Leaving Connor with Shelby, who was now hiccupping and shuddering as if she were the bereaved fiancée, he strode across the lawn and pulled her away from Drew's body.

"Hey," he murmured, angling down to look her in the eye. "You okay?"

She nodded, grateful for the strength of his hand, which she realized she was clutching hard enough to break a few bones. She wasn't okay, and he knew it, but she wasn't going to faint and she wasn't going to throw up and she wasn't going to scream. For now, that was the most she could hope for.

The whole scene was like a Norman Rockwell painting as imagined by Wes Craven—the sky was a bright, clean swath of blue, the garden borders were an artist's palette of colors against the jewel green grass, and the miniature spire and white trim of the guesthouse were solidly American gothic, homey and comforting. The problem was, a group of relative strangers had wandered into the picture, half dressed and pale with horror, and a twisted corpse was sprawled in the center of it all.

"It's just . . . I can't believe it," she said weakly. "He's dead. It's just . . ."

"Impossible," Tyler said grimly. "I know. But it's not just possible, it's true. The question is, why? What the fuck happened last night?"

Just then Bobby staggered onto the terrace, looking not far from the walking dead himself. He was green instead of gray, but when he saw what everyone was looking at, the blood drained from his face.

"Oh my God," he rasped. "Oh my sweet good God. What the hell . . . I mean, what . . . ?"

He glanced around wildly, settling his gaze on Whitney, who hurried over to him, her heels slapping viciously at the stones.

"Drew's dead, Bobby," she said. Her mouth was set in a tight line. "Why don't you go back inside? You look awful."

"But I . . ." He broke off, tears welling in his eyes as he stared back at her, and bit his bottom lip. "I just don't know . . . oh, shit. *Shit!*"

"Bobby, go," Lake snapped at him, getting up from a lounge chair. "Paige is standing right there, and after Shelby's hysterics, she doesn't need to see you freaking out." She was holding on to her own shock and rage by a very thin thread, Maggie thought.

"You don't know . . ." he said, shaking his head, and then he started to cry in earnest. Whitney hissed something at him, too low for Maggie to hear, and jerked him around toward the doors, giving him a shove when he didn't move.

At least Paige seemed oblivious to the rest of them. She was finally sitting, perched on the edge of the terrace with her feet in the grass. The tears had slowed, but they'd left glistening tracks on her cheeks, and Ethan was still beside her, still murmuring what Maggie assumed was soothing nonsense. Lucy had dropped into a lounge chair a few feet away, and Maggie cringed at her blank, devastated stare. So much for nothing worse happening.

Nell was edging toward Drew now, her hair falling against one cheek as she tilted her head, examining him as if he were some lab specimen laid out for observation. She caught Maggie and Tyler watching her and drew her mouth into a moue of grief as she marched toward the house.

Marty had disappeared, presumably to break the news to Sybil, and Tony was still notably absent. Maybe Whitney had waylaid him inside. Connor had steered Shelby into the house, as well, his expression grim. But Lake was still on the terrace, crouched against the wall, her arms wrapped around her bare knees.

"I just don't get it," she said, shaking her head. "I mean, what the hell happened? It doesn't . . ." She choked back a sob as the tears started, and looked up at Maggie with glassy eyes. "I just don't understand."

"No one does," Tyler said, letting go of Maggie's hand to crouch beside her. "I know you were a friend of his . . . Do you want me to, I don't know . . . ?" He let the thought trail off and glanced back at Maggie, his brow furrowed in a combination of helplessness and concern.

They were both clueless here. Neither one of them knew anyone very well, aside from Lucy and, in Tyler's case, Paige and Drew.

"No, it's Paige we have to worry about," Lake said, drawing the back of one hand across her wet cheeks. "And we have to . . . call the police."

"I can do that," Lucy said, appearing at Maggie's side. Her hair looked as if she'd combed it with a blender—she'd been running her hands through it without thinking. "But maybe you can help Ethan get Paige inside. She shouldn't sit there looking at . . . him." The last word was squeaked out in disbelief.

"Right," Lake said, standing up and sniffling hard. "I'll do that."

She walked away, leaning over Paige and taking one of her arms as Ethan stood and took the other. They led her through the French doors slowly, helping her up the step, and she obeyed like a sleepy child. She was in shock—the paramedics would have to come, too.

Then the three of them were alone, and they turned to stare at the body in the grass.

Lucy broke the silence. She wrapped her arms around her middle, shaking her head in rueful desperation. "I am so fired."

"I think he must have fallen from there," Tyler said, pointing up at the charming balcony on the third floor of the guesthouse fifteen minutes later. The white railing enclosed a space roughly twelve feet by five feet.

They were sitting at a wrought-iron table on the terrace, doing what Maggie had begun to think of as guard duty. When Lucy had gone in to call the police, Tyler had told her to keep everyone else inside, because they'd probably tracked up the lawn and the rest of the site pretty badly already. He and Maggie had been elected to watch over Drew's body. *As if he's going anywhere,* Maggie thought.

"But what was he doing on the balcony?" Maggie asked him. "Whitney said last night that he was afraid of heights."

He squinted up at the balcony again, shading his eyes with one hand. When he was concentrating that way, his profile took on the ferocity of a hawk. "Yeah, she did. But is that really what you'd consider a height?"

"It's at least twenty-five feet off the ground," she told him, pulling her bare feet underneath her. "I'd consider that a height, sure, especially outside. Some people who are really phobic can be too scared even to take an escalator."

"Really?" Tyler looked askance at her, and she nodded. "Okay, so that's bad. That means someone convinced him to go out on the balcony, where he probably didn't want to be."

She followed his gaze back to the guesthouse, picturing the scene and shuddering. If someone had threatened him . . .

"And I'm guessing someone pushed him," Tyler added,

frowning now, crossing his arms over his chest. "Why else would he fall backward like that?"

Oh, God. She closed her eyes, trying to breathe deep. Worse? This was beyond worse. This was beyond trouble. This was murder, most likely.

This is what happens when you don't have a plan, she thought. Not that you could plan for murder, of course, but someone should have thought about . . . well, *something.* The fact that Drew hadn't seemed ecstatic about the PR blitz staring him in the face. The fact that someone had invited his nasty producer with her eccentric bird, and one costar who appeared to hate him and another who was ready to strip off her clothes if he looked at her the right way, even in front of his fiancée.

God, his fiancée. She imagined Paige inside, still white with horror and disbelief, and remembered the girl she'd met just yesterday afternoon, so excited about her wedding plans and the hotel she wanted to open, and her soon-to-be husband's comeback in the movies . . .

Maggie swallowed hard, trying to stem angry tears. She should have seen it coming yesterday in the car. Not murder, exactly, and certainly not that it was Lucy's fault, but disaster had been written all over this weekend. She'd just ignored it. She'd made her own plan—antiques and beach time and free food and design porn.

Tyler reached across the table and took her hand. So much for planning. She hadn't had a sensible thought in her head since she'd seen him yesterday afternoon.

And part of her didn't care. It was the part that wished they were still upstairs, tangled in her bed, sleepy and naked and touching each other.

Okay, it was a shallow, selfish, pouting part of her, but it was there. Even if she'd promised herself last night would be the only night. The end. Another hour or two in the morning wouldn't have counted.

"We should go in there," Tyler murmured, and she realized he had cocked his head at the guesthouse.

"Oh, no," she whispered back fiercely. "No. Absolutely not."

"Why? The police aren't here yet," he argued, stroking the back of her hand with his thumb. Mesmerizing her, or trying to.

She jerked her hand away. "But they will be. Any minute. It's a crime scene. God, I can't believe I'm saying that. A *crime* scene, Ty. We can't disturb it."

"We won't. We'll be careful. We'll look, not touch." He took her hand back, leaning toward her, his tone smooth and confident. He might have been discussing the breakfast menu. "I just want to see if anything's in there. Anything that points to someone here as a murderer."

"And what are you going to do if there is?" she argued back. "Make a citizen's arrest? *No.*"

"Come on, Maggie." His eyes were innocent, earnest even, but she set her jaw and shook her head.

"I know you're curious," he said, scraping his chair closer. "Didn't you ever see *Risky Business*? Sometimes you just gotta say what the fuck."

"Didn't *you* see it?" She snatched her hand back again, incredulous. "Don't you remember Guido the Killer Pimp? The Porsche in the lake? 'Who's the U-boat commander?'"

He arched a dark brow at her, his mouth quirked in the beginning of a grin. "But it all worked out in the end, right? Princeton. The girl. Joel scored, Maggie."

"You are completely insane," she said cheerfully, getting up. "First you buy a hotel on a whim; now you want to be Sherlock Holmes."

He raised both brows this time, confused. "What does one thing have to do with the other?" He followed her to the edge of the terrace, taking hold of her elbow. "Actually, don't answer that. I think I'm afraid of the answer. Just do me one favor—stand guard on the porch while I go inside."

"Oh my God." Even as she said the words she was following him, shaking her head, her heart hammering in her chest, but following him just the same.

That was the problem. She did want to see inside the house. She did want to poke around for a clue to who might have paid a visit to Drew last night. But the Maggie she usually was would never actually do it. That Maggie knew the rules, and followed them. That Maggie would have already been planning her statement to the police, her trip home, and a gracious combination thank-you/sympathy note to Paige.

And with Ty, that Maggie vanished.

She ran across the grass behind him, slamming into his back when he stopped to try the door, using his shirt to avoid leaving a print.

"Were you a criminal in another life?" she hissed, looking over her shoulder to make sure no one was coming. "Where did you learn that?"

"TV," he said. "That's where you find out all the good stuff. I can fly a plane in an emergency, too."

She jabbed him in the ribs with her elbow, and he grunted.

"Well, I think I could, at least. There, it's open." He turned around. "Are you coming? Or are you doing sentry duty?"

She swallowed hard. "Go," she said, and followed him inside.

It was dim and quiet, and she blinked to adjust to the dark after the glare outside.

Everything about the house was miniaturized—the entry hall was about the size of a postage stamp, and the living room just to the right was cozy, just big enough for a comfortable sofa, a club chair, and a bookcase fitted with a TV and a compact stereo. It was like the three bears' house, with a medium-sized chair for Paige and a big couch for Drew.

And room for a coffee table littered with bridal magazines, Maggie noticed with a pang. Videos in plain black cases were stacked on the floor beside the sofa, and two black-and-white pictures of Drew and Paige, arms around each other, soft-focused under a cherry tree, were framed on the wall.

Maggie stood in the tiny hall, arms wrapped around her middle. This was wrong. They were snooping, and they had no right to be, even if their intentions were good. And any-way, aside from some larger-than-life fingerprints, and possi-bly a convenient signed confession, she had no idea what she was looking for. "Find anything?" she called to Tyler, who had continued down the hall to the kitchen.

"Dirty laundry. The real stuff, not the metaphorical kind," he said, walking back into the hall. "Let's go upstairs."

But as soon as they'd turned toward the steps, the wail of a siren echoed through the open front door. It was getting closer, too.

"Shit," Tyler muttered, grabbing her hand and pulling her outside. Closing the door behind him, he gave Maggie a gen-tle shove in the direction of the patio.

They were seated at the table—slightly out of breath, but seated—when the French doors opened and two blue-uniformed patrolmen walked onto the terrace. The others, or most of them, were close behind.

The first officer stopped two feet from Drew's body, lean-ing over to squint at it before unhooking his radio from his belt. He was standard issue police—big and brawny, with a pair of mirrored sunglasses jammed beneath a heavy brow.

"Dispatch, I have a 10-55d. Go ahead and alert homicide, and send an ambulance, too."

The second officer stopped at the table and took off his sunglasses. They were much hipper, classic Ray-Bans. "I need you two to step toward the house, please. We're going to se-cure the scene."

"Certainly," Maggie said, getting up and nudging Tyler's ankle with her foot. He wasn't moving, frowning up at the policeman instead.

"What will happen now?" he asked. "And is someone tak-ing care of his fiancée? She was in shock, I think."

"An ambulance should be on the way, sir," the officer told him, folding his arms over his chest. He was just as big, if not as brawny, and his blond hair was brush cut. "And what happens next is we figure out how the victim died."

"His name was Drew Fisk," Tyler said, and stood up. He took Maggie's hand, and they walked over to the others. Lucy, Ethan, and Lake were standing just outside the doors, but the others had gone back inside and were gathered at the big ballroom window.

Connor was sober, Whitney was frustrated, Lake was grieving, Marty and Ethan were still shocked—a whole range of emotion was visible. The only thing Maggie couldn't tell as she walked into the house was which one of them had hated Drew enough to kill him.

Chapter Nine

"More coffee?"

Tyler shook his head, and Lucy nodded in sympathy. One more cup and he'd probably lift off the ground spontaneously.

In the two hours since the patrolmen had arrived, the "accident" scene had been secured, the techs had shown up with their cameras and other equipment, and a pair of detectives had split everyone into groups, sending some of them into the drawing room, some into the library, and some into the family room off the kitchen.

Tyler had drawn the family room with Connor, Lake, Lucy, and Maggie. And they were all going crazy with the waiting in their own unique ways.

He stood up and stretched. If Connor cracked his knuckles one more time, he was going to slug him. Hard. Right in his movie-star nose.

Maggie looked up from the table where she had spread out what looked like a rainbow of Post-it notes and odd scraps of paper. She was helping Lucy cancel tonight's party, which wasn't the easiest task she could have chosen to pass the time—when Lucy wasn't brewing another pot of coffee, she was fluttering around the kitchen, cell phone to her ear, or muttering random things like, "Caterer!" and "The tent is a wash."

Tyler had no idea what she was talking about most of the time, but he felt sorry for her anyway.

Maggie gave him something that passed for a smile as he walked past her, stopping just long enough to trail his fingers through her hair. She looked exhausted, despite the nervous gleam of caffeine in her eyes, and he didn't blame her. They'd fallen asleep for good sometime around four, if the clock was right, and Shelby's screams had woken them before eight.

And it wasn't as though they'd been sitting around meditating all night, either.

He repressed a frustrated groan and walked over to the window overlooking the pool. The water glittered in the morning sun, an unbroken sheet of blue glass, and the dunes were visible in the distance, prickly with beach grass.

He hated this. Caging him was the best way to piss him off. Even when the cage was as elegant as this one, the sensation was too much like handcuffs.

The detectives had made it clear barely a minute after they'd introduced themselves that no one was leaving the house or the premises until they had a lead on what had happened. It didn't matter that he'd been invited for the weekend, and had been planing to stay—now he *couldn't* leave. Couldn't take Maggie out to lunch, couldn't rent a boat out on the bay, couldn't stroll down to the beach for all he knew. Police department orders.

And Maggie hadn't been any happier about it. He'd seen that expression again, the darting, furtive glance that was checking for an exit loophole, if not an escape hatch. The difference was, she didn't want to be caged with him, no matter what had happened last night.

He looked over his shoulder at her, but she was deep in Post-it note land, that delicate brow furrowed, muttering as she sorted them into multicolored piles, which obviously went way against her grain. A glass of ice water sat untouched on the table beside her, dripping perspiration onto the smooth oak surface.

If he watched her for much longer, he'd be tempted to grab her up and kiss her until that frown disappeared. Until her eyes widened in startled pleasure and she opened up to him, naked and wet and . . . Maybe it would be a better idea to empty that glass of water over his head, now.

He couldn't remember a weirder weekend. Well, there were two, actually, but they were weird in different ways. This one, well . . . all he'd been expecting was a diversion, a few days away from the steamy salt air and the boredom of his desk. Paige was sweet, and her praise of Moonstone had been so genuine, he'd been flattered she'd wanted his advice about the hotel she wanted to open. "Something stable, for Drew and me," she'd said. A luxury retreat that could be a retreat for them, too, from Hollywood and the press. *In case this movie doesn't work out* had been the unspoken end of that sentence, he was pretty sure.

Now it didn't matter. Drew was dead.

He wondered if Drew had known it was coming, what he'd thought about in that last half second before he'd blacked out. Paige? His career? A simple *Oh, shit?* Had he wanted a drink, or to kiss his fiancée one last time?

Had he known he was going to die?

Tyler's gut clenched at the idea. It was too close to home, too sickeningly familiar. He'd worked his way past it a long time ago, taking every moment as it came, welcoming every opportunity and living as though regret was a dirty word.

Until he met Maggie.

Five years and he'd never gotten her completely out of his mind. That was the thing, and it wasn't just a bruised ego. It was the fact that no matter what it was, he couldn't make it go away. He dreamed about her roughly once a week, and for the first six months after she disappeared, he'd spotted her dozens of times on the boardwalk or walking down Duvall Street. In Mallory Square one night, he'd actually grabbed a girl by the elbow, positive that the dark hair and the subtle sway of her hips proved it was Maggie, and almost got a lungful of pepper spray.

And that wasn't like him. He didn't stay put, even before that other weekend that had changed everything, the one that had convinced him to scrap the bar exam and buy the hotel. Even now, he wasn't always there. Moonstone was in good hands, because he'd chosen those hands himself, and because he liked to take off on the spur of the moment.

It had been years since he'd had anything like a real relationship. A couple of weeks at most and he was itchy, ready to move on, even if he was only moving on to a ski slope in Colorado or a couple of days in L.A. instead of to another woman.

He just wasn't a digging-in kind of guy. So the idea that one woman—a woman he'd spent only three days with, naked or not—had implanted herself in his brain was infuriating. And confusing as hell.

And last night hadn't exactly cleared things up.

Fuck it, he did need more coffee. If he rocketed out of the room, that would be a good thing.

Maggie was trying to make sense of another of Lucy's scrawled notes when the detectives walked in.

"Sorry to keep you waiting, folks," the male said, striding into the room and dropping inelegantly into the nearest chair. "Quite a crowd here today."

"Betsy Szabo," the female said, shaking Tyler's hand first, and then making her way around the room. Her long, faded blond hair hung in a braid down her back, and her gray suit was hopelessly wrinkled.

What was more, she looked as if she'd been crying.

"Would you mind if we used the table here to ask each of you some questions?" she asked, gesturing at the pile of notes and lists Maggie had organized.

"Of course." She grabbed up the first of them before the detective could—police investigation or not, she wasn't sorting through that mess a second time today. When this was over she was buying Lucy a proper FiloFax.

Regina wasn't coming to help her, of course—no one was coming in or going out, at least for now. No one but the police, of course. Since she and the others had been herded into the family room, she'd watched the officers at work on the lawn, snapping photos, marking out what she assumed was evidence, and finally loading Drew's sheeted body onto a stretcher, all of them glancing up at the house from time to time.

Wondering about the people inside, and what they knew of Drew's deadly fall and the hours that had preceded it, Maggie thought. Just like she was.

"We can start with you, since you're right here," the male detective said, pulling out a chair with a heavy sigh and flipping open his notebook. "Joe Vaughan, by the way. And you are?"

"Maggie Harding." She sat down, smiling uncertainly when Detective Szabo sat beside her and laid a hand on her arm.

"Did you know Drew—I mean, Mr. Fisk—very well?"

Maggie blinked at the reverence in her voice. "No, not well," she said. "I just met him yesterday."

Vaughan narrowed his eyes at her—bloodshot, suspicious little eyes, too small in his fleshy face. "How did you come to be invited this weekend, then?"

"I'm a friend of Lucy Petrillo's," Maggie explained, gesturing at her friend, who waved uncertainly at them from across the kitchen counter. She was still on the phone. "Lucy works for Fountain Publicity, the firm that was handling the party tonight. Paige agreed she could invite me along."

"Nice of her." He managed to make that sound questionable, too.

"You must have been excited, huh?" Szabo said, her eyes focused on a point just past Maggie's left ear. Imagining herself at last night's dinner party, probably.

"I'm a designer, so I was interested in seeing the Redmonds' house." When the other woman stared at her in disbelief, Maggie added weakly, "And meeting Drew and the others was very nice, too."

Vaughan made a note on his pad, and Maggie frowned. If they thought she was the chief suspect here, the police department had more problems than they could handle.

"How did Drew"—Szabo caught herself and shook her head—"I mean, how did Mr. Fisk strike you? Last night, I mean. Emotionally. Did he seem depressed? Upset? Unhappy?"

"Well, I didn't know him, so I can't tell you what he was like usually," Maggie said carefully, "but last night was a little . . . awkward. By the end of the evening I think he was angry and frustrated."

"Really? By what?" The detective rested her elbows on the table, leaning closer, but the posture made her look like an eighth grader at a lunch table, drooling over a piece of gossip, instead of a woman conducting an investigation.

What the hell was she supposed to tell them? She knew what had seemed off to her last night, but it was all speculation, an outsider looking in and possibly misunderstanding everything she heard.

She realized Connor was staring at her, his mouth set in a grim line, and she looked away. Was she supposed to tell these detectives that yesterday afternoon it had seemed to her that Connor would have thrown his own party if Drew dropped off the face of the earth?

"Ms. Harding?"

"Sorry, I was just trying to remember what happened when." *And what I should mention while Connor is listening.* "He seemed a little put off by the crowd, although I don't know if you can really call fourteen people a crowd, and at one point before dinner he wandered into the conservatory to play the piano. And during dinner . . ." She glanced at Connor again. Lake was sitting beside him, her legs curled beneath her, gray smudges of exhaustion under her eyes.

"Even before dinner, Shelby was . . . well, flirting with him. He didn't seem to take it very seriously, but then Whitney made a comment about his past relationships after dinner, and he seemed furious."

Connor grunted, and Lake looked up, her eyes wide. She seemed to be holding her breath, waiting for Maggie to reveal something else. *But I don't even know what I'm revealing now, except that most of the people here weren't especially interested in being polite to Drew or Paige.*

"Was he . . . drinking?" Szabo had lowered her voice to ask this, and she bit her bottom lip. "He'd been in rehab, you know, twice. He really wasn't a very happy—"

"Betsy!" Vaughan barked. "We're talking about last night, not his childhood."

"He wasn't drinking," Lake said softly. "Not that I saw, at least. But he was angry. Shelby was practically drooling on him, and Paige was upset. Whitney's little remarks about his past didn't help."

"What about his past?" Vaughan asked, twisting around to face her.

"Well, he wasn't exactly a monk," Connor put in. His laugh was a sharp burst of contempt. "A few years ago, you'd be hard pressed to go ten feet in L.A. without running into someone he slept with—or someone who claimed to have slept with him."

"But Paige had to know that," Maggie said. "Didn't she?"

"I'll ask the questions." Vaughan's tone was sharp. There was an awkward pause before he said, "Was Ms. Redmond aware of his reputation?"

"Yes," Lucy said, dropping her cell phone on the counter and crossing the room to collapse into the chair opposite Connor and Lake. "At least that's what she told me. But it's not something that needs to be discussed at a dinner party, you know?"

"Especially not with Shelby doing her best to make it clear she'd like a turn with him," Connor grumbled. "Fucking twit."

"She kept cooing about how sweet he was on the set," Tyler added, running a hand through his hair. It spiked up like exclamation points. "And she mentioned at least twice in front of Paige how much she liked his trailer better than hers. As in, she'd spent a lot of time in his trailer, and she wanted everyone to know it."

Then everyone joined the Shelby bashing. Betsy Szabo's lips parted as she listened, Maggie noticed. Her notebook lay untouched on the table, and her eyebrows lifted higher with each gossipy new tidbit.

Joe Vaughan had opened his mouth to speak at least twice before he seemed to realize he had lost control of the situation, and then he held his hand up, snapping, "Quiet!"

In the abrupt silence, Maggie waited for one of the others to giggle, or for Vaughan to start assigning detention.

"I'll take statements from each of you, but one at a time," he said gruffly. "Until then, shut the hell up already."

"Do you have anything else to add, Ms. Harding?" Szabo asked stiffly, uncapping her pen. She was expecting a few demerits, for sure. "Anything else you noticed about his behavior?"

"Not about his behavior," Maggie said, "but I do know that after we screened the movie last night, Paige went up to the master bedroom here in the main house, and Drew went back to the drawing room. If he joined her, I didn't hear him—my room is down the hall in the east wing."

"You screened the movie?" Szabo's tone was faintly jealous, but she flipped to a new page in her notepad, all business, when Vaughan glared at her.

"Tell me a little bit about the others," he asked Lucy. "Whitney . . ." He checked his notes. "Craig. And Tony Angelino."

"What about them?"

"What do they do, exactly?"

Maggie felt a flicker of apprehension at his voice. It was too casual, too bland. *Oh, you've got to be kidding,* she thought.

"They produced *The Truth About Simon,*" Lucy said, confused. She wrinkled her brow, sitting forward. "Didn't Paige explain who everybody is?"

"She did, yes," Vaughan said, stuffing his hands in his pockets and pacing toward the French doors. "But I didn't want to bother her with too many little details. She's grieving."

Lucy shot Maggie a look that said, *Well, duh,* and Maggie shrugged helplessly.

"What does a producer do?" the detective went on, gazing out the windows, his voice still carefully neutral. "Do they . . . read scripts, for instance?"

Connor rolled his eyes with a groan and threw his back against the sofa. "Let me guess—you have one, right? A hard-hitting look at an unsolved case and the gruff yet warmhearted detective who finally solves it?"

Lake bit back a smile, but she didn't stop him, and Maggie didn't blame her. Szabo's fan-club-president act seemed sweet compared to this.

"No," Vaughan snapped. When he turned around, his florid cheeks were even redder. "I mean, yeah, I have written a screenplay, but it's not a police drama. It's a . . . police comedy."

"Oh, that makes all the difference." Tyler's voice was wry. He arched a dark eyebrow at the cop from the depths of a club chair by the fireplace. "I'm sure no one will mind you asking about *that.*"

One more word from any of them and the purple vein in Vaughan's forehead was going to explode. But before he could protest, a cell phone in his jacket pocket shrilled.

"Vaughan," he barked into it, striding toward the far end of the room. "Yeah, I know. It was bound to happen." He paused, listening. "Well, handle it. Post someone outside for the duration. Right."

Flipping her notebook shut, Szabo followed him. "What's up?"

"The word's out that Fisk is dead," her partner said bleakly. He regarded the rest of them with distaste. "And the media frenzy has begun."

Chapter Ten

"Vultures," Maggie whispered. She was crouched behind a hedge with Tyler, eyeing the crowd beyond the iron gates. "Don't they know someone is dead?"

"Of course they do," he said. "That makes it even juicier. How? Why? Murder or an overdose? It doesn't matter. It makes good copy for the *Star*, and even better gossip for the water cooler."

There were at least fifty people out there, and half of them seemed to be reporters. Maggie had stopped counting the boom mikes a while ago, because the crowd was too fluid— they were all angling for a closer look, edging others out of the way to press their noses between the heavy bars of the gate. The major networks were all represented, too—the traffic on Gin Lane had to be a nightmare with all the vans parked haphazardly, half on the grass and half on the pavement.

"What if it was just an accident?" she said, watching his face. "It could have been, you know. Maybe we're all freaking out for nothing. Last night got a little ugly, so we're all jumping to conclusions. I mean, people don't just go around killing each other." Her shoulders sagged when he gave her a rueful smile.

"Well, they're not supposed to, anyway," she insisted. "I mean, this isn't some mafia hit or a drive-by shooting."

"It must be nice to live in your world, Mags," he said, circling her waist with one arm. "Your world sounds very peaceful."

"Okay, maybe I'm a little naïve, but it doesn't seem like a crime of passion," she said, shrugging him off to cross her legs more comfortably on the grass. It was surreal to be hiding in the bushes when they had a house roughly the size of a small airport at their disposal, but they'd both wanted to check out the crowd, and the atmosphere inside was so thick with tension and grief, she'd barely been able to breathe. Paige had been given a Valium after the detectives left, and Lucy had put her to bed, but the others had stalked around the house all afternoon. When Whitney had turned on the local news, Maggie had had enough.

"Why?" Tyler said, stretching out beside her. "Because he wasn't shot? Because it's . . . well, bloodless?"

She considered that. "Maybe. It's just that we heard Paige go upstairs last night, and she seemed as shocked as any of us this morning. She's not the actress in the family."

"But she does have a motive," Ty argued. "Jealousy."

Maggie pictured Paige as she'd met her yesterday, her face open with excitement, all golden good looks and simple, elegant grace. Not exactly your typical murderous type, not that Maggie knew anyone who fit the description. But then she brought up the image of Paige after the screening, drawn and three shades paler, her doe eyes suddenly too big for her face, wounded and confused.

"Maybe," she relented, even though she felt guilty even saying the word aloud. "But there are a lot of other people to consider."

"Such as?"

She thought about that, and frowned at him again. "I don't know. I mean, I don't know any of them well enough to guess. Shelby wouldn't kill him—at least not until she'd slept with him."

"And she'd get a lot more mileage out of being his girlfriend on the side than from being his killer," Tyler pointed out.

"True." In the gathering twilight, Ty's face was shadowed, but she could just make out the dark stubble on his jaw. He'd never shaved this morning. It made him look slightly dangerous.

Like he wasn't dangerous enough, to her, at least, fully groomed.

Behind them, a twig snapped, and then a voice called out, "Hey! You there! Did you know Drew?"

A second voice shouted, "Can you tell us what the police are saying?"

Maggie scrambled to her feet as Tyler grabbed her by the elbow, dragging her away from the pair of reporters who had trudged through the foliage on the other side of the fence and found them.

"No comment," Ty said tersely, and Maggie called back over her shoulder, "Do you have no sense of scruples?"

"You're the ones hiding behind the hedge," one of them called back, sticking his mike up against the fence. "What's going on in there? His fans want to know!"

A flash went off, momentarily blinding her, and she threw her arm up in front of her face. Down the lane, brush crackled as the rest of the crowd caught on, running toward the reporters.

"Don't say anything else," Ty warned her, hurrying her along the hedge until they found the break near the driveway. They crashed through it and ran along the pavement. "So much for being sneaky."

"If that's what celebrities have to go through every day, I'm glad I'm not famous," she said. He was still holding her by the elbow, and she tugged it out of his hand gently. His hand was a warm, heavy weight on her bare skin, and his body was comforting beside her, huge and solid.

But thinking that way lay madness. When they were allowed out of here, he'd head back to the Keys where he belonged, and she'd go back to Manhattan, to her comfortable little apartment, and her neat desk at the office, with its color-coded files and the fragile pot of ivy she'd been babying for two years now.

Enjoying the feel of him next to her was a habit she was going to have to break. Even when imagining her life at home suddenly made the inside of her chest feel hollow.

"We should scrounge up some dinner," he said, opening the front door. "I'm starved."

"Scrounge?" she said, tilting her head up to look at him. "I guess we can't exactly call for take-out, huh?"

"Probably not." They walked past the dining room and turned into the hall toward the kitchen. "We'll just see what we can find and throw something together."

"I'm a recipe kind of girl," she told him dubiously.

"I'm beginning to get that." Without warning, he looped an arm around her shoulders, pulling her close. "But I'm trying to teach you the joys of living dangerously."

"I'm not wired that way," she said, knowing it was a lie, at least when it came to him.

He opened the door to the pantry and walked inside. "Oh, I think you are."

"It's a short. I'm having it fixed."

He snorted and ran his fingers along the shelves. "We could be cooped up here for a year and not starve. There's enough pasta here alone to feed a small army."

"Pasta's good," Maggie said, examining a jar of garlic and basil sauce that seemed to have been imported from Italy. "It's easy, at least."

She jumped at a heavy thud on the other side of the wall, and Tyler grabbed her again. Then he reached out and switched off the light, pulling the door almost shut.

She was about to ask him what the hell he thought he was doing when she heard voices. He was listening hard, a dim, indistinct shape in the dark.

She strained to listen, too, tracing the voices in the vague map of the house in her head. They were coming from the stairs on the other side of the wall, stairs that led up to the bedrooms in the east wing.

"What is the matter with you?" It was Whitney's voice, sharp with exasperation. "You can drop the act now—it's getting a little old."

"You don't get it, do you?" It was Bobby who answered, and he sounded only slightly less drunk than he had last night. He'd disappeared after the police had left, and Maggie bet if they searched his room they'd find an empty bottle or two.

"Get what, for Christ's sake?"

"I didn't do it, you stupid bitch," he shouted. Something thudded against the wall again, and Maggie shrank away with a start. *Do* it? Did he mean kill Drew?

Something scrabbled on the polished stairs, and then a ringing slap landed on someone's cheek. Tyler gripped her hand tighter.

"What . . . mean?" Only some of Whitney's words were audible through the wall now, but her tone came across loud and clear. She was furious and shocked.

"I didn't kill him, you idiot! I fucking passed out! You don't understand . . . I've known him since we were kids, just about, and he's like . . . he's like a brother to me. He was, I mean. Christ, I can't fucking believe this. I didn't do what you wanted, and he's dead anyway!"

"Shut up!" That much was clear enough, too.

Maggie held her breath, glancing up at Tyler. Bobby might not have killed Drew, but Whitney had wanted him to. *Whitney.* The producer of his new movie, a woman who had staked at least part of her future income on his success. It didn't make any sense.

She heard a noisy squawk and then something beating frantically against the wall—Bogart. Bottles of olive oil clinked against huge cans of tomato paste and pumpkin pie filling.

"Let go of him!" Whitney's voice was shrill now, and

Maggie started again when something that sounded very much like a body hit the wall. She reached out to grab a teetering bottle of balsamic vinegar.

"It's all over," Bobby was moaning now, his voice raw with fury and shock. "All of it. And I can't even tell him . . ."

"You're not . . . anything." She frowned when Whitney's words faded in and out. "Nothing . . . on."

Bogart cried, "Come on!" and Maggie heard them clomp upstairs, Bobby muttering and Whitney hissing at him.

She glanced up at Tyler again when it was quiet, and he reached out and flicked on the light.

"Well, that was interesting," he said dryly.

"I don't understand," Maggie whispered, sitting down on the top ledge of a stepladder. "Why would Whitney want Drew dead? He's the star of her new movie."

"Maybe that's just it," Tyler said. He was still holding a bag of fusilli, and he turned it over in his hands absently. "Maybe the publicity around his death would sell a lot more tickets."

"No one's that greedy," Maggie said, but her voice sounded uncertain even in her own ears. "Anyway, it doesn't really matter. She may have wanted Bobby to kill him, but he swears he didn't. And I think I believe him—he was so shocked this morning, he looked ready for smelling salts."

"But Drew is still dead," Tyler argued. He raked a hand through his hair again. "And with those two planning his murder, it seems a little too coincidental that he fell accidentally, don't you think?"

"Probably." She pressed the heel of one hand to her forehead. A nagging, dull pain had set in right behind her eyes. This weekend had turned into a modern-day version of Alice down the rabbit hole. Every time she turned around, something morbidly fascinating was going on.

Tyler tilted his head down, looking at her with concern. She was suddenly too tired to protest when he said, "For now, let's take care of you. Eating first, sleuthing later."

* * *

"It's awful," Maggie said. "Just awful."

"The pasta?" Tyler said, scraping the bottom of his bowl with a dripping fork. "That's the last time I cook for you."

She rolled her eyes at him. "No, not the pasta. *That.*" She pointed at the huge TV across the room. Tyler had switched it on while they were waiting for the sauce to heat, and one of the celebrity "news" shows had featured nothing but reports of Drew's death, interspersed with clips from *Hollywood High* and some of his movies.

"With his comeback in *The Truth About Simon* set for later this summer, Drew Fisk's career seemed on the upswing again," the ruthlessly cheerful host said. Her red hair didn't move even when she turned to face another camera. "Now, of course, that career is over, and his fans are left to mourn what might have been."

"Oh, God, turn it off," Maggie groaned. "Drew was a very nice guy who went through some bad times, but they're making it sound like we missed the second coming. And they don't seem too concerned with how he died, either."

Tyler took her bowl and put it in the dishwasher with his own before flipping off the set. She'd loaded an odd assortment of other dishes into the machine while he cooked—it looked as though at least a few of the other guests had come down to forage for food while she and Tyler were outside. She'd found four or five Frosted MiniWheats stuck to the inside of a bowl, and the remains of some of the party sandwiches that had been delivered yesterday and a single-serving lasagna on the counter, still in its black plastic tray.

Lucy had come down briefly, looking more tired than Maggie had ever seen her. She'd made a pot of tea for Paige, filling an insulated carafe, and had nibbled a few pieces of pasta with butter before going back upstairs. "I talked to her mother," she'd told Maggie, "and she's coming as soon as she can." Ethan wouldn't stop hovering, though. Lucy had finally snapped at him to make dinner for himself and Nell

and let Paige get some sleep. Maggie wondered if the sandwiches or the lasagna were his.

She and Tyler hadn't turned on many lights, and the family
room stretched away from her, a dim, shadowy expanse of
angles and corners, the furniture hulking in heavy, motionless groups, a breeze stirring the sheers at the window overlooking the pool. She shuddered, wrapping her arms around
her middle. Someone had committed murder here last night,
while she and Tyler and the others had been upstairs asleep.
Well, at least some of them had been asleep.

"You want a drink?" Tyler said. "Or a game of pool?" He
reached over and smoothed a stray hair off her forehead. It
was so hard not to lean into his hand. *Don't be nice to me,*
she thought. *I'm all wrong for you.*

"I suck at pool, remember?"

"Right." He grinned. "I could teach you, though.".

"Maybe tomorrow. I think I'm going to go upstairs."
Alone. Please. Don't tempt me anymore.

"Well then, I'll join you," he said easily, switching off the
light as they walked into the hall.

Whoever said telepathy worked had obviously never
tested it on her brain, Maggie thought mutinously, hating
how much she loved it each time his arm brushed against the
bare skin of hers. She was going to have to dress in long
sleeves and pants tomorrow.

They had just turned the corner into the upstairs east wing
hall when they heard voices, and they both froze just two feet
from her bedroom door. It was Nell and Ethan this time,
Nell's lighter feet pounding up the stairs ahead of her husband's.

"I don't even know why I came," she hissed. "If I dropped
dead, you probably wouldn't even notice."

"Nell, don't be absurd," Ethan answered. For a man in the
middle of an argument, he sounded remarkably cool. Maggie
could picture him, pushing those fussy glasses up on the
bridge of his nose, his forehead creased in distaste. Ethan
didn't strike her as the fighting-in-public type.

"Absurd? I was gone for three hours this afternoon, out by the tennis courts. Did you even notice I was gone?"

"Of . . . of course I did," he said, the surprise in his tone making it far too clear that he'd had no idea where she'd been, and had never once missed her. "But Paige's fiancé is dead, Nell. We're her friends. I'm just trying to help her through this."

A door slammed, and the elegantly framed Picasso on the wall beside Maggie quivered. She reached up absently to steady it, wondering who had ended up on the other side of that door and who would be bunking on one of the sofas tonight. Not that it would be a hardship—if she wasn't mistaken, the drawing room sofas were upholstered in imported raw silk. The Axminster carpets didn't look too uncomfortable, either.

Beside her, Tyler held a finger to his lips, and she froze, listening as, around the corner, Ethan said, "Nell, open the door. *Nell.* I'm not going to ask you again."

Silence. The stillness practically hummed with the force of Nell's rage, even from down the hall.

Without warning, Ty grabbed her arm and the doorknob to her room at the same time, and she found herself shoved over the threshold into the darkness, where she banged her ankle on the secretary just inside the door.

"Ouch," she whispered, pulling her head back when she realized she was talking into his shirt. It smelled like salt water and sea pines, but beneath it was the unmistakable scent of hard, hot Ty muscle. She allowed herself one deep, irresistible lungful before she said, "Turn on the light."

"Shhh." His hand snaked out and clapped over her mouth, but before she could wriggle away—or bite him in protest—she heard Ethan's muffled footfalls on the antique runner in the hallway as he headed for the back stairs, just down the hall from Maggie's room.

When Ty removed his hand, she ducked under his arm and reached for the lamp on the secretary. He closed the door and leaned against it.

"Sorry about that," he said when she turned around, blinking in the bright glare of the light. "Stealth is usually the way to go when you're eavesdropping."

"Which we shouldn't have been doing," she said, tucking her hair behind one ear. One day, she had to figure out how to say something like that without sounding like a prim maiden aunt.

"Why not? We just did it an hour ago." He strode past her and sprawled on the bed as though he had every right to be there. Of course, after last night, there was no good reason for him to think otherwise. Her brilliant plan to resist his charms wasn't going very well so far.

Especially when he was so out of place against the busily feminine and floral comforter. He was too big, too dark, too male. He was crushing the sprigged lilacs into dust, not reclining on them.

And rather than ordering him off the bed, what she wanted was to strip away the fussy linens, and then strip his clothes off him. Not necessarily in that order.

Stop staring, she told herself. As a distraction, she went to the window, peering down at the lawn and out at the dark, quiet bulk of the guesthouse. Amazing to think that just twelve hours ago, they'd all been gathered on the grass, staring at a dead body.

"Because this really isn't any of our business," she said finally. Well, there was a lame answer. It really wasn't fair. They'd spent the night in what some people would have called sexual gymnastics only to wake up to murder this morning, and he was as calm and collected as ever. Then again, she couldn't blame a little surprise homicide for her own case of nerves—Ty was the one who'd thrown her off balance the minute she saw him across that hangar-sized ballroom yesterday afternoon.

"We're not talking about tax returns, Maggie; we're talking about murder," he argued, and she turned around to find him toeing off one shoe and then the other.

She swallowed hard. She hadn't said the part about stripping his clothes off out loud, had she? *Keep going, big boy,* a lusty little voice in her head whispered, while her good sense rapped a metaphorical ruler across her knuckles and demanded, *Get him out of here while you can still remember your own name.*

"Exactly," she said quickly, nodding. "Murder. We're in the middle of a murder investigation. And that's no time to . . . to eavesdrop," she finished helplessly.

Obviously, she'd lost every shred of her intelligence somewhere in the sheets last night. The plan had been to get him out of her system, hadn't it? One night, full stop, no more temptation. No more impulse kissing. No more accidentally-on-purpose touching. No more wondering if he still tasted as good as she remembered.

What a dumb plan.

"If you ask me," he said, shrugging out of his shirt and staring up at her, "it's the perfect time to eavesdrop. Aren't you curious about what the hell happened last night?"

"Of course I am," she said, realizing that her voice sounded far away in her ears. She was having a hard time taking her eyes off his chest. The ruler came down again, hard. *Stop it.* "But we don't—I mean, *I* don't know these people. Eavesdropping doesn't get you too far if you don't know what anyone's talking about in the first place."

"Not if you listen hard enough. Like we did before dinner." He grinned, and she could see the devil in his eyes. "I'm not stooping to a drinking glass against the wall, though—it's strictly serendipitous eavesdropping for me. And I think I'm done for the night." He narrowed his eyes at her thoughtfully. "You don't talk in your sleep, do you?"

God, I hope not. "Of course I don't." She scrambled for something else to say when he climbed off the bed and walked toward her, cupping his hands on either side of her waist and leaning down to kiss the line of her jaw. "But I . . .

I don't think . . . I mean, maybe it would be better if you stayed in your room tonight."

"Why?" His voice was muffled in her hair now, and she shivered when he blew it aside to trace a hot path down the side of her neck with his tongue.

Why. *Yes, why?* "Because we're . . . we're in the middle of a murder investigation. It seems . . . I don't know . . . rude."

"We're not in the middle," he argued, sliding his hands beneath her shirt and up her back. Oh, that was good. Too good. "We're on the sidelines. Actually, we're way up in the nosebleed section, in the bleachers. At least for now."

He was right, of course. After the chaos of the crime scene officers and the detectives' questions—not to mention Bobby's minibreakdown and Nell and Ethan's argument—the house was finally quiet. There was nothing for them to do now. Nothing related to the murder, anyway.

Maybe if she gave in and spent one more night with him, she'd get him out of her system for good. In a permanent, definitely-not-going-off-the-deep-end way. Since he was tugging her shirt over her head, it seemed like the sensible thing to do, at least at the moment.

She groaned as a thrill of anticipation skittered up her spine—he was unfastening her bra now, his hands huge and warm and so very strong. There was no arguing with those hands, not when the two of them were stuck in this house anyway for the duration, with nothing more pressing to do than exactly what they were doing. *And will be doing more of soon, and probably most of the night,* the bad girl's voice in her head reminded her.

She curled her fingers into the belt loops of his shorts, pulling him closer, and tilted her head up to look at him. His eyes were dark blue now, just like they'd been last night before he'd kissed her into blissful incoherence. There was no arguing with his mouth, either, she thought as it came down on hers, hot and hard.

Suddenly, he broke off the kiss, and when she opened her eyes, he was fumbling in one of his pockets, frowning.

She sighed and held out the foil-wrapped condom she'd found in his back pocket. Arguing was definitely over. She was way ahead of him.

Chapter Eleven

Tyler rolled onto his side with a satisfied groan. Beside him, Maggie drew in a shuddering breath and reached for the sheets. Her cheeks were still flushed, her lips still dark and plump. He smoothed a hand over her brow as her eyes fluttered closed, and she smiled.

His heart was still hammering in his chest, and his legs were tingling with the power of the orgasm that had roared through him, but he felt peaceful enough to drift off to sleep for days without worrying about anything.

Not murder, not the hotel, the staff of which expected him back tomorrow night, not what was going to happen when it was time to leave and he and Maggie had to say good-bye again.

Not when she was so peaceful, too, sprawled in the circle of his arm, her breathing finally slowing, her body warm and soft against him. Not when she was, consciously or not, giving him the chance to study her.

"Mmmpf," she murmured, snuggling closer, rubbing the top of her head against his shoulder.

He laughed, leaning down to press his mouth to her hair. It smelled like apples, and something a little spicier. "Say again?"

"I don't think I'm very good with actual speaking at the moment." She groaned, stretching again, dragging her toes along his calf. "Every cell in my body is still stunned."

Not surprising. They'd wrestled each other out of their clothes, suddenly frantic once she'd handed him the condom. Pill or no pill, it was safer for both of them, and Maggie had made putting it on a lot more fun than not using one at all.

The memory of her sitting astride him, her eyes dark with abandon, her hair wild around her face, rippled through his gut, and his cock pulsed at the image. It was only minutes ago, and he was nearly ready to start all over. Because she felt so good, for one, tight and hot and so incredibly wet as he slid inside her, but mostly because she let go so completely when they made love.

As if inhibition was a word she'd never heard of. As if the moment was all that mattered. As if she was made of nothing but impulse and need and desire. Watching her come made him high in a way he'd never experienced anywhere before.

She wasn't all about plans and lists and doing the right thing at the appropriate time. He'd found her wild side, and he intended to keep an eye on it, at least while they were here.

"Still awake?" he murmured, sliding his hand over her shoulder to cup one breast.

"Barely." She opened one eye to look at him. "Why?"

"If you can keep your eyes open for ten more minutes, I'll have a surprise for you," he said, leaning down to circle one damp nipple with his tongue.

She groaned softly. "Does it require getting out of this bed?"

"It will be worth it, I promise."

She yawned and curled onto her side as he got up. "I'll give it my best shot."

He patted her ass, hard, as he headed into the bathroom, grinning at her surprised "Hey!" and leaned down to turn on the tap in the huge tub. It was built for more like four than two, an elegant expanse of tile with a separate shower. He checked the water temperature and then poked through a basket on the shelf above the toilet, coming up with three different packets of bath salts, a vial of scented oil, and two bottles of foaming gel. Paige wouldn't have any trouble running a hotel—she was practically doing it already. He'd found two of his favorite magazines waiting for him in his own room, as well as three brand-new DVDs of recent movies.

Pomegranate, jasmine, something called appleberry, and green tea and cucumber were his only choices, scent-wise. He shook out the last one under the running water. Vegetables were at least marginally manlier than fruit.

The room was steaming up already. He took down two huge, fluffy towels and laid them on the counter, then dimmed the lights and found a conveniently placed book of matches to light the candles lining the top shelf and the back of the toilet. He stood back to take a look at his handiwork. Perfect. As long as Maggie was still awake.

"Definitely worth getting out of bed for."

He turned around and found her in the doorway, naked and still flushed, a pleased smile on her face.

"It was supposed to be a surprise," he said, holding out his hand.

"It was. Until I heard the water running." The smile broadened into a grin, and that adorable little mole on her cheek bounced higher.

"After you," he said, standing back to let her climb in—and to admire the view from behind as she lifted her leg to test the water with one cautious toe. She had the most delicious ass, curved just right, and just lush enough to squeeze.

"It smells wonderful," she said, sliding in and shuddering as the steaming water washed over her. "Actually, it smells a little bit like . . . salad."

He shrugged sheepishly. "Yeah, well." Climbing in, he faced her and unfolded his legs along hers, resting his feet against her hips. "Consider it marinade."

"Whatever it is, it feels good," she said, leaning back and sliding lower, the water covering her breasts and shoulders. "I would kill for a tub like this at home."

Home. He repressed the urge to ask her what her apartment was like. He wanted to know everything, but he was sure if he started asking, she would clam up and this moment would be over before it had even started.

Something innocent, then. Something she'd brought up herself.

"Can I ask you something?" he said softly, taking one of her feet in his hands and stroking it beneath the water.

Her mood changed immediately—just a slight shift, a barely noticeable tension in her shoulders. But she opened her eyes to look at him, and the reflected candlelight glittered in them. "Sure."

"What did you mean when you said your sister was going to join the circus?"

She froze, staring, and then burst into laughter so quickly, she splashed water out of the tub. "I'm sorry," she said, taking a deep breath as her shoulders stopped shaking. "That was the very last thing I expected you to ask."

He grinned, taking back the foot she'd dislodged. "I've had pictures of clown shoes and rubber noses in my head since you mentioned it."

"Well, Jeannie did try to join," Maggie said, floating her hand on top of the water, making ripples. "Remember when we were talking about being afraid of heights? Jeannie is. Well, was. She thought tightrope walking would cure her."

"In the circus," he said, fascinated.

"Uh-huh." She shook her head fondly. "But what she didn't know was that you kind of have to be born into stuff like that. So she took time off from work and learned to skydive instead."

"To cure herself of her fear of heights."

She sighed. "That's my sister."

Interesting. Sounded like Jeannie Harding wasn't afraid to live dangerously. "Do you have other siblings?"

"Four." She looked up with a weak smile. "Jeannie, Matt, Emily, and Theo. I'm number five."

"What does Jeannie do now?" he asked, curious.

"She's taking hypnotherapy courses and working part-time at a dog groomer's." It cost her an effort to say it out loud, he could tell. Her cheeks were flushed again, but the water had already cooled.

"What about the others?"

"They're not here," she teased, pulling her foot out of his hands and nudging it between his thighs.

He groaned at the jolt of arousal as her toes kneaded his cock, then slipped lower, gently pressing against his balls. *Not so fast, sweetheart.* He wasn't ready to give up yet.

Family wasn't the sexiest subject in the book, but that was exactly why he'd wanted to broach it. Sex was easy, at least between the two of them. She could look at him slantways and he'd be hard within seconds. It was the other stuff they'd never explored, and no matter how often or how fully she bared her body to him, he wanted at least a peek at her soul.

"I know," he said, grabbing her foot back and holding it tight. "The others are a country group. The Harding Family Singers. No, wait. The Harding Family Hoedown! Much better."

"We're from New Jersey," she said dryly, splashing him. "But strangely enough, Emily is a singer. She teaches music and sings in piano bars. Torchy stuff, standards."

"What about your brothers?"

She tried to tug her foot away, but he held firm. Sighing again, she said, "Matt works at a bookstore in Seattle and is writing an environmental newsletter in his spare time, and Theo bartends when he's not trying out for reality shows."

He laughed. "A well-rounded group. What about your—"

"Don't even get me started on my parents," she warned him, attacking with her other foot. She planted it against his belly.

"You don't sound like a proud little sister," he said lightly.

"I am proud of them," she argued, shaking her hair away from her face. It had gone wavy in the humid air. "They just

. . . scare me. They let life blow them all over the place. They don't have a *plan*. Not for more than five minutes anyway."

"Ah. The famous plan." He leaned back, letting her hostage foot loose and grabbing the other one. "You're big on planning, huh?"

"There's nothing wrong with being prepared," she said stiffly, sitting up and drawing her knees toward her chest. Her eyes still shone with candlelight, but she was frowning again. "Or with having a goal and sticking to it."

"Not a thing," he agreed. "But there's nothing wrong with being flexible either."

"Well, my siblings are so flexible, they're like the Stretch Armstrong of families," she said, shaking her head. "Last year, Jeannie was into cosmetology. This year it's hypnotherapy. Next year it could be feng shui. And she wonders why she never has any money in the bank and her marriage broke up."

Hmmmm. He let that slide, knowing she would back off completely if he dug too deep. "Did you always want to be a designer?"

"Well, mostly," she said carefully, not looking at him. "When I was a kid, I wanted to be an artist, but it's not exactly a stable career, you know? In college, I decided to focus on interior design, so really, it's the best of both worlds."

Compromise never sounded like the right choice to him, not when it came to how you lived your life, but he had a feeling she didn't want to hear that. She sounded so stubborn, so practiced, as if she'd made the decision long ago but was still trying to convince herself it had been the right one.

Which meant she probably wasn't happy, at least not the way she could be. She'd never given up everything to go after what she wanted, he bet, so she'd never faced the possibility of losing it all.

She'd never had a moment to imagine that her life was over, and it wasn't the life she'd wanted to lead.

He fought down a hot spark of anger. Now was not the time to tell her she wasn't as smart as she thought she was.

And it probably wasn't the time to suggest that she needed to loosen up, either. It was her life, after all. It was just that the way she apparently lived it made it a lot clearer why she'd fled that hotel room five years ago.

And it wasn't going to be easy to change her mind about doing it again.

Change her mind? About what? A future with him? A lifetime? That wasn't what this was about. Was it?

No. It was about this moment. This tub, and the things they could do in it.

"You're wrong," he said softly, leaning over to spread her knees apart, dropping light, damp kisses on the top of each one. "The best of both worlds is getting clean—and getting down and dirty at the same time."

"That sounds promising," she murmured. She looked relieved and aroused at the same time, her lips parted, her eyes wide. She leaned toward him, too, and he caught the scent of her—damp, warm, and definitely a little bit like salad.

"The best thing is, you can get down and dirty so many ways," he told her, nudging her thighs apart until her knees hit the sides of the tub. She eased down, letting her arms go slack and leaning against the headrest, her breasts bobbing just above the water, the nipples rosy and erect now.

"Just start with one," she breathed, closing her eyes as he slid his fingers over the mound between her legs, gently circling the heel of his hand against the wet curls.

"For now," he said. Like he could think past this minute anyway, with her breath catching in the slender column of her throat as he pressed harder. She was already letting go, forgetting their conversation to savor the pure sensation.

He scooted closer so he could lean down and cup one breast in his other hand, weighing it carefully before he lowered his head, licking the underside and the soft slope of the top before circling the nipple with his tongue. He swirled around it lazily as he massaged the plump mound of flesh between her legs, slowly, letting the pleasure build.

She was speeding up, though, arching her hips, thrusting against his hand, and to distract her he drew her nipple into his mouth, fastening his teeth around it gently.

She groaned when he bit down, just hard enough to spike the sensation, and her arms thrashed, slapping the water. He blinked the stray droplets away, suckling her hard, ignoring a sudden stab of pain in his hips. He wasn't built to sit like this, legs spread around her, but he was enjoying himself too much to move. When he turned his hand around, thrusting his middle finger inside her, he grinned around the rigid bud of flesh in his mouth at her sudden jolt of pleasure.

"Tyler," she groaned, wiggling farther down in the tub, trying to take him deeper, but he wasn't going to let her set the pace. She was too close already, and he wanted this to last.

"Patience," he murmured against her breast, nuzzling its wet surface. It was slick and smooth, heated beneath the cooler skin of water. Given the chance, he would lick her dry, head to foot.

He slid another finger inside her, and she shifted to accommodate it, a soft, surprised noise escaping her mouth. When he nestled his thumb between her lips, brushing against the swollen knot of flesh inside it, she gasped.

He set the rhythm then, kissing her breasts so lightly, nothing more than a whisper of his mouth against her skin, and thrust his fingers deep, then deeper, in and out, as his thumb circled her clit. She groaned, and he felt her orgasm start as her thighs tightened. She teetered there for a moment, right on the edge, riding the sensation as long as she could.

Then it broke, rushing over her in a wave that made her whole body arch. Her mouth fell open, an astonished O of pleasure, as her head fell back. The fragile flesh around his fingers pulsed, and he caught his breath, arousal kicking in so hot and urgent that he wanted to haul her out of the tub and onto the floor, where he could bury himself inside her for the next two days, at least.

Instead, he held on, gentling his fingers, easing her down

as she gasped, waiting for the moment when her eyes would open and she would see his face.

When it did, he smiled. She was so flushed and steamy and thoroughly satisfied, she looked like some wild underwater creature from a really sexy planet.

"So," he said, grinning, "that's one way . . ."

"It's a good thing sex works off calories, because it makes me hungry," Maggie said, buttoning a loose white shirt. Her fingers still felt weak and tingly—Tyler hadn't stopped with just the first way to get down and dirty. "Although," she added, watching him zip his jeans, "it's really a vicious cycle. Maybe there's something dietetic downstairs."

He snorted. "Good sex calls for good snacks," he said, crossing the room and pulling her against him roughly. "We deserve something sinful."

She grinned against his shirt. They did. And something to drink, too. She felt as though she'd run a very long, if extremely pleasant, marathon.

She pulled on a clean pair of shorts and shook out her damp hair. Tyler had washed it when the water had finally grown too cold and they'd stood up to turn on the shower. She'd never met another man who could make shampoo such a turn-on.

"Come on," he said, opening the door. "I think I saw some chocolate cake in the fridge."

"I feel a little funny doing this," she whispered as they crept into the hallway. It was well after midnight now, and the house was dark and silent. "I mean, I don't usually raid the kitchen when I'm a guest somewhere."

"We've been left to our own defenses by murder," he argued, his voice low as they started down the stairs. "I don't think Paige is going to begrudge us a few leftovers."

That was probably true, of course. Paige most likely had no idea what or if anyone had eaten since this morning, and more likely didn't care.

Following Ty down the stairs, she wondered if Paige had had a plan. Maybe meeting Drew had been a complete surprise. Maybe she'd wanted to go to cooking school, or learn photography. Maybe she'd wanted a job, although that was a little hard to imagine when she clearly didn't need one and spent her time doing useful things like volunteering for charity already.

Either way, everything she'd counted on happening in the next few months was over—the wedding, the honeymoon, maybe even finding a house of their own. Even if Paige had charted out everything to the last detail and color-coded it from here to eternity, it wouldn't matter much now.

On the other hand, Maggie's plan was finally working. She'd been going to the gym—maybe not four times a week, but once at least, and that counted. She'd reupholstered the chair she'd found on MacDougall Street and painted the kitchen a delicious buttery yellow. She'd finally found a deli that had perfect sweet and sour chicken, and she'd been dating again. Dan Rothman. He was a very nice podiatrist she'd met when Lucy thought she was getting a bunion last winter. She'd taken on three new clients in the last month, and two more were this close to signing with her. And she was thinking about getting a cat.

Suddenly, it seemed as though there should be more to the plan than decent take-out food, a possible pet, and a guy who examined people's feet, even if he didn't mind watching the occasional chick flick and never forgot to call her back.

Tyler put his hand on the small of her back as they turned the corner into the hall that led to the kitchen. It was so dark, she couldn't see her hand when she held it out, but somehow his gesture seemed more sexy than protective. Dan had waited till the fifth date to kiss her good night, and that was apparently as far as he was willing to go, even now that they were on date seven.

She let herself relax into the warmth of Ty's touch, not

even bothering to argue with herself. They were here for the duration, whatever that might be. She was going to enjoy it, and him, until it was over.

As they walked into the kitchen, Tyler stopped so suddenly, she almost gasped. He stepped in front of her, and she wriggled beneath his arm, squinting into the shadows.

Then she wished she hadn't. Someone was standing by the window in the family room that overlooked the back lawn, frozen in place, the faint moonlight glinting off a highball glass in one hand.

Her pulse sped up crazily, and Tyler wrestled himself in front of her again, taking two more cautious steps onto the cool Italian tile that surrounded the center island.

The figure never moved. It was a man, she thought, still trying to make him out, and it had to be someone staying in the house—no stranger was going to break in and then pour himself a double shot before absconding with the valuables.

Finally, he drank from the glass, and when his head tilted back, she saw an indistinct gleam of light on a pair of glasses. Ethan. If he turned around, the moonlight would reflect off the top of his head.

But he didn't. He remained motionless, his gaze fixed on the lawn and the shadowy outline of the guesthouse beside it. Right where Drew had been found this morning, she thought. He might have been standing there for hours, he was so firmly fixed in place.

Grabbing Ty's hand, she jerked her head toward the hallway. He followed her, his scowl evident even in the darkness. When they'd walked as far as the entry hall, she whispered, "Ethan. He got kicked out of his room tonight, remember?"

He nodded, but he glanced back over his shoulder as he did. "He's staring at the guesthouse," he murmured.

"I noticed." She felt for his hand and slipped hers inside it. "Let's skip the snack, huh? He looks like he might snap if we startle him."

"Let's see if there's anything to drink in the drawing room," Ty argued. "I'm not cupping my hands under the faucet all night."

She sighed and let him lead her down the hall again. Yesterday afternoon, she'd been impressed with the house's combination of grandeur and charm, but right now it seemed like the perfect place to film a murder mystery or a horror movie. All those expensive architectural details cast weird shadows, and there were too many doors and corridors. She wasn't exactly unhappy about having Tyler's hand to hold at the moment.

She clapped a hand over her mouth when something in the drawing room crashed with a brittle tinkle of glass, and even Tyler jumped. *Don't scream*, she told herself. *In the movies, screamers always get it first.*

The thing to do was hide under the nearest desk or possibly in a closet. Until morning, at least. But for some reason Ty was charging toward the source of the noise, and she was following. Standing in the dark hall alone with creepy Ethan in the family room and someone in the house guilty of murder wasn't an option, either.

"No good choices here," she muttered out loud, hanging on to the back of Ty's shirt. They rounded the corner into the drawing room just as the alarm went off, a shrill electronic whine loud enough to make her eardrums bleed.

Footsteps pounded down the hall, and this time she did shriek, grabbing Ty's shirt. But it was only Ethan, skidding to a stop in the doorway.

"What the hell is going on?" Despite the confusion creasing his brow, his voice was so mild, he might have been asking if Ty could fix him a drink.

Ty turned on a light, shaking his head. "There's no one in here, but a window is broken." He had to raise his voice over the shrieking alarm.

Ethan knew the security code and disappeared into the

front hall to turn off the alarm, but by then Connor had come running into the room with Lake right behind him.

Lucy was next, her hair wild and her threadbare "Georgia Peach Bowling League" T-shirt barely covering her neon green panties.

"It's nothing," Ty said. "Well, it's something, but it's over. Someone tried to break in. Maybe one of the fans outside the gate."

Without warning, the alarm stopped, and the room was plunged into silence. But the shrill ghost of it hung in the air. Maggie's ears were still ringing with it.

Lake ran a shaky hand over her head, ruffling her short blond hair. "Well, that was a crappy way to wake up. It took me an hour to fall asleep, too."

"You want a drink?" Connor said quietly, walking toward the bar and looking over his shoulder at her.

"No. But if you want to watch TV with me, I wouldn't say no." In the dim light from the single lamp, she looked breakable, her shoulder blades sticking out like wings and her legs as long and thin as a colt's.

"You got it," Connor said, putting an arm around her. As they walked out, Maggie heard him say, "Ten bucks I find an *I Love Lucy* rerun. I have, like, radar for that show," and Lake's relieved giggle.

He seemed like a different person to Maggie. Yesterday he'd been as arrogant and self-absorbed as any movie star cliché. But Drew's death had hit him hard, and she hadn't heard one nasty or sarcastic word from him since they'd discovered the body. Except about Shelby, of course, who deserved it.

"It's like a nightmare," Lucy said, shrugging helplessly as she walked back into the hall. "At least Paige didn't wake up."

A moment later Maggie heard her on the stairs, telling Marty and Whitney to go back to bed, and then Ethan came back into the room.

He stared at the shards of broken glass on the polished wood, his glasses halfway down his nose and the little hair he had tufted around his ears. He bit his bottom lip nervously before he looked up at them, hands stuffed in his pockets and his shoulders hunched forward. He reminded Maggie of a frightened turtle.

"What is it?" Maggie asked him with a sigh. She'd bet money she didn't want to hear the answer.

"I don't think it was a fan," he said quietly. "Paige told me someone tried to break in earlier this week, long before Drew died."

Chapter Twelve

The sun made everything feel better, Maggie thought the next morning. Brighter, naturally, but just plain better, too. Things didn't go bump in the daylight, especially not true-blue, cloudless Hamptons sunshine. Murder was really much better suited to after dark. It was ten A.M. now, and she and Lucy had escaped the awkward crush in the kitchen, where everyone was trying to fix what passed for breakfast at the same time.

Lying on a cushioned lounge chair by the tennis courts, she turned her face up to the sun and groped blindly for her mug of coffee. She could hear the rhythmic clink of Lucy stirring cream into hers.

"Regina had a few interesting things to share about Lake," Lucy said. The Sunday papers, with their screaming head-lines, were spread around her on the ground. She'd been giving Maggie all the gossip her boss had shared in their marathon of phone calls yesterday, and Maggie had explained what she and Ty had overheard between Whitney and Bobby.

At the moment, though, Maggie was resolutely keeping her eyes closed. Maybe if she ignored Lucy's voice—the same way she'd been ignoring the yellow crime scene tape festoon-ing the guesthouse—this whole bizarre situation would go away. She didn't want to know anything nasty about Lake. She liked her. But she'd liked Bobby, too, at least until he got too drunk to walk, and he'd wound up being Drew's would-be murderer, even if he hadn't gone through with it.

"Maggie?" Lucy said. Maggie could hear the scowl in her voice. "Are you asleep?"

She opened one eye and tilted her head at her friend. "No, sadly." When Lucy stared at her, she sighed. "What about Lake?"

"Turns out she and Drew had a thing a while back," Lucy said, setting down her coffee cup and tucking her legs underneath her. "A very hot and heavy thing, before Lake was well-known. Or known at all, I guess."

"Really?" Sitting up, Maggie glanced back at the house, recalling Lake's face when Maggie told her Drew was dead. She was grieving for a former lover, not just a casual friend.

"Really really," Lucy said, raising her eyebrows. "Regina said that Drew was really heavy into drugs at that point, and Lake was a big partier, too. At that point, her career was pretty much working the L.A. club scene, the parties, trying to meet whoever she could to score a bit part here or there. Then she met Drew, and they started partying together."

Maggie opened her mouth without any idea what to say to that, then closed it again. She wasn't judgmental, but she was surprised that she'd never heard about that period in Lake's life. She was everywhere right now—she'd starred in three movies last year alone, and had two more set to come out this fall. She was truly the It Girl of the moment, compared to Shelby's transparent It-Girl-in-Training act.

"It's weird, right?" Lucy said, scrunching up her forehead over her coffee cup. "I mean, I thought I would have heard something about it before now, but I guess since she wasn't really working back then, there weren't a lot of pictures taken. The paparazzi hate the unknown girlfriend shots."

"Which means she's probably worked pretty hard to cover it up, I guess," Maggie said.

"Exactly. Regina said when Drew went into rehab that time, it was a big wake-up call. She wanted to clean up her image and stop using, and she didn't want to trade on his name."

It fit, Maggie thought. At least it fit the little Maggie knew of her since they'd met. She was honest and down-to-earth and friendly, not a diva. She didn't seem to have any illusions about creating a Lake Healy, Movie Star persona because she was just Lake Healy, on ordinary girl who happened to act. And was adored by millions of fans, of course, but that wasn't really her fault.

"What's strange is that she's here at all," Maggie said thoughtfully. "I mean, with all the publicity she must get just when she walks out her door, and the PR Drew's movie and this weekend were supposed to attract, why would she want to link herself to him again?"

"That's what I don't understand," Lucy said, setting down her empty cup and stretching out on her chair. Her bare legs were slightly orange with self-tanner—she'd never learned how to put it on right. Last summer, she'd looked like an Oompa Loompa for a week. "She's not even in this movie with him."

"I know," Maggie said absently. She was remembering Lake and Drew talking in the drawing room that night, comfortable and oblivious to the others. And then Lake disappearing, not only during the after-dinner drinks, but for the whole screening, as well.

It made her a suspect. Well, possibly. It didn't make her look innocent, that was for sure. But while Lake might have wanted to get rid of Drew before he could use her new stardom to attract more publicity for himself, she couldn't really imagine Lake pushing Drew off that balcony. She'd loved him, or something like it.

That was the problem, Maggie realized, reaching for her cold cup of coffee. It was too hard to put the pieces together because there were simply too many. She'd been trying to relax all morning, letting Ty take his time showering and shaving—and giving herself some time to decompress from

another night of nonstop naked fun. She'd been trying to en-
vision the Kirklands' living room, which was her next project,
mentally matching fabrics with paint colors and rearranging
the furniture, but every time she closed her eyes she saw Drew's
twisted body on the lawn.

And what she really wanted to do was get out her notepad
and start making a list. Including, but not limited to who to
question about what, who had a history with whom, where
everyone had been last night after the party broke up, and
who stood to gain the most from Drew's death.

She wanted to plan, damn it. Because whatever the police
were doing, leaving them all here to whisper and sulk and
probably think up alibis was ridiculous. If she were running
this investigation, she'd be doing a much more efficient job
than Vaughan and Szabo were, and she wouldn't be trying to
sell a screenplay at the same time.

"I'm not even sure if Paige knows about their relationship," Lucy said idly, reaching up to pile her mess of curls behind her head. She was wearing the most absurd pair of
sunglasses Maggie had ever seen—huge rectangular frames
with lavender-tinted lenses—but they actually looked pretty
good on her. "Paige said she and Drew have been honest
about everything, but that's only as far as she knows, you
know? If he's admitting to drug use and rehab and other
fairly seedy stuff, she's not going to notice if he hasn't filled in
all the girlfriend gaps."

"He might have kept quiet about it because Lake asked
him to," Maggie said. "He seemed like a nice guy. And no one
really needs to know every sordid detail of her boyfriend's
past."

Except me, she thought mutinously. This was the other
problem. The more time she spent with Tyler, the more she
wanted to know about him. Girlfriends, lovers, casual flirta-
tions. Hell, she wanted to hear about his elementary school
crushes.

But you won't, she told herself, *because you won't ask.* It would be pointless. It didn't matter. Tyler wasn't hers, not really, and when the police finally let them go, they would say good-bye.

It was sensible. It was smart. It was a plan. A plan designed to keep her heart from getting broken. If they stayed together, Tyler would probably eventually want to do impulsive things all the time, like buying other hotels, or golf courses. Or islands! He'd want to move to Fiji, or Switzerland, or adopt six children in one fell swoop, and then God only knew what would happen to their lives.

She couldn't live like that. It wasn't *her*. She'd told him so. She wasn't wired that way.

But when he strolled down the lawn a minute later to tell them that the police had arrived, she took one look at his lopsided, still-sleepy smile, and his wonderfully touchable body in dark jeans and a plain red polo, and she wished, just for a second, that she knew a decent electrician.

Everyone had gathered in the drawing room. Joe Vaughan was pacing in front of the fireplace, and Betsy Szabo was sitting stiffly in one of the striped armchairs beside it.

"Is that everyone?" Vaughan barked.

"Yes," Lucy said waspishly, settling on the arm of the nearest sofa. "We didn't know you'd be taking roll."

Maggie elbowed her and sat down. He was a police officer, not the principal. Mouthing off would get her a lot worse than detention.

"Someone claiming to be Mr. Fisk's brother was picked up early this morning on a drunk and disorderly call. Can anybody verify who he is? He didn't have any ID on him, and he's not exactly what you'd call coherent." He looked at Paige, who was curled in the corner of one of the sofas.

She was still too pale, and her hair was combed back indifferently into a loose ponytail. She looked hollow, Maggie thought, and when she spoke, her voice sounded as if it had been scraped up from the pit of her stomach.

"Drew has a brother named Jack," she said dully. "He's an alcoholic and a user, and Drew always tried to take care of him, but he disappears a lot. Drew thought he might be bipolar, too, but he's never been diagnosed. Someone . . ." She paused and took a deep breath, studying the carpet before she looked up at the detective. "Someone tried to break in a few days ago. We thought it might have been him."

"If it was, he tried again last night," Tyler said, and Paige whirled around to look at him.

"What are you talking about?"

"It's okay," Ethan said quickly, putting a hand on her shoulder. He was hovering over her like a bodyguard, standing at attention beside the sofa. "I didn't want to upset you, because nothing happened, really. Some glass got broken, but no one got in—the alarm went off."

She pressed a shaky hand to her forehead. "I need to know everything, Ethan. I can't believe I didn't wake up. It's those stupid pills . . . I'm not taking one tonight, no way."

Lucy jumped up and went to sit next to her, sliding an arm around her back. "It's okay, Paige, you don't have to," she murmured. "We just thought you needed the rest. I'm sorry."

"And in the meantime, anything unusual should be reported to us immediately," Vaughan said, scribbling in his notepad. "You should have mentioned the earlier break-in attempt, too. Until we find out what caused Mr. Fisk's death, we need to know everything that goes on, Ms. Redmond."

Finally, Maggie thought as Paige nodded at him. She wished she could shout, *One of them is responsible,* but she had a feeling the cop was already catching on. He'd been scrutinizing the group since she and Lucy walked in.

Marty and Sybil were sitting together in the loveseat near the bay window, and Tony was at the table at the other end of the room, paging through *Variety* too quickly to actually be reading it. Whitney was pacing with Bogart on her shoulder, and Lake and Shelby had staked out seats beside Maggie. Bobby was sprawled in a chair near the French doors, his face gray and his hair raked back in uneven spikes. His feet were bare beneath a ratty pair of jeans. Everyone was unhappy, but for what seemed like wildly different reasons— Shelby was clearly bored, Bobby was hung over, Tony was restless, and Marty and Sybil simply looked uncomfortable, like guests who had overstayed their welcome but had no place else to go.

Connor, on the other hand, had taken a seat near Tyler and was listening intently as he described what had happened last night. The comb marks were still fresh in his hair, and he had pulled on a plain white shirt over a pair of chinos. He looked like a Boy Scout.

Nell was sitting as far away from Ethan as possible, clear on the other side of the room from his post beside Paige, her silky hair falling over her face like a curtain as she bent over one foot, methodically removing her toenail polish. The smell of it was sharp and acidic.

"We'll have to dust for prints outside there," Vaughan was saying when Maggie turned her attention back to him. Tyler was pointing out the broken glass beneath the sash of one of the long windows that faced the side yard. Sunlight sparkled off a deadly looking piece as he nudged it with the toe of his shoe.

"Where was the other break-in attempted?" Vaughan asked, turning back to Paige.

Ethan answered. "The guesthouse, Detective. But no one got in."

Vaughan raised an eyebrow. "Were you there?"

"Well, no." Ethan flushed. "But—"

"Then maybe Ms. Redmond could tell me what happened."

Paige sat up, her hands clasped together in her lap. "Drew and I were asleep upstairs in the guesthouse, and we heard something banging against the side of the house, and then what sounded like the doorknob around back. He got up and went downstairs, and he must have frightened whoever it was because I could hear something crashing through the bushes, and then one of the chairs on the terrace turned over. And that was it," she finished.

"I'll take another look around out there," Vaughan said, watching as Szabo flipped to a new page in her notepad and scribbled something. "In the meantime, I may need you to come down and identify the man we have in the holding cell—he's still sleeping off whatever he was on. The tox screen won't come back until later."

Maggie shifted on the sofa to look up at Tyler. His face was a mirror of the knot in her stomach. If Vaughan thought Drew's brother had managed to get onto the property Friday night and kill him, he wasn't going to look much farther for another explanation. But it didn't make sense that he would have come back last night, unless he was so out of it that he didn't even realize he'd killed Drew.

Either way, they needed to tell the detectives what they'd overheard Bobby and Whitney discussing. Even if Bobby claimed he hadn't gone through with it, he wasn't exactly a paragon of morality. He'd agreed to Whitney's plan, after all, whatever it was.

Paige had agreed to go to the station with the detectives and went upstairs to change her clothes. In the meantime, Vaughan pulled Maggie and Tyler into the hall.

"You're free to go," he said gruffly. "Just the two of you. Neither one of you has any direct link to the victim, and all of your references checked out."

"Lucy has to stay?" Maggie asked, surprised.

"She's working for his fiancée, for him, really, and there could be all kinds of reasons she didn't want him around." But Vaughan looked dubious even as he said the words, and Maggie sighed.

"So it's a murder, then?" Ty said quietly. "Not an accident?"

The silent corridor hummed with tension, but Vaughan finally conceded, "It's been ruled a homicide, yes." Checking the battered silver Timex on his wrist, he started to walk away.

Not so fast, mister. "Why?" Maggie asked. "Can you tell that someone pushed him?"

"We can tell that there was blunt force trauma to his temple," Szabo said, coming up behind the other detective. Her face sagged like a basset hound's. Someone had killed her fantasy boyfriend, and she still couldn't believe it.

Vaughan was obviously unhappy she had shared that last bit, and Maggie switched topics quickly. "If I wanted to stay, would that be all right?"

"You can come and go as you please now," he said, but he narrowed his eyes. "Why would you want to hang around?"

Yes, why? What the hell was she doing? She'd wanted to leave since the moment she got here. But now things were different. Things like the man standing beside her, smelling so very good and reminding her with every unintentional brush of his arm against her that she was enjoying being with him far too much.

There was also the fact that Detective Vaughan wasn't solving the case very well, but it didn't seem diplomatic to tell him that. "Well, Lucy's my friend, and I hate to leave her alone."

"Sounds okay to me," Vaughan said, and as he started to walk away, he glanced at the framed Miró on the wall with a smile that seemed to say he was just a screenplay away from a house like this.

"Oh, and one more thing," Maggie said, looking at Ty. He nodded, and together they whispered the most salient details of Whitney and Bobby's heated conversation.

"I know it might not matter, since he said he couldn't go through with it, but it seemed like something you should know," Maggie told him.

"Yeah, well, I could have known last night if you'd called

me," Vaughan barked, making furious notes on his pad. "What the hell were you two doing, trying to send me a message by ESP?"

Tyler cleared his throat and looked at his shoes, and Maggie bit back a smile.

Finally, he jerked his head at his partner. "Tell Ms. Redmond I'll need a few more minutes," he said. He marched back to the drawing room, and Maggie had the uncomfortable feeling that someone was in for another round of questioning. When it came to Whitney, she hoped it was under a bare bulb with only the bad cops in attendance.

It would be even better if she got to watch.

But in the meantime, Ty was watching her, and she knew she was going to have to answer a few questions herself. She'd surprised him, all right. She'd surprised herself. And now she didn't know whether to kiss him or slug him, since it was all his fault. She was becoming spontaneous and spur-of-the-moment already.

"Nice of you to keep Lucy company," he said, leaning against the wall and crossing his arms over his chest.

"It's the least I could do."

"I'm staying, too," he said, his eyes bright with amusement.

Well, of course he was. As if she'd had the slightest doubt.

As if she hadn't been secretly hoping he would, despite the fact that every minute she spent with him was going to make it harder to say good-bye.

"To keep me company?" she said as casually as she could.

He let his grin start in one corner of his mouth and spread so slowly, she had to stop herself from fidgeting until he answered.

"All day long," he said. "And all night, too."

Chapter Thirteen

Paige's mother arrived in the middle of the afternoon, a sleek black Town Car delivering her to the front door, where Lucy and Paige were waiting. Maggie and Tyler were spying on the scene from the long line of tulip trees that edged the drive.

"It's not really spying," Maggie insisted, peering carefully around a fat tree trunk as Mrs. Redmond put her arms around her daughter. A younger woman with brown hair twisted into a chignon got out of the car next. "It would be awkward to interrupt a family reunion. Although I can't figure out who that other woman is. Paige doesn't have a sister, does she? Anyway, it's not our fault we were walking the grounds when they arrived."

"Oh, I agree," Ty said, crouched on the ground at her feet. "Especially not after you quizzed Lucy about what time Mrs. Redmond was expected."

"Shut up," she said, kicking him gently. "I hate tennis, and Shelby has permanently claimed the pool. It's not like there's anything else to do."

"Okay, see, there I beg to differ."

She kicked him again, and he grabbed her ankle playfully. She tugged it out of his hands. "Be quiet—they're going inside already."

She didn't even know what she wanted to see, exactly.

Maybe how Paige and her mom interacted. Maybe just what Mrs. Redmond's luggage looked like. Either way, she couldn't help thinking that there was no way to figure out who had killed Drew without knowing more about him, and since he was, of course, dead now, the next best source of information had to be Paige, who was closest to him.

The problem was, she hadn't seen much of Paige since the body had been discovered, and she was pretty sure Paige wasn't up for a girlish chat about her dead boyfriend. And even though she didn't really know Paige either, she was sure Drew's fiancée was blameless.

No one who had committed murder could grieve the way she was.

The four women went into the house, and Ethan appeared like magic on the veranda to collect the luggage. That was another relationship worth investigating. Nell and Paige might have been friends since childhood, but Nell obviously couldn't care less about what had happened, while Ethan was playing Assistant Chief Mourner and Official Hand Holder. Had he been Paige's friend since childhood, too?

"What are you thinking up there, Miss Marple?" Ty said idly. "Is the stakeout over, because I'm getting a cramp in my leg."

"Miss Marple wasn't the stakeout type," Maggie said, stepping away from the tree as the driver steered the car toward the garage. "You can get up now."

"Thanks, boss." He straightened up and put his arm around her, pressing her back against the tree. "I've been staring at your legs for fifteen minutes, you know. You have very sexy legs." He leaned down to kiss her, but she wiggled out from under his arms.

"Do you think Ethan's relationship with Paige is weird?"

"I think it's a weird time for you to ask that question," he said with a heavy sigh, "but yeah. Weird doesn't even begin to describe it. I think Dr. Phil has written books about relationships like that."

"I know." She paced away from him, biting her bottom lip. "And I didn't tell you about Lake yet."

They'd scraped together lunch from the uneaten party food with some of the others after Vaughan and Szabo had left with Paige, finally taking theirs out to the wrought-iron table on the terrace when Sybil's constant, twittered questions to Marty went from irritating to nails-on-a-chalkboard painful. "But why do we have to stay?" "For how long?" "Can I send for more clothes?" "Are you sure Esmeralda is feeding Cricket and Queenie?"

The sun and the steady breeze off the ocean had been so peaceful in comparison, she and Tyler had eaten their sandwiches in silence, and she'd fallen asleep in a lounge chair afterward for a little while. Tyler had awakened when her nose was getting pink, and when they'd heard chants and shouts at the end of the driveway, they'd decided to investigate. With Paige's mom due to arrive any time, Maggie had figured they could kill two birds with one stone.

They'd been so busy watching the group of mourners being interviewed by reporters, she'd forgotten to tell him what Lucy had shared that morning. Twenty women carrying handmade signs with Drew's face plastered to them, all of them singing the theme song from *Hollywood High,* was too mesmerizing.

So now she told him what Regina had revealed about Lake's relationship with Drew, and he grunted in surprise.

"Didn't see that coming," he said. "But I can't imagine her killing him. He would have had a million chances to use their relationship for the PR already, but he never did."

"Yet," she reminded him. "Drew seemed like a good guy to me, too, but this movie is the biggest thing he's done in years. Plus, he's already gotten second and third and fourth chances from Hollywood and his fans—between rehab and that brawl at the club in L.A. two years ago, I bet he had everything riding on this movie's success."

"Okay," Ty said, slipping his arm around her again, and steering her toward the house. "But when?"

"Lake disappeared after dinner, and she never came down for the screening. She could have been waiting in the guesthouse the whole time."

"I didn't realize that." He frowned, but then he shook his head. "Still, I don't buy it. I don't know her, either, but I don't get that vibe from her. She was genuinely shocked to find him out there yesterday morning, and I think she's genuinely mourning him now. My money's on Ethan."

"Ethan?" Maggie tilted her head up to look at him. "He doesn't look like he could kill a spider, much less a human being. And in cold blood."

"But maybe it is a crime of passion, like you said last night," he argued. They had reached the veranda, and he lowered his voice as he opened the door. Inside, the air was cool and still, and Maggie had to let her eyes adjust to the dim light. "Ethan is obviously in love with Paige. Maybe he wanted Drew out of the way."

"But what about Nell?" Maggie said. "Are you saying she's next?"

He didn't answer, and she looked up to see Bobby ambling toward them across the polished marble floor.

"Taking a walk?" His voice was colorless, and he still hadn't changed or showered, as far as she could tell.

"Took one," Ty said easily. "Now we're back."

"Yeah, well, you're both crazy." Bobby snorted inelegantly, but his eyes were still heavy with grief. He jammed his hands in his pockets as if they were about to escape otherwise. "If that detective had said I could get out of this high-class prison, I'd be in the car before he finished the sentence. This whole scene is so fucked up, I can't take it."

And it wouldn't have been if he'd actually killed Drew as planned? Maggie thought, but she kept her mouth shut.

"The police will figure it out," Ty said, taking her hand

and pulling her closer to him. "Soon, I bet. Until then you should just relax. Jump in the pool. Watch a movie."

Bobby stared at him, and finally nodded. "Yeah. You're right. I should." Then he walked off in the direction of the drawing room.

Probably heading for the bar, she thought. That didn't bode well.

"This photographer will self-destruct in approximately one more day," she whispered to Ty, who gave her a mirthless laugh.

"If not sooner," he said. "Come on." He turned left into the hall that led past the library and took her into the billiard room, where he closed the door behind them.

"I told you, I'm awful," she protested, running her hand over the smooth green felt surface of the table and admiring the mahogany woodwork.

"We're not playing now, although it might be fun to teach you one day," he said with a wicked smile. "I was just looking for someplace we could be alone without a bed in it. My willpower is taking a beating this weekend."

His? She flushed and leaned against the table. "You're not the only one," she mumbled.

He pretended not to hear her, but his grin could have powered a small city. He dropped into a club chair against the plaid-papered wall. "You've got me thinking about who killed Drew, and I wasn't finished when Bobby walked in."

She folded her arms over her chest. The air-conditioning was blasting, and in this dark, curtained room, it felt more like February than June. "The problem is, there are too many possibilities. I think we can leave off Shelby, since she's really not smart enough—or talented enough—to pull off killing him and feigning shock at the sight of his body. I wish I had a piece of paper. We need to go through this methodically. List all the people in the house, their possible motivations, where they were the night he died, especially since we know now that someone hit him—"

"Whoa!" Ty held up his hands, laughing and shaking his head. "You really are a Type A, aren't you? I just thought we could, you know, talk about it."

She blinked. "Oh."

He stood and walked over to her, smiling fondly. "You look like you just heard Christmas was cancelled. How about this for a plan? We go out."

"Out?" she said dubiously, glancing at the window, beyond which lay the mob of mourners and reporters.

"Yeah," he said easily. "We're not under house arrest anymore. We can hit up one of the Hamptons hot spots, engage in a little selective eavesdropping, ask a few pointed questions . . . everyone in town is probably talking about Drew's death. We can sleuth, and we can eat a decent meal. What do you say?"

He was pretty hard to resist when he was making pleading puppy-dog eyes at her. She relaxed into his arms and smiled up at him. "You had me at 'plan.'"

Three hours later, Maggie was standing in front of the meager contents of her closet in bra and panties, mentally kicking herself. She could picture the dress she'd love to wear—hanging in her closet at home. The downside of being an efficient packer was that emergency clothes were the first thing to go if the suitcase was too full.

Of course, she hadn't counted on staying for a couple of extra days. "No one expects the Hamptons Inquisition," she muttered, fingering the sleeve of the dress she'd planned to wear to Saturday night's party.

It was a delicious mocha, with a sexy halter top and a skirt that stopped just short of her knees. It was an old favorite, and it looked good on her, but she wanted Tyler to like it. She wanted Tyler to love it.

It was their first real date, in a way. Yeah, they'd spent plenty of time together, both five years ago and this weekend, but in both cases it was usually naked, sweaty, not-much-conversation time. Like they had after they'd come upstairs before. Three-thirty was too early to go out for dinner even for senior citizens, and Tyler had come up with quite a few better things to do to pass the time.

All of which she'd enjoyed immensely, she thought with a tingle of memory in her breasts and between her legs. But now they were going out to dinner, which was not clothing optional and meant an hour or two of conversation, one on one. Impossibly, she was nervous about it.

She thought about the red dress at home, which she was suddenly positive would be the answer to all her problems, when the bedroom door opened without warning.

"I like that look," Ty said, shutting the door behind him. That slow, Big Bad Wolf grin spread across his face again, and he dropped onto the edge of the bed with a murmured, "Mmmm mmmm."

She shot him a dirty look before turning back to the closet. A moment later, he said, "I don't think the clothes come out on their own, you know."

"Funny." She sighed, uncomfortably aware of the heat of his gaze on her ass. Two more minutes and she'd give in and strip, and leave the dinner out for another night.

"What's the matter?"

"I can't decide what to wear. I hadn't planned for a night out."

She could feel him rolling his eyes, and then he was standing up and pawing through the few things she had brought.

"This," he said, handing her the mocha halter dress. "This I'd like to see on you."

"Really?" She raised her eyebrows. "On?"

"We can discuss off later," he drawled, and sat down to watch. His eyes widened when she took off her lacy white bra.

"I thought you were getting dressed," he said. His voice was already husky.

She turned around to take another bra out of the dresser.

"That one won't work with the halter top," she explained, smiling. If she bottled Ty's appreciation of her body, she'd have a permanent pick-me-up for every bad day.

"Why do you need a bra at all?" he said. His voice was getting lower every second, and he was suddenly standing up. He took the second one out of her hands, examining the construction, then tossed it across the room.

"Be daring," he whispered, sliding his hand over her breast. The nipple hardened against his palm, and she caught her breath at the urgent stab of need. "Wouldn't it be exciting to go without, just for one night?"

There it was again, that thrill of impulse, that naughty go-for-it voice in her head that she heard only at times like these. The Dr. Jekyll Maggie would have been concerned about wardrobe malfunctions and breast support, but Mr. Hyde Maggie was too turned on to care.

"I think I can handle that," she said, her voice just as husky as his. She held out her hand, but he picked up the dress and shifted her around, sliding it over her head for her. He zipped up the low back and let her adjust the halter top before she turned around.

"You like?" she said.

"Oh, I like," he said with that wicked grin. "Dare I ask what kind of shoes you're wearing?"

"Those," she said, pointing to the high-heeled black ones on the floor.

"Very nice," he said approvingly, and watched as she stepped into them. "Oh, yeah, they work."

"Stop it," she said suddenly, laughing. "You're making dinner out seem like a really dumb idea."

He held his hands up and stepped back. "I'll be a good boy, I promise. Are you ready?"

She sighed. Men. "I have to put on some makeup and brush my hair. Just give me five minutes."

"Only if I can watch," he said, following her into the bathroom.

She could feel his breath on her bare back as she fumbled through her makeup case for eyeliner and mascara. In the mirror, his face was intent as he watched her uncap a brown pencil and line her upper lashes.

"What's that for?" he asked, kissing her shoulder.

"It's supposed to define them," she said, a bit breathlessly. It was hard to concentrate with his lips on her skin, and the rest of him much too close.

"And this?" he asked, reaching around her for the tube of mascara.

"That," she said, snatching it away with a little laugh, "is a necessity. And stop nibbling me. Unless you want a trip to the emergency room instead of dinner. Where you'll be the one explaining why my eyeballs look so long and lustrous and my lashes don't."

He grinned and stood back, but as she pulled out her lipstick she caught his gaze in the mirror. He watched as she slid the glossy deep red stick over her lips, and she felt her heart stutter nervously. When he looked at her like that, it was hard to remember her own name.

"Ready?" she finally said to his reflection. One more moment of exchanging smoldering gazes and she was going to take her dress off again.

He drew in a deep breath. "More than," he said with a gleam in his eye, gesturing widely at the bathroom door.

She let the warmth of his hand on her bare back a moment later tingle through her. It curled deep, a steady, aching little pulse. She wondered if he'd settle for fast food.

They took Lucy's rental car, since Ty had flown into East Hampton on the seaplane charter.

"Have fun," Lucy said glumly from the door of the garage. "And don't worry about us. We'll be fine, stuck here with the leftover party food and the murderer on the loose."

"We can stay, if you want," Maggie said, her hand on the car door. *Upstairs, of course. Naked.*

Lucy sighed and flapped a hand at them. "No. Go. Have fun. At least I'm off duty with Mrs. Redmond's assistant taking over the phone. But bring me back something wrapped in a tinfoil swan."

Tyler laughed. "I promise." He opened the driver's side door and peered inside with a purely male growl of appreciation in the back of his throat. Then his head popped up again. "Screw the Hamptons. Let's drive into the city. No, wait. Let's drive to Baltimore."

"There's nothing quite like the love of a boy for his V-8 engine, is there," Maggie said dryly, getting into the car.

"See you later," Lucy called as Ty got in and turned the key in the ignition.

Maggie waved as he backed out of the garage and pulled into the driveway. Lucy waved back, then frowned as Ty jerked to a stop.

"What are you doing?" Maggie asked him.

"It would be a crime against everything good to keep the top up on a day like this," he said. "And there's been enough law breaking already."

The roof disappeared little by little, and Maggie tilted her head back, breathing in the rich scents of the flowerbeds bordering the drive and the salty tang of the ocean. It was a relief to escape the air-conditioned sanctum of the house.

Until she realized that it was going to entail braving the mob outside. Tyler leaned on the horn as the gates opened, but instead of backing up, the crowd swarmed forward. Everyone was shouting, and at least half of the people gathered seemed to have mikes and cameras.

"Can you tell us what's happening inside?"

"How is Drew's fiancée holding up?"

"What are your names?"

"It's Tyler Brody, the Florida hotelier, with an unnamed woman," a reporter planted near the right headlight said into his mike.

I'm not unnamed, Maggie thought irritably, but under the circumstances, she thought it was probably best to stick to the no-comment rule. Even when a fortyish woman in an enormous black T-shirt with Drew's face silk-screened onto the front leaned into the car and grabbed her shoulder, shouting over the other voices, "Do you have anything of his? Did you see his body?"

Maggie shrank toward Drew, who was still honking furiously, edging the car forward inch by inch. Maggie glanced at him and pointed at the lack of a roof with raised eyebrows.

"Okay, so putting the top down was premature," he growled. Waving another trip of reporters out of the way, he gunned the engine and shot out onto Gin Lane as Maggie grabbed the dashboard and held on.

"Do you have a death wish?" she shouted over the wind as he sped down the street, veering around a parked caterer's truck and two bicycles on the narrow shoulder.

She peeled her gaze away from the windshield long enough to see him give her an odd look, but all he said was, "No. I have a date wish. And I pictured just the two of us, not a press conference."

She managed a grin, but then he was gunning the engine and making a left-hand turn at a speed that defied the laws of physics.

"We've still got company," he shouted, jerking his head backward.

She glanced over her shoulder and saw a news van following them, with a lime green Volkswagen in its wake. Ty gave the car more gas, and she lurched in her seat, white-knuckled.

A date was one thing. A high-speed chase was another. Talk about not in the plan.

"We'll lose them up ahead," Ty assured her. How could he grin like that when he was doing sixty in a twenty-five-mile-per-hour zone, with the media and several crazed Drew Fisk fans in hot pursuit?

Clutching the dashboard with one hand and the center console with the other, she nodded without a word. He drove the way he lived, ignoring all the yellow lights and speeding down the off-ramps without so much as a turn signal. And for the weekend, at least, she was along for the ride.

Chapter Fourteen

"What do you think?" Tyler asked Maggie, winding his arm around her waist in the crush of people beside the bar.

"I think I just saw one of my former clients," she whispered over the rim of her martini glass. "Not one of the ones I liked, either."

He laughed, letting his fingers rest on the small of her back. She was slightly flushed, and her skin was warm. She'd recovered pretty well after they'd lost the caravan of paparazzi and mourners and he'd pulled into a French restaurant the tourists and the locals both loved, although she had grilled him about his driving record and his insurance premiums for a little while. But the waiter had seated them at a table in a secluded corner, and sometime between the arrival of the wine and the basket of warm parmesan bread, she'd relaxed.

She'd asked him about the hotel and its staff, about where he lived, where he grew up, and somewhere along the line they'd ended up talking about inconsequential stuff, playing the Batman or Superman, Wilma or Betty game, and debating which rocked harder, old U2 or new U2.

He couldn't remember when he'd had a better time, even when she argued in favor of *The Deer Hunter* over *Taxi Driver* for her favorite Robert DeNiro performance. Seriously misguided. But there was a lot that they hadn't touched on, things that did matter—or maybe only mattered if they were thinking past the next few days.

Like the scar on his forehead, which he'd glossed over when the waiter appeared with dessert, and the story behind it. Later, he'd promised himself. Maybe. With Maggie, it was so hard to decide what would scare her off and what would draw her closer.

He'd suggested this club afterward, because he'd heard it was a magnet for all the celebrities and celebrity seekers who flocked out here in the summer. If they were going to find out anything about the other guests at the Redmonds', this was the place to do it.

Now Maggie turned in the circle of his arm, looking over her shoulder.

"I think I just saw Billy Joel," she whispered fiercely.

He followed her gaze and squinted into the crowd at the other end of the cavernous room. The club was a converted barn, fitted with varying levels of dance floors and three separate lofts with long tables. The lighting was low and the music was loud, and he was beginning to wonder how they were going to eavesdrop on anything other than pickup lines when Maggie grabbed his hand and pulled him toward the steps leading to the nearest loft.

"We need to mingle," she said as they pressed past a group of scantily clad twentysomethings coming down the stairs, giggling.

"Okay," he said, amused. He couldn't pick out any likely candidates from the throng of people up on the loft, but he was interested to see what Maggie was planning. If he knew her at all, there had to be a plan.

He followed her to two seats, where they squeezed in next to two obviously wealthy couples in their thirties. Diamonds dripped from one woman's ears, and her husband's watch looked more expensive than Tyler's car.

Eyes wide, Maggie asked, "Did you hear about what happened today at Paige Redmond's?" She raised her eyebrows in some kind of a signal.

"No," he said uncertainly, curious. What the hell was she doing?

"Her mom showed up and kicked everyone out of the house," Maggie said, leaning closer. "She said this is what happens when you get involved with 'people like that.'"

"Really?" He had no idea where to go with the story, since he couldn't imagine how she would explain hearing it in the first place.

But the woman on Maggie's other side broke in, eyes bright. "No, no, she couldn't kick anyone out; the police have them there until they pin down a suspect. It's all so Agatha Christie, isn't it?"

"Oh, yeah," Maggie said, edging closer, conspiratorial. "But I heard from a friend who works for the network that someone did leave . . ."

"Well, I heard that the police have cleared a few of the guests, but most of them have to stay—too many motives, you know. My cleaning woman is dating someone on the police force."

Maggie made an impressed face, and Ty coughed to cover a bark of laughter. Maybe he should recommend her to Whitney and Tony for a role.

"What kind of motives?" she asked, lowering her voice.

"Well, the Margolises are broke," one of the men said. He had the kind of leathery, permanent tan that meant money and year-round golf, and he seemed bored with the topic already. "Drew was their biggest client for a long time, but too many stints in rehab means not enough time in front of the camera, you know? They treated him like a son, if you like to think of your kids as cash cows."

The logic didn't work, Ty thought—being broke gave them more motive to see him alive and acting than six feet under.

The man's female companion was already adding, "And

he and Bobby Gleason go back a long way. Who knows what kind of dirt Drew might have had on him?"

Well, they already knew something was going on there, Ty thought, knocking back the rest of his rum and Coke. They could set the gossip chain on fire if they shared some of the things they'd seen and heard the last few days

"What about . . ." Maggie paused, frowning, as if she was thinking hard. "What's her name, Shelby? Shelby . . . ?"

"Shelby Byrne," the woman said, rolling her eyes. "She's one of those party girls turned actresses who learned everything she knows about acting on the casting couch. Or, more likely, kneeling in front of it."

Tyler nearly choked on his drink, and Maggie was trying to cover her surprise by pretending she had something in her eye. She looked up at him a moment later, and he could tell she was trying not to laugh. He shrugged mildly, eyeing the woman, who was still talking.

"My friend Jane knew her for a while," she was saying, twirling the straw in her drink viciously. "She's older than she says she is, for one, and she's had so much work done, she's practically all silicone now. You should have seen her a few years ago—nothing to write home about. She should thank the gods of plastic surgery that Botox was discovered, if you ask me."

"I heard she really had a thing for Drew," Maggie ventured cautiously. It wouldn't be easy to credit that piece of gossip to her "friend from the network" but the other woman didn't seem to notice.

"Oh, she does. Well, did. On the set of *Simon,* she apparently did everything short of issuing an engraved invitation for him to sleep with her, but from what I heard he really did love Paige. I don't know why, but there you go. Love is a weird thing."

Maggie was bristling now, and Tyler grabbed her hand across the table.

"Isn't that Lucy?" he said quickly, pointing downstairs. "Let's go say hi."

Don't look so confused, he thought, standing up, and watched as her brow furrowed in surprise before she understood what he was doing.

"Oh, yeah, we should," she said, grabbing her glass and scraping back her chair. "Nice gossiping with you," she said to the others with a friendly laugh, and one of the women waved as they headed for the stairs.

"Nice save," she whispered as they moved down to the main floor.

"You looked like you were going to slug her," he said mildly. "Which probably would have given us away. Or gotten us arrested."

"Well, I don't know what that crack about Paige meant," she said as they found a place to stand near the bar. The speakers were blasting something with a heavy bass line, and he could feel the vibration through the floor.

"Who wouldn't fall in love with her?" Maggie went on, standing on tiptoe to shout into his ear. "She's beautiful and kind and smart and generous . . ."

"And rich," he added. "Don't forget that."

"That's not why Drew wanted to marry her," she insisted, shaking her head, but even in the dim light he could see the flash of doubt in her eyes.

"I don't think so either, but there are people who would do anything to get their hands on money like hers."

"You mean someone else wants her money?" she asked, frowning. "And that someone killed Drew?"

"It's a possibility, I guess," he said. "One of the many."

She sighed and took a long, slow drink of her martini as she glanced around the room. The dance floor was crowded with bodies, most of them women only half dressed in cropped tops and tiny skirts, and body-skimming dresses in sheer, floaty fabrics.

It was hot and close, the smells of old sawdust and perfume and alcohol combined into something dark and rich. Beside him, Maggie was swaying a little bit, her bottom lip caught between her teeth, her eyes sparkling with the gleam of the flashing lights over the dance floor.

In another minute it would be too late, and she would turn to ask him something or announce that she had to go to the ladies' room. And after an entire evening spent close enough to touch her, but not to touch her intimately enough, he wasn't going to let the chance slip by.

Taking her glass out of her hand and setting it on the bar, he steered her toward the floor. When the song ended, the speakers pulsed with something mellower, sexier, and he allowed himself an inward sigh. Dancing was always a good thing, but slower was better.

She smiled as he pulled her against him, and she wound her arms around his neck. Oh, yeah, this was exactly what he wanted. He let his hands slide down her back and then over her ass as the song spiraled into its lazy chorus. She felt so good, alive and warm and so soft beneath his hands. When he lowered his head to nuzzle her ear, he could feel her heartbeat in the vulnerable hollow of her throat.

She arched her neck as he ran his tongue along the heated pulse, pressing herself closer, her belly against his groin. He drew in a ragged breath—if they'd been back at the house, his hands would have been under her dress already, stroking her warm velvet skin.

She took her bottom lip between her teeth when he moved against her in time to the music. Her nipples were rigid now, the silk of her dress whispering over them as he pressed his chest to hers, and suddenly her fingernails were digging into his shoulders—just hard enough to remind him where they were.

He pulled away just as the song ended, and she gave him a shaky grin.

"Let's get some air," she said, shouting as another song

started. It was some kind of metal/rap combination that everyone on the floor was jumping up and down to as Maggie led him to a set of doors flung open to a rustic deck.

"I'm so hot now," she said, fanning herself as they sank onto the corner of a bench.

"Me, too." He raised his eyebrow, and she flushed even pinker, letting him wind his arm around her shoulders. "You ready to go back to the house?"

She slid her hand along his thigh, echoing his earlier words. "More than."

But as they stood up, she froze, turning her head toward a noisy conversation a few feet away. Club girls, it looked like to him—in their mid twenties, professionally tan, in a combination of designer dresses and knockoff shoes. He saw them all the time in the Keys, now that it had become a party spot nearly as hot as South Beach.

Reaching blindly behind her for his hand, Maggie inched her way toward them, listening.

"I'll go get drinks," he murmured, leaving her to look out over the railing at the dunes in the distance.

A minibar had been set up on the deck, and he asked for two cold Coronas. Over his shoulder, he could hear one of the girls giggling, and a light snort from one of the others.

"Julie always had a thing for the other guy, but I liked Drew. Plus, Drew always had something to get the party started, you know?"

He turned around and crossed over to Maggie, who was pretending to be caught up by the view. Handing her a beer, he squeezed lime into his own and took a long drink. If these girls didn't deliver something juicier than the usual gossip, he was hauling Maggie out of here as soon as he finished. He could still smell her hair and the slightly musky scent of her skin, and if he wasn't careful, his mouth was going to start watering.

Maggie elbowed him as one of the other girls said, "I was at his house once when this one girl totally lost it—she was doing coke, I guess, and we were all out by the pool, you know? And she just . . . like, *lost* it. Started taking off all her clothes and running around, and then she hit Drew with one of the deck chairs, and this other guy finally smacked her so she would shut up. It was ugly."

"Was she the one who disappeared or whatever?" another girl asked, even though she sounded too bored to care.

"I think so. Although . . . I don't know, it might have been someone else. Hey, look! Brad's here!"

They hurried inside in a cloud of perfume and the sound of at least two cell phones ringing.

Maggie took a drink of her beer and looked up at him. "Do you think they were talking about Lake? I know she didn't 'disappear,' but she did disappear from that scene, if what Lucy's boss said is true."

"Depends on how long ago it was," he said, "and those girls were only in their early twenties. We'd have to figure out when Lake started getting parts."

Maggie shook her head. "I can't really believe they were talking about her, though. I just can't picture her . . . going off the deep end like that."

"Drugs do strange things to people," he said, but he knew what she meant. Maybe it was just too painful to imagine graceful, intelligent Lake naked and screaming, out of her mind with fury.

He shook off the thought and took Maggie's hand. "We were on our way home before the gossip patrol interrupted us," he said. "Had enough sleuthing for one evening?"

She smiled, and set her beer down on the railing. "For now."

Chapter Fifteen

"I'm not ready to go in yet," Maggie said as they shut Spindrift's garage door a half hour later. The crowd had gone home for the night, leaving teddy bears and wilted carnations and handmade signs fastened to the gates in their absence. As she looked up at the house in the darkness, she wondered if Paige would want to keep them.

Only a few lights burned inside, although she could hardly see the whole thing from where she stood on the driveway. "You know, driving up to this place on Friday I thought it was one of the most beautiful houses I'd ever seen, and now it just seems creepy."

"You want to walk down the beach?" Tyler asked, coming around the car to slide his arms around her. She sighed and snuggled into him, resting her head on his chest.

He was so *comfortable*. As though he'd been made to fit her. She drew in a shuddering breath when he pulled her closer, so they were truly fitted together, length to length, all of his hard, muscular angles softened by her curves.

Okay, maybe comfortable was the wrong word, she thought, that familiar curl of desire licking at her again. That was what was so dangerous. He felt comfortable, he felt right, but he wasn't. Because he was dangerous, at least for someone like her. Part of her believed that if she had told him to drive into Manhattan tonight, he would have.

"Maggie," he murmured, "are we going down to the beach or upstairs?"

"The beach," she said decisively, lifting her head and looking at him. "We've been here for two days and I haven't even seen it yet."

"All right," he said, "letting go of everything but her hand. But I can't promise I won't ravish you right there in the sand."

Yup, he was dangerous. Because she didn't doubt him—and she was secretly looking forward to it.

They went around the garage and headed toward the lawn, but they only got as far as the terrace when someone called, "Who's there?"

She jumped, turning her head to see a flicker of light on the far side of the stones.

"It's Maggie and Tyler," she called, and Tyler squeezed her hand as he stepped in front of her.

"Connor?" he said.

"Yeah, it's just me," came the answer. "Sorry to startle you." A second smaller glow bounced in the dark, and Maggie caught the sharp tobacco scent of cigarette smoke.

"Can we join you?" she said.

"Sure. I'm just brooding." He punctuated the words with a rueful laugh.

Tyler pulled out a chair for her, and she sank into it gratefully. Her feet were killing her. Why did sexy shoes always have to mean pain?

"What did you think of the Hamptons' nightlife?" Connor asked, stubbing out his cigarette in a heavy glass ashtray and sliding another one out of a pack on the table.

"The restaurant was phenomenal," Maggie said, settling back in her chair and trying to slide her shoes off without anyone noticing. "The shrimp was so fresh, mine was practically still flopping around."

Connor laughed with a little more mirth this time and took a long drag of his cigarette. "Tables, right?" he said.

"I've been there. Actually, Drew and I took Paige and Lake there Thursday night." In the flickering candlelight, his expression was sober, and sad.

"Were you . . . friends?" Maggie asked him. The way he'd talked about Drew on Friday, it didn't seem likely, but since they'd found Drew dead on the lawn, Connor had definitely changed.

Of course, that could be because he killed him, she thought, shivering as a breeze off the ocean swept over the patio.

"We weren't, not really," he said, "any more than you consider someone you simply work with a friend. I mean, it happens, sure, but not with Drew and me. And despite how I must have sounded on Friday afternoon"—he gave Maggie an embarrassed smile—"I didn't hate him. I just hated how . . . how much everyone seemed to love him, no matter what he did. There are other people who have fucked up, you know, doing less than he did, who just got cut off. Cut out. No more jobs, no more PR, not even a guest spot on some crappy sitcom. I was jealous of him, I guess."

He looked up from his contemplation of the cigarette slowly burning down between his fingers. "And then I saw him lying there, dead, and I thought, what a waste. He really was talented, and he finally had his shit together, you know? And now he's gone. And I feel stupid for envying him anything, because I forgot about what he went through—the drugs, the drinking, rehab. This business isn't easy, and I've always known it. I'm lucky I didn't fall into some of the same traps."

There wasn't much to say to that. Beside her, Tyler stirred, looking back at the house, and then Connor suddenly got up, stubbing out the cigarette.

"I'll go brood in my room and let you two enjoy the moonlight," he said with a wry smile. "And, Maggie," he added, looking back over his shoulder when he had walked just a few feet away, "I'm sorry I was such an ass, too."

She smiled at him, aware of Tyler's sharpened interest. Amazing how you could sense when a man picked up the smallest sign that someone had tried to poach on his territory.

"What did that mean?" he said, frowning.

"That he was an ass on Friday," she said simply. "Seemed pretty clear to me."

"I think there's something you're not telling me," he said, following when she got up, picked up her shoes, and headed toward the door.

"You're right," she said with a secret little smile. "I didn't tell you that I changed my mind about the beach. I want some tea, and then I want to go upstairs. With you."

He was considering and rejecting several things to say; she could see it in his scowl and the faint tightening of his jaw. But he gave in and followed her inside without a word. Jealous men were kind of sweet when they knew better than to make a big deal of it.

Inside, the house was hushed and dark. Even the carpet felt cool on her bare feet, and she shivered again. Paige kept the place as air-conditioned as a mausoleum.

There was a soft lamp burning in the drawing room to her right, and far down the hall to her left, the low gleam on the tiled floor meant at least one light was on in the kitchen, but otherwise the hall was dark.

"The electric bill must be a bitch," Tyler said with a shrug, fumbling on the wall for a switch.

"Well, it's not like they can't afford it," she whispered. "Come on. We can make it down to the kitchen without getting lost."

But as they made their way through the shadows, she stopped suddenly. Ty crashed into her back, and she dropped one of her shoes.

"Shhh!" She held up her finger, pointing at the corridor to the right, which led past the dining room to the conservatory.

Someone was playing the piano. Well, not playing, exactly, but picking out odd notes at random.

Taking her hand again, Ty led the way down the hall. Her heart was pounding, which was silly. She didn't believe in ghosts, not that she thought Drew was the haunting type anyway, and whoever was in there was simply someone staying in the house, not a random piano-playing burglar.

Of course, someone staying in this house is a murderer, she thought as they neared the open door to the conservatory, and grimaced.

Ty stopped just outside the door, craning his head inside, and she peered around him. She could still hear the gentle plink of the piano keys.

The only light in the room was coming from the driveway, where security lights were aimed at the front of the house, but she was pretty sure she recognized Nell seated on the piano bench. She looked up when a floorboard creaked.

"Who is that?" she said idly. Her words were slightly slurred, a watercolor impression of her usually precise diction.

"It's Tyler and Maggie," Tyler said. "We heard the piano."

She didn't reply, picking out the notes to "Happy Birthday" instead.

"Are you okay, Nell?" Maggie asked, edging toward the piano. Now that her eyes had adjusted, she spotted a bottle of cognac on the bench beside Nell. An empty glass rested on the music stand, the last sticky coating of alcohol puddled in the bottom.

"Oh, I'm great," she said, looking up. Her hair fell forward, a black curtain over one eye. "I'm fine. I'm a prisoner in this house for the duration. Why wouldn't I be?"

"I know it's hard . . ." Maggie started, but Nell's hollow laugh stopped her.

"Yeah, it's hard," she said, picking up the bottle and splashing a generous amount into the glass. "Of course it's hardest for Paige, but it's not exactly an unexpected vacation for the rest of us, is it? Not with daily interrogation by the East Hampton Police Department the only activity on the schedule."

Tyler cut his gaze toward her, and Maggie raised her eyebrows. Nell seemed to be talking more to herself than to them, and the longer she talked, the more coherent, if not charitable, she seemed.

"Did you have things you needed to do this week?" Maggie ventured.

"Other than being stuck in this house, you mean?" Nell said with a wicked little smile. "Of course. Ethan has work, of course, although you'd never know it mattered to look at him."

"What does he do?" Tyler asked, sitting in the closest chair. Maggie sat down next to him, her shoes still dangling from one finger.

"He's the publisher of the *Knickerbocker Review*." Nell's icy tone implied that this was something they should have known, or at least have been told. "The literary magazine? They've expanded into a small press, as well."

Strangely, she also sounded proud. Maggie didn't know much about Ethan Winship, but she'd assumed he had come from money. His carelessly rumpled hundred-dollar chinos and stuffy good manners didn't scream middle-class suburbia. Maybe he had used family funding to start the magazine, but the admiration in Nell's voice made Maggie wonder if he'd succeeded on his own merits afterward.

And if Nell was proud of Ethan, she probably loved him. That was harder to believe, given the interaction Maggie had seen between them, but maybe what she had taken for resentment and humiliation was true jealousy—a woman scorned, or at least ignored. It wasn't as if Ethan bothered to pretend he didn't care for Paige.

She couldn't keep any of it straight anymore. Her head was pounding from the wine they'd had with dinner, and the drinks afterward, and she was suddenly exhausted. Sitting in the dark with a half-drunk, bitter woman she barely knew was no stranger than being asked to a weekend party that was interrupted by murder—especially when a man she knew only slightly more intimately was sitting beside her, his hand on her thigh. Either way, she was tired of it all. Weird had become the new normal, at least this weekend.

And suddenly she wanted the old normal. On any other Sunday evening, she would have been settled in her apartment in her pink cupcake pajamas, with a pot of tea and a bowl of ice cream, a DVD queued up and her laptop with its cartoon fish screensaver on the sofa beside her so she could catch up on e-mail and work. She'd be comfortable, waiting for her mother's usual Sunday night call, her clothes already laid out for the next morning and the coffee maker programmed.

She sighed. When she thought about it, it was too Bridget Jones for words. A little more organized, and minus the neuroses, of course. Comfortable, yeah, but a little bit lonely. A little bit, well . . . pathetic. She could have been writing a novel, or writing letters to underprivileged children or something. She could have been downloading pictures of hot actors, like Lucy did. She could have been posting on a message board with possibly hot guys, also like Lucy did.

She was the anti-impulse, she realized. She'd turned down a date with a perfectly nice and perfectly nice looking guy just two months ago because she wasn't sure where a relationship with him would lead. He was an advertising consultant, or something like that, and once she heard he traveled at least two weeks out of the month, she'd said no thank you.

So she'd started dating Dan the Dull instead. Because he was reliable.

Tyler was looking at her strangely, and Nell seemed to have forgotten they were in the room—she was picking out what sounded like a Sheryl Crow song on the piano.

She laid her hand on Tyler's, and heat rushed through her when he smiled.

Tyler. He was the kind of impulse she'd avoided all her life. And when he looked at her that way, she didn't want to avoid it anymore.

At least not tonight.

"I think we're going to bed," she said suddenly, standing up. "Tyler?"

"Uh, yeah," he said, scrambling up beside her.

Nell waved her balloon glass at them, never looking up from the piano. Cognac sloshed down one side, and Maggie heard it hit the keys with a soft splash.

"What happened?" he said when they were in the front hall, lengthening his stride to keep up with her.

"Nothing," she said, shrugging. "It was just getting too *Twilight Zone* in there to take. I mean, any minute she was going to start playing the tune from some horror movie."

"Yeah, that was a little weird," he agreed. "Connor, too. Before dinner Friday night, all he could talk about was some movie he made that never got enough attention, and how *The Truth About Simon* was crap compared to that one, blah, blah, blah. Talk about your timely epiphanies."

Epiphanies. Maybe she'd just had one, she thought, turning away from the stairs and heading down the hall to the billiard room.

"Can I take you up on your offer now?" she asked over her shoulder.

"What offer?" he said, confused.

"To teach me to play." She opened the door and reached inside for a light switch. Warm yellow light spilled from the billiard lamp over the table, illuminating the neatly racked balls.

"Now?" he said, frowning.

"Why not?" she dropped her sandals and walked over to the rack of cues on the wall. Selecting a likely looking one, she took it down and twirled it between her palms. "I need to broaden my horizons. I've never played before, not really, and you offered to teach me. And, as luck would have it, there's a lovely table moldering here all unused and lonely. What do you say?"

"I say it's hardly moldering," he said dryly, taking a cue for himself and then leaning against the table, arms folded. "And I also say this is a little more like the reckless, unpredictable Maggie I met all those years ago."

Good, she thought, checking in each netted pocket for the cue ball. *I want to be impulsive. I want to embrace the crazy and see what it feels like.*

But when she looked up at him, she wanted more than that. In the soft light, his face was shadowed, his eyes an indistinct gleam under his brow, and his mouth curved in a wicked grin that emphasized the hard line of his jaw.

God, she wanted him. All of him, every sharply defined angle and smooth plane of that delicious body, every grin and every wicked laugh, even every amused quirk of those damn eyebrows. He wasn't afraid of anything. Maybe he could teach her not to be.

"I'm feeling reckless," she said, laying her cue down on the table. "In fact, I'm feeling so unpredictable, I think I've changed my mind again."

"Oh, yeah?" he said. Impossibly, his grin widened.

"Yeah," she said, locking the door to the hall. She turned around and faced him. He'd laid his cue beside hers and perched on the edge of the table, just one foot on the floor, his arms still crossed over his chest. Something about his posture screamed "challenge," as if he didn't really believe she was going to try anything here in the billiard room, door locked or not. Maybe it was that eyebrow again, which looked dubious despite his grin.

Try me, she thought, and walked over to run her hand along his thigh.

"I'm not in the mood for pool anymore," she said, nudging him sideways until he was seated squarely on the edge of the table, his thighs spread just wide enough for her to drag her fingers along the seam of his crotch. He was hard already. "But the table will probably come in handy."

"Oh, yeah?" he echoed. His voice had gone husky, and his eyes were smoky now, a dark, deep blue.

"Mmm hmmm." She tugged his shirt free of his pants, sliding her palms over his chest. His stomach muscles twitched as her fingertips grazed the hot skin, exploring lower.

She undid his buttons quickly, throwing the shirt open so she could kiss him, starting near his collarbones and working her way down. His skin was faintly salty with sweat, but he tasted as good as ever—better, even. She licked each flat disk of nipple, and their small, hard little points, smiling against his chest as a low growl of pleasure rumbled in his throat.

She smoothed her hands over his ribs as she worked her way lower, finding his belt buckle and opening it. She undid the button next and slid the zipper down, reaching inside to find the fly in his briefs. When her fingers closed around the hot, rigid length of him, a soft shudder of breath escaped her.

She loved this—holding him, tasting him, feeling the power of his need pulsing in her hand. She loved being able to make him speechless, even just for a minute, and know that everything he was feeling, she was giving him.

What was more, she loved that he trusted her. If she'd cornered Dan like this, even with the door locked, she was pretty sure he would have run screaming into the night after a lecture about appropriate times and places.

Not that she'd ever, for even a moment, wanted to do this with Dan.

Ty groaned as she bent down to take just the tip of his cock between her lips, sucking him lightly, stroking her tongue around the sensitive slit. She slid her hand down to cup the weight of his balls as she took his erection farther into her mouth, licking the velvet underside. A vein throbbed there, tickling her tongue, and she sucked harder, breathing in the dark, rich scent of him as she did.

His thighs tensed as she took him deeper still, working her finger into the vulnerable spot just behind his balls, and he groaned louder. He let go of the pool table's edge to grip her shoulder, his fingers hard on the bare flesh.

"Maggie," he growled, and a shudder ran through the length of him, vibrating in his cock.

She held on, working her tongue around him, her heart pounding as she felt him take a ragged breath. He was so close, and the intensity of it burned between her legs, a steady, licking flame.

But suddenly he was wrenching her away from him. She stumbled backward, confused, and then she saw the look in his eyes. Dark blue had turned almost black, hot and deep and undeniable.

He wanted inside her, and that was fine with her—she was slick with wetness already, and the flame of heat between her legs had become a hollow ache.

But when he reached for her, she turned around at the last second, leaning against the pool table, sliding her skirt up over her behind at the same time.

She couldn't see his face, had no idea what he was about to do, but that was part of the excitement—she was more vulnerable than ever this way, but she trusted him completely. Here, in this moment, body to body, he would never hurt her. He would make her fly.

Another ragged, incoherent groan escaped him, and the sudden contact of his hands on her waist made her shiver. He pushed her panties down and slid two fingers between her legs, slicking her wetness over the lips.

Her turn to groan. She trembled as he nudged her forward, spreading her legs and arching her ass up to give him room, and then he was inside her, thrusting slowly.

Oh, God. Her knees jerked, unsteady, and she gripped the table with both hands, holding on as he took her deeper. The angle was new, and she wriggled to adjust as each stroke touched places she hadn't known existed till now. Good places, wonderful places—she barely registered the gentle smack of his abs against her ass until his hand slid around her thigh. He eased one finger into her damp curls, and then between the slick lips, finding that swollen, aching knot of flesh and circling it slowly.

"Ty . . ." It didn't sound like her voice—it was too raw, too desperate, but the pleasure was washing over her too fast.

His lips found the back of her neck, leaving soft, whispery kisses against her nape, until the rhythm of his cock inside her was too urgent.

It was almost frightening, the power of the sensations—her knees were weak, and her heart was hammering so frantically she could hear the blood pounding in her ears. If she closed her eyes, everything but the places they touched burned away, and the whole world was dark, throbbing heat, a coil of pleasure that wound in on itself, tighter and tighter . . .

Until it snapped, and she gasped as the orgasm flooded through her, wave after wave of hot, sweet satisfaction. Tyler shouted as a violent shudder rocked his body and he spilled inside her, his mouth on her shoulder and his arms holding her tight.

She let out a trembling laugh as they sank to the floor together. No matter how high he took her, he was always there when she came down. So far, at least.

The scary thing was the way he made her wonder if she would ever be content to stay earthbound again.

Chapter Sixteen

"You're crazy," Lucy said, handing Maggie a cup of coffee the next morning. "As in the-men-in-white-coats-should-be-called crazy."

"I'm not crazy," Maggie whispered fiercely, stopping to smile at Lake, who had wandered into the kitchen yawning. "I'm sensible. I'm practical. I know my limits. And Tyler is definitely outside them."

"How?" Lucy asked, frowning as she stirred a third spoonful of sugar into her coffee. "Let's see, because he's just too homely to take? No, that's not it. I know, because he's a deadbeat! No, wait, he's totally successful. Must be because he's such a big fat jerk. Except, hold on, he's not! Mostly because he puts up with you, otherwise known as Miss Changes Her Mind Daily." Her cell phone rang, a chirpy electronic rendition of "Girls Just Wanna Have Fun," and she carried it over to the bay window to answer it.

Maggie sighed and sank onto one of the stools at the counter, staring bleakly at her coffee. Paige's mother Vivian patted her shoulder as she bustled past with another bowlful of eggs. She'd announced that she was making an old-fashioned breakfast last night, or so Lucy had told Maggie, and that she was embarrassed that Paige's guests had not been fed properly since Friday evening.

Given that Paige's fiancé had been murdered since then,

Maggie didn't think anyone was really complaining, but it did strike her that almost everyone had come downstairs on the early side this morning, sniffing for the sizzle of bacon. Vivian hadn't disappointed them. She'd set one platter of sausage links and bacon on the long kitchen table already, and was getting ready to make another plate of scrambled eggs.

Vivian Redmond looked to Maggie as though she'd been born wearing Chanel, and considered full-price stuff from Talbots her lounge-around wear, so it was difficult to reconcile her with the Ozzy and Harriet type who had fastened an ancient apron over her linen blouse and jeans. Her champagne blond hair was twisted up in a topknot, though, and she was wearing a string of pearls, so the effect wasn't completely Suburban Grandmother.

She didn't look old enough to be a grandmother anyway, Maggie thought, smiling as the older woman banged through the cabinets for another platter. She was as down-home and friendly as her daughter—or at least as her daughter had been until Saturday morning. The daughter in question was curled up in one of the armchairs in the adjacent family room, staring blankly over the top of a coffee mug at the pool.

Not that Maggie could blame her. She was feeling a little overwhelmed this morning herself, and she was simply dealing with a weekend fling gone wild, not a dead fiancé.

Lucy clicked off her phone and gave Maggie a c'mere wave from the other side of the room. She picked up her mug and sidestepped Vivian and a baking sheet of croissants to sit beside her in the wide window. It was another bright blue day outside, and the sun glinted off the smooth surface of the water in the pool.

"Regina," Lucy said. "She was reading the morning headlines to me and, I think, having a coronary at the same time." She groaned and grabbed Maggie's knee. "Distract me with your neuroses again, please?"

Maggie slapped her hand away as she bit back a smile. "I'm not neurotic. I told you, I'm—"

"Sensible. I know." Lucy grinned and shook her curls out of her eyes as she sat up straight. "I don't know too many sensible people who stage a seduction in the billiard room of a stranger's house."

"I knew I shouldn't have told you that," Maggie said waspishly. "I could mention a certain disastrous incident that took place in the rest room of the Astor Place Barnes & Noble . . ."

"Okay, okay." Lucy raised her eyebrows, tilting her head at Paige in warning. "But I still don't know what you're so freaked out about. You've had nothing but a big fat grin on your face since Saturday morning—well, you know, except for when we found Drew's body."

Maggie rolled her eyes. "That is so not true."

"Oh, yeah?" Lucy snorted. "Do the words 'tousled hair' and 'hickey' mean anything to you?"

"I do not have—" Maggie protested, until she caught Lucy grinning at something behind her, and she turned around.

"Morning, Tyler," Lucy said demurely.

"Good morning," he said, resting his hand on Maggie's nape. "Something smells good down here, huh?"

She turned her face up to him. She'd crawled out of bed early, even though she would have been perfectly happy to lie snuggled against his warm body all day. Actually, she'd gotten up *because* she would have been perfectly happy to stay there all day. Getting used to him was a really bad idea, which was what she'd been trying to explain to Lucy with so little success.

He'd showered and shaved, and was wearing a faded navy polo over a pair of jeans. His damp hair was still sticking up in places, and he smelled like soap and the clean, crisp shave gel she'd found in his dop kit last night when she'd been poking around for floss.

And he looked good enough to eat. *No breakfast for me,*

Mrs. Redmond, I'm just going to nibble on this man over here. Don't mind us.

It was a shame she couldn't actually say that, she thought as Tyler nudged her until she scooched over to make room for him. It was a shame she couldn't actually *do* that.

It was really a shame she had to try and keep her distance from him today, before she melted down completely and packed herself in his suitcase.

"Anything wrong?" he murmured close to her ear. "You were up and gone awfully early."

"Nope," she said brightly, inching away. "Just hungry. And I had to call the office. And, uh, read the paper."

Since the newspaper was still lying neatly folded on the counter across the room, he angled his head around to look her in the eye, but just then Vivian called, "Come sit down, everyone! Breakfast is ready!"

"Oh, good," she said, getting up and pointedly not looking at him. "I'm starved."

"Well, there's plenty of food," Paige said, falling in beside her as they took seats at the table. "Mom likes to cook when she's nervous or upset, so we can all probably figure on gaining five pounds until this is over."

"It's very sweet of her," Maggie said, unfolding her napkin.

"And it looks delicious," Tyler added. He'd taken the seat on the other side of her, naturally. And the traitorous part of her was glad he had. It would just be easier to ignore him if he wasn't so agreeable and easygoing and sexy. Why couldn't he cooperate and start acting like a jerk?

Vivian sat down at the head of the table while Marty, Ethan, Nell, and Lake found seats. Tony and Whitney were already piling their plates at the other end, and Bobby was staring into a steaming mug of coffee.

Everyone was busy passing platters and helping themselves to eggs and hot croissants when Connor wandered in.

"Morning, everybody," he said, pouring himself a cup of coffee. "What smells so good?"

"You name it," Lake said, smiling over a forkful of eggs. "Mrs. Redmond made breakfast."

"Call me Vivian, please," the older woman said with a pleased smile. "Oh, Connor, there are no seats left. Let me get up and—"

"Don't you dare," he interrupted her, shaking his head. "I'll be fine at the counter. The cook deserves a place at the table."

"Well, if you insist." Vivian looked at her daughter with interest. "Aren't you eating, dear? Try a croissant at least."

"I'm really not hungry, Mom," Paige said, flushing when the others at the table turned their attention to her.

"You haven't eaten enough to feed a mouse in days, Paige," Lake said softly. "An anorexic mouse, come to think of it."

Paige opened her mouth in protest, but the phone rang at the same time. Stella Durden, Vivian's assistant, appeared from out of nowhere and snatched up the cordless receiver, carrying it out into the hallway.

There was a moment of startled silence before Whitney said dryly, "She's efficient, isn't she?"

From his perch on her shoulder, Bogart parroted, "Efficient. Efficient!"

"Yes," Vivian said, eyeing the bird warily, a forkful of eggs forgotten halfway to her mouth. "I hired her a few years ago when Paige's father died, because I needed someone to keep me organized between the funeral and the house in the city and the charity events we'd scheduled that season. She's been with me ever since."

"Maybe she has a twin," Tony quipped, breaking a croissant in half. "Who doesn't mind bird sitting."

Whitney scowled at him, and Maggie coughed to cover a laugh. Everyone else was busy with their plates, except for

Paige, who was still sipping her coffee absently. Without makeup, and with her hair pulled into a loose ponytail, she looked a little bit like an orphaned ten-year-old.

"Just the papers again, ma'am," Stella said, returning to the kitchen with a grim sigh. "I, of course, told them we had no comment. Again."

Maggie blinked. She was as British as tea in a tweed-patterned cup, very crisp and stiff upper lip. She was even carrying a clipboard, and two different-colored pens hung from a black cord around her neck.

Stella was her kind of girl.

"I'm going to finish up the letters, ma'am, and then I'll start on the"—she lowered her voice discreetly—"funeral arrangements. Mr. Fisk's mother did say it was up to you and Paige, is that right?"

"Yes, she did. She's going to fly up tomorrow or the next day, I believe." Vivian's gently friendly tone had shifted to one that was more clipped, Maggie noticed, and it hadn't escaped Paige's attention, either. She glanced up at her mother with wounded eyes, and then pushed her chair away from the table sharply and got up.

Maggie braced herself for a scene, but the Redmonds were too well bred to provide one. Paige simply set down her cup and walked out of the room, and Vivian turned back to her breakfast with a sigh.

Everyone waited a moment longer, eyes wide, just to be sure they weren't going to miss fireworks, before picking up their forks again. The silence was deafening.

It was broken by the shrill buzz of the front gate from a panel on the kitchen wall. "Detectives Vaughan and Szabo," Vaughan intoned through the speaker. "Open the gates, please."

"My, he's impatient, isn't he," Stella said with a frown, but she buzzed them in and clicked off in her sensible low heels to wait at the front door.

"He's not quite impatient enough, if you ask me," Vivian said, pushing her plate away and getting up. "I would have thought by now they'd have . . ." Her voice trailed off as she glanced at the faces around the table, and her unspoken words hung in the air: *found out who killed Drew.* Of course, that translated into *arrested one of you for murder,* so no one chimed in as she left the kitchen, color high on her patrician cheekbones.

"This started out a lot better than it ended," Tyler murmured with a nod at the table. "The croissants were good, though."

Maggie shot him a disapproving glare. She wanted to know what news the police had to share, and he was piling more bacon on his plate.

So she looked up at Lucy, who was twisting a stray curl around one finger nervously.

At the same time, they said, "Excuse me for a minute."

"Where are you going?" Tyler said, his mouth full of bacon.

"To the ladies' room," Maggie told him, unable to resist wiping a crumb off his chin.

He arched an eyebrow. "Together?"

"Women always go together, you know that," Lucy said with a little laugh, standing up.

"At home?"

"It's a big house," Maggie said weakly, and followed Lucy into the hall before he could ask any more questions.

"I think they're in the library," Lucy whispered, stopping beside the doors to the ballroom and listening. When they heard the purposeful click of heels on marble, they ducked into the empty room.

"I think Stella's going to get Paige," Maggie whispered, and a moment later they heard the two of them walking back down the hall, Stella's crisp voice subdued.

"I'm sure she didn't realize how it sounded," she was saying to Paige. "Mrs. Fisk sounds like a lovely woman."

Lucy and Maggie exchanged another glance, and as soon as the coast was clear they tiptoed down the hall. The door was ajar, which was lucky, but they couldn't exactly stand right there and eavesdrop. Maggie couldn't believe she was doing this in the first place, but after last night she wanted this murder solved. Every minute she spent with Ty made her want to spend all her minutes with him, and that wasn't going to work. Sticking around had been such a bad idea. If she'd left when the police gave her the go-ahead, she wouldn't be in this position, literally or figuratively.

And she was, literally, being dragged into the closet beside the library door, wrinkling her nose as she ducked her head beneath a bunch of coats.

Figuratively, she was between the proverbial rock and hard place. The rock being Tyler, of course.

Lucy elbowed her, and she dragged her attention back to the voices in the library. Vaughan was droning on about something. It would have been easier to hear if she wasn't surrounded by camel hair and musty wool. She leaned closer to the partially open closet door, resting her chin on Lucy's shoulder.

"What do you mean, an alibi?" Vivian was saying.

"Jack's whereabouts on Friday night have been verified," Betsy Szabo said. "He was at a bar in Westhampton with someone named Cheryl DeFiore, and they returned to her rental, where her roommates agreed that they spent the night."

"What about Saturday?" Paige said, almost too quietly for Maggie to hear.

"Saturday he claims he entered the grounds from the beach end, and that he did try to break into the house. Apparently he forgot that the alarm would sound if he broke a window."

Vaughan added, "You really should consider improving the security system. Anyone could walk up the beach and onto your property."

"We never needed much security before," Paige said dully. "And Jack won't bother us now. Not with Drew gone."

Maggie's heart twisted. She sounded so beaten. Her entire future had been wiped out with one vicious push on Friday night, and instead of curling up with a few pounds of chocolate under the covers, the way Maggie figured anyone would have, she had a house full of guests, some of whom she didn't even know.

And one of them had killed the man she was going to marry.

As Vaughan explained that he would need to question everyone again, Maggie nudged Lucy out of the closet and down the hall. They needed to do a little sniffing around themselves. Detective Vaughan certainly wasn't getting anywhere fast, and Paige needed to know who had killed Drew so she could bury him properly and get them all the hell out of her house.

Besides, if Maggie was going to try to convince herself that she hadn't stuck around just to be with Tyler, she could at least try to figure out which weekend guest was hiding a murderer behind his or her Gucci sunglasses.

"Is he going to question me again?" Lucy whispered. "I don't know what else to tell him. But he's beginning to grate on me less and less. I think I may have Stockholm Syndrome."

Maggie rolled her eyes and dragged Lucy farther down the hall as they heard footsteps emerging from the library. "What about Whitney and Bobby? I think we need to look into that a little further."

"Why?" Lucy argued. "Bobby said he didn't do it. And Drew's dead anyway. She can't kill him again."

True. Maggie frowned and bit her lip. Still, she wanted to know why Whitney had hated Drew so much. "Why did she want Bobby to kill him, though? Maybe there's more to this. Maybe someone else is in danger."

Lucy looked doubtful, but she shrugged. "We could always do a little Internet sleuthing. See if we can dig anything up."

Maggie nodded, linking her arm through Lucy's. At least it was a plan of sorts, and one that didn't revolve around Tyler. Behavior mod, they called it. She'd wean herself off him slowly. She hoped.

"Point me to a computer and I'll get Googling."

Chapter Seventeen

Tyler took a deep breath and dove off the board into the pool. The shock of the cold water hit him hard, and he surged up and out, shaking droplets of water out of his hair and ears, gasping. The sun was hot again today, but it was still only early June—the water wouldn't be really warm until sometime in August, this close to the ocean, with the salty breeze rippling across the pool's surface all morning.

Didn't matter. It was a good thing, in fact. If he dove in a few hundred more times, maybe the freezing jolt of the water would dull the edge of his frustration.

When Detectives Vaughan and Szabo had started questioning the others, he'd helped Vivian clean up the kitchen, although Stella had pursed her lips in disapproval. A guest was clearly not supposed to be hanging around with a dish towel, asking where the baking sheets should be put away.

But he'd found himself with nothing else to do. First Maggie and Lucy had disappeared; then the others had been herded into the drawing room for the latest round of good cop/bad cop, Hamptons style. So he'd called the Moonstone and checked in with Simon and Bethany, the hotel's managers. No problems, aside from a honeymooning couple who'd been caught on the back lawn, apparently determined to consummate their union everywhere they possibly could, and another fight between two of the restaurant's wait staff, who'd started and stopped dating at least three times in the past month.

He'd even called his father, just to make sure he wasn't worried, although Ben Brody was certainly used to Ty taking off on the spur of the moment by now. When he'd finally convinced his dad to move to Key West, Ty had warned him that he wasn't always around, but Ben didn't seem to mind. He'd taken to the Keys' lifestyle right away, shedding his usual Oxford cloth shirts and ties for polos and plaid shorts, with a jaunty straw hat that made Ty cringe. At least he wasn't wearing black socks with his sandals. He'd even found a girl-friend, although the term was a little weird for a widow in her late sixties. It was better than "lady friend," he guessed.

Then he'd read the papers, which were plastered with pho-tos of Drew and Paige, as well as the Hamptons house and the crowd of mourners and celebrity-seekers at the foot of the drive. When he'd flipped on the TV in the deserted family room, Fox News, CNN, and MSNBC were all covering the story, interspersing speculation about the crime, the date of the funeral, and Paige's future with clips of a much younger Drew on *Hollywood High,* brooding handsomely.

It was enough to make him nauseous. The anchors were all busy wondering which celebrities would show up at the service, when it was finally held, and putting on their best se-rious faces when they mentioned Drew's drug problems and time in rehab, but none of them seemed to care that he was just a guy. A guy who had stumbled into acting, sure, and had hit it big for a while, but also just a human being, like anyone else, whose problems with drugs were a lot more than juicy gossip-page stories. A guy who had a family, and probably a mortgage, and who liked to play the piano and kick back on the couch with his girlfriend and eat potato chips right out of the bag. A guy who was about to get mar-ried, and who was trying to restart his career.

Who put his pants on one leg at a time, as the old cliché went. It was such a waste. He'd had a life, and all it mattered to the people who'd made him famous was that it gave them something to talk about this morning. He'd turned off the TV with a growl then, wondering where the hell Maggie had wandered off to, when Vivian had reappeared in the kitchen.

Doing the dishes wasn't high on his list of favorite ways to pass an hour—and he'd had plates go green and fuzzy on him in the past as proof—but Vivian was tense and upset, and the remains of breakfast were a disaster. Plates and silverware were piled on the counter, or left at the table. There were two frying pans glistening with congealing bacon grease, and half-full coffee cups everywhere. For a moment, he'd felt a little guilty he hadn't cleaned it up already.

And Vivian had seemed grateful for the company, especially with Stella answering the buzzer for the front gate at least a dozen times. There were so many flower arrangements on the dining room table and the kitchen counter now, the whole place had begun to smell like a funeral home. Then he'd asked a tentative question about Paige and Drew. Vivian's shoulders had stiffened as she stood over the dishwasher, piling plates and bowls in the bottom rack, and Stella had shot him a warning glare.

Which had meant sleuthing was out. And Maggie, wherever she was, was still gone.

He cut through the pool fiercely, slicing at the water, still irritated. Wandering around the house looking for her was too pathetic to consider. Especially since he hadn't had to until now.

He climbed out of the pool, shaking off water, and stood looking up at the house, frowning. Last night had been incredible, both in the billiard room and after, and then this morning she'd awakened and left while he was still barely awake.

Not left, escaped. Run away. Again.

And he couldn't figure out why. He knew she'd enjoyed dinner last night. She'd been flushed and glowing all evening with the wine and the food, and she'd been ready for some more one-on-one time with him even before she'd led him into the billiard room.

That was where something had changed. He grabbed his towel and scrubbed at his wet head before tossing the towel back on the lounge chair and striding over to the diving board again. The sun felt good on his bare back, but the shocking rush of adrenaline when he hit the chilly water would be better.

The way she'd turned the lock on that door, purpose and desire hot in her eyes, wasn't new. He'd seen that all those years ago, and he'd seen it this weekend, too. But when he'd lifted her away from his cock, desperate to be inside her before he came, she'd done the one thing she'd never done before—she'd turned around.

The sight of her bare ass, round and soft beneath the raised skirt of her dress, was far from a turn-off. And he was too far gone to argue about positions, much less about what they meant—the wet heat of her mouth had driven him to the urgent, screaming edge of orgasm a couple of minutes earlier, and the moments it took to work her panties down her legs seemed too long. It wasn't until this morning that he realized it was the first time they hadn't faced each other when he was buried inside her. He was used to kissing her, to licking the slender column of her throat, to feeling her lusciously warm breasts pressed against him.

He was used to looking into her eyes.

With her back to him, her dark hair flipped over one shoulder and her hands clutching the edge of the table, she could have been anyone. And he could have been anyone to her.

He took a deep breath and dove into the pool again, closing his eyes as he plunged into the water. He nearly touched the tiled bottom before he somersaulted, pushed off, and swam to the top, sputtering as he broke the surface.

This wasn't even working anymore. Now he was tired and

cold and wet, and he was still confused. Or maybe just pissed off. It was hard to tell. The only thing he knew for sure was that he *wasn't* sure why he'd decided to stay.

Because Maggie was, he thought as he swam to the edge of the pool and turned around to rest his elbows on the ledge. Because after five years, he'd finally found her—or at least run into her accidentally—and two nights in bed with her wasn't enough. Yet.

The thing was, he wasn't sure it was ever going to be enough. And he didn't know how to feel about that.

Finding her again had been a . . . bonus. A way to convince himself that she hadn't run off last time because she was tired of him, or because he just didn't do it for her. It was an ego stroke, with the added appeal of a few more tangible strokes thrown in for good measure.

It was a hell of a better way to spend the weekend than making polite conversation with people he didn't know, talking up the Moonstone to potential guests with fat checkbooks and plenty of friends with the same. But that was all it was. He should have been in a cab to the airport the minute Vaughan lifted the house arrest. He did have a life to lead, after all, and a business to run.

Oh, yeah, because the place is going to hell without you. Not likely. Simon and Bethany probably wouldn't notice if he didn't show up till next month. That was exactly what he'd counted on when he hired them. It was what he'd wanted when he bought the place. A business that would run itself after a few years, with the right staff, giving him the freedom to . . . do what exactly?

He climbed out of the pool again and stalked over to his towel. It was the middle of a gorgeous, sunny early summer day, and he was standing by a pool with a view down to the beach. And he was soul-searching. Something was wrong with this picture.

He turned his head when he heard feet rustling the grass

and saw Shelby, looking like an overripe piece of fruit about to burst its skin. Her pale purple bikini was more like a suggestion than an actual swimsuit.

"Oh, good, company," she sighed, throwing a towel and her sunglasses on one of the lounge chairs and reaching up to twist her hair into a loose knot. The movement pushed her breasts forward, which he had no doubt she intended it to do. They looked bizarrely like grapefruit, too round and firm to be real, and he turned his attention back to drying off. Breasts were supposed to come in all shapes and sizes, and he'd always been happy with the ones he got to meet, no matter how big or small they were. The last thing he wanted when a woman took her shirt off was a handful of silicone.

Maggie would never do that.

He glanced up as if someone had spoken to him, startled. No, she wouldn't, but it didn't matter. Because they were going to say good-bye in a few days. Maybe today, in fact.

He ignored a sharp stab of disappointment at the thought.

Shelby was pouting, maybe because her cleavage hadn't inspired the appropriate reaction from him. Stretched out on the lounge chair, she had turned her face up to the sun, but her brow was still slightly furrowed.

"What did Detective Vaughan have to say?" he asked, shrugging his T-shirt over his head.

She made a face. "Don't even ask. He's such an ass. Like I would really kill Drew. Hello? Trying to have a career here. Not so possible in *prison.*"

And if she weren't trying to have a career, killing him would have been an option? Ty stifled a grunt of contempt and slung his towel around his shoulders.

She shaded her eyes with one hand, pouting. "Don't leave. I just got here. And I'm so *bored*. I wish I could go shopping or something. Not that the Hamptons is exactly good for that—God, I would give anything for an hour on Melrose right now."

The Hamptons had some of the most exclusive—and expensive—boutiques in the country, but try telling that to the spoiled L.A. princess. If he didn't leave now, he was going to get homicidal himself.

"I have some calls to make," he lied, striding past her and up the lawn.

"Hasn't anyone around here ever heard of a cell phone?" she complained as he walked away.

She didn't seem particularly bothered by Vaughan's questioning, he thought as he went into the house, aside from resenting her captivity. Which probably meant she didn't have anything to be guilty about. She wasn't talented enough to pull off the innocent act this long.

Lake had emerged from questioning while he was still in the kitchen with Vivian, as subdued and slightly worried as she had been all weekend. Whitney had come out and immediately taken her cell phone onto the terrace, where she had paced back and forth, a script in one hand and that god-awful bird on her shoulder. Tony had followed only a few minutes later, and Ty assumed he had gone upstairs—he had lumbered around silently most of the weekend, from what Ty could tell no differently than he usually did. The others had still been waiting their turns when Ty went out to the pool.

He found Ethan and Nell in the family room when he went into the kitchen for a bottle of water. Nell was curled on a loveseat reading another magazine, and when she looked up her expression was as icy and brittle as it had been since Saturday morning. Ethan, on the other hand, looked like a wounded puppy—he was circling the room, glancing out the windows and into the hall, as if he was waiting for someone.

The air was heavy with the scent of roses—another arrangement had been left on the counter. Ty opened the fridge and peered inside, wondering if it was too early for a beer. Behind him, Nell snapped, "For God's sake, sit down, Ethan. Or go away. You're driving me crazy. If Paige needs you, I'm sure she'll ring a bell or something."

In the stunned silence that followed, Ty glanced over his shoulder to see Ethan furrowing his brow at his wife, which made his delicate wire-framed glasses slide halfway down his nose. He pushed them up again and cleared his throat, then sat down and picked up the remote control.

"I'm sorry," he said, so quietly Ty could barely hear him. "I'm just restless."

"Aren't we all." Nell punctuated the wry words with the vicious flip of a page.

Ty grabbed a cold bottle of water and left, shaking his head. Being cooped up was getting to everyone, including him.

And you chose to stay, he reminded himself, wondering for the thirty-fourth time where the hell Maggie was. He took the stairs two at a time, wishing his room was closer to hers, and nearly smacked into her when he rounded the last step and turned onto the second floor.

"Ty!" She glanced at his towel and then down at his damp trunks. "You were swimming?"

"Didn't have anything else to do." Perfect. He sounded like a surly ten-year-old boy.

She flushed, color flooding her cheeks. "Oh. Well, I'll let you . . . get dressed."

He didn't want to get dressed. He wanted to be naked, with her, somewhere other than here. The embarrassed look on her face had melted the edge of his frustration already.

"Come with me," he said, taking her hand and tugging her in the direction of his room. She didn't protest, for which he was grateful.

Inside, he shut the door and skinned off his T-shirt. "Where did you and Lucy disappear to?"

Her bare arms were folded beneath her breasts, and the expression in her eyes was guarded. As if she was afraid he would come too close, or touch her.

And he wanted to touch her very much. In her sleeveless white blouse and those chocolate-colored above-the-ankle pants women seemed to wear all the time now, she was too cool, too crisp.

He wanted her soft and warm and a little sweaty, somewhere where no one had been murdered and she had nothing to think about but the ways he could make her sigh with pleasure.

The way it had been at the Moonstone, five years ago.

She sat down in the chair near the window abruptly, arms still folded, her ankles crossed neatly above a pair of flat brown sandals. "We were . . . snooping."

No wonder she looked so guilty. That wasn't on her rigid list of rules. He sat down on the bed, interested. "Where?"

"On the Internet."

He snorted. "That's not snooping," he said with a gentle laugh. "That's what you do when the workday gets boring."

"Oh." She bit her lip to hide a smile. "Well, I guess. Anyway, we were looking for dirt on Whitney. And we found some. I think."

"Yeah?" He raised his eyebrows. "Such as?"

She settled back in the chair, relaxing a little bit, although she couldn't seem to keep her eyes off his chest. He was tempted to strip off his wet trunks, especially since they were probably making the comforter damp, but he had the feeling she would bolt if he did. Whatever had made her disappear so quickly this morning, and after breakfast, too, was obviously still blowing around in her head.

And that made his own frustration float to the surface again. He'd spent the morning pissed off at her for disappearing, and angry with himself because he couldn't figure out why he cared so much, and after two minutes in her company, he'd been willing to let it all go if she'd just let him kiss her. But at the moment that seemed like the one thing that would scare her most, even if she didn't realize how obviously she was appreciating his body.

"Well, it's not really about Whitney so much as about Drew and Bobby, but since Whitney was the one who wanted

Bobby to do the dirty work, I'm assuming it's all connected somehow . . ." She trailed off, frowning, and he realized her gaze was riveted to his bare legs.

He let a warm little glow of pride flicker in his chest before he said, "What's connected? You're leaving out major pieces of information here."

She finally looked up at him, and her eyes were dark and worried. "We dug up a couple of stories about a girl who committed suicide three years ago, right before Drew went into rehab for the first time. Bobby and Drew were both mentioned as friends of hers in the stories."

"But no mention of Whitney?"

"No." She shook her head and leaned forward, her hair swinging over her shoulder. "We gave up on finding anything but industry-related news about her after a while and started to look for stuff about Bobby instead. We're only figuring it's connected because Bobby was the one who was apparently going to do the deed for her." She stopped, frowning, and looked so upset he crossed the room and crouched in front of the chair to take her hands in his.

"But what?" he said softly.

"It just feels . . . wrong." She turned her eyes up to his, and they were so sad and confused, he would have pulled her onto his lap if they wouldn't have ended up on the floor. "We're snooping around in these people's business. And I'm beginning to feel like we're doing it just to be nosy instead of to help. We're not the police."

"Whoever killed Drew had no right to do that either," he argued. "And we're not talking about anything that's not public knowledge, one way or the other."

"What about what that woman told us about Marty and Sybil?" she asked, watching as his thumb stroked the back of her hand.

"I bet three dozen people in Hollywood know their finances are a mess," he said. "If they don't have a full client roster and Drew hasn't been working, it wouldn't be too hard to figure out. My only problem with suspecting them is that it benefits them far more if Drew is alive and working than it does if he's dead."

"Unless they figure nice and prominently in his will," she said, sighing. "Although I don't know how much money Drew had left between the rehab and the drugs."

He stood up and grabbed his jeans and polo shirt off the bed, then stripped out of his trunks. "The problem is," he said, zipping up the jeans, "too many people possibly had a reason to want him dead. Which is sad in itself. Drew seemed like a good guy to me. One with some problems, sure, but a decent guy. Yet most of the 'friends' invited this weekend aren't exactly unhappy to see him six feet under. I don't envy Detective Vaughan."

He turned around and found her gaze fixed on the place his ass had been a moment ago, until she looked up guiltily and blushed again.

"My thinking is, we can forget all about Drew's murder and hole up in here for a while, or we can really try to give figuring it out another shot," he said, pulling her to her feet. No matter how hard she was trying to convince herself otherwise, the sight of him was definitely not turning her off. He let his hands linger on her wrists, then he dragged her closer, chest to chest, breathing in the sweet smell of her hair and enjoying the giving softness of her breasts against him.

She resisted for about half a second before letting him kiss her and then pulled away to say with a dreamy sigh, "My body is definitely voting for holing up here, but my imagination is wondering what you have in mind. In terms of snooping, I mean," she said, slapping his hand away from her breasts with a little grin.

"Damn," he murmured, leaning down to kiss her neck and her throat, tasting the faintly salty tang of her skin, sliding his palms over her ass and up her back, feeling for a bra strap. "The plan that involves staying here is much better. One of my best, actually. You sure about this?"

"I'm sure," she said primly, but she was biting back a grin at the same time. "What do you have in mind?"

He sighed and let go of her. "Some real snooping."

Chapter Eighteen

Standing inside Whitney and Tony's room three hours later, Maggie decided that she had finally lost control of the situation completely. Internet sleuthing was one thing, but pawing through Whitney and Tony's bags was another.

Tyler, of course, felt differently about it.

"Don't just stand there," he whispered with a frown, opening a dresser drawer. "We don't have much time until dinner."

His plan, if it could be called that, was to wait until just before dinner, which Vivian had announced she was cooking. When everyone was gathered downstairs, she and Ty would sneak up to the producers' room and poke around for anything incriminating. Or, more likely, anything that looked vaguely dubious.

Which they'd done, with Lucy in on the plan and standing guard at the bottom of the stairs. Or, to be more precise, sitting guard in the stiff little Louis XIV chair in the hallway, near the stairs, pretending to talk on her cell phone. If Whitney, Tony, or anyone else looked as if they were heading for the second floor, she was going to warn Maggie and Tyler. Somehow.

That part really hadn't been worked out satisfactorily, in Maggie's opinion.

"Maggie, come on," Ty said, turning around. He looked

like a gentleman thief tonight, in black trousers and a charcoal button-down shirt, although maybe it was just the situation. Thieves probably looked a little more intimidating and immoral. Ty just looked . . . sexy. As usual.

She sighed and ventured farther into the room, glancing around cautiously. Whitney and Tony had been given the room overlooking the backyard, on the other side of the ballroom from the master, and it was just as spacious as she assumed that room was, although the two of them had managed to make it look as though they were crammed into a space the size of a prison cell anyway.

Bogart's cage was set up on a dresser near the window, an enormous silver affair with a Gothic top and an array of perches, toys, and Bogart's own contributions. Apparently Whitney wasn't any more fastidious about cleaning it than she was about picking up the rest of the room. It looked as if she and Tony had been in residence for a month, based on the amount of clothes tossed over chairs and on the floor, and Tony's collection of scripts and 8x10 casting glossies piled on the desk and the floor beside it. A dirty dish had been left on a bedside table and a bowl crusted with potato chip crumbs on the long bureau, and an empty bottle of wine sat on the floor beside the unmade bed.

"Apparently she's used to maid service," Maggie whispered, toeing a pair of boxers gingerly.

"I don't think their laundry is going to turn up any useful clues," Ty said dryly. "Do you see her purse? Or a briefcase?"

"Not yet." Maggie stepped around an empty wineglass and squinted into the shadows on the other side of the bed. Whitney had left only one light burning on the desk, and Ty didn't want to turn on any others.

Which was making the huge lump under the burgundy-striped comforter look menacing.

She tiptoed toward the bed, feeling foolish. *It's not like it will be another body,* she told herself. *Everyone's downstairs.*

Still, she snatched the covers away and jumped back quickly.

A purse! She didn't feel any less foolish, but at least she'd found something.

"Ty," she whispered, glancing back to see him holding up a black-and-white photo of what she assumed was a young actress. With really white, really perfect teeth inside her lipsticked smile. "Ty! I found Whitney's purse."

He put the photo down on the desk with a guilty smile and peered over her shoulder. "Go for it," he said.

"You do it." She thrust the black leather bag at him. "I'm not cut out for the pen."

He snorted and sat down on the bed, pulling out a dead cell phone, a full case of cinnamon Altoids, car keys, two lipsticks, a brush clogged with frizzy blond hair, a pair of silver hoop earrings, a black hair band, and a pair of sunglasses.

"She should really use a case," Maggie pointed out. "They're completely scratched."

"Focus, Mags," Ty said, reaching in to pull out the only other things that might prove interesting—Whitney's wallet and a Palm Pilot.

"Start with her wallet," Maggie said, moving the lipsticks and the hairbrush aside to sit down. "It's more . . . personal."

"I think you'll do fine in the slammer," Ty said, eyebrow arched. "You look in the wallet, and I'll browse through this thing."

The wallet was sleek black leather—Kate Spade, Maggie noticed with a twinge of envy—or at least it had once been sleek. It was soft and worn now, as well as scratched. Inside, Whitney had six dollars and—Maggie counted—forty-seven cents, but twelve credit cards, ranging from Visa to Diners Club, with a few more mundane store cards for places like Sears and Nordstrom. There was a library card, an ID to get onto the Paramount lot, a couple of stamps, a receipt from Office Max, and a few photos.

None of Tony, Maggie noticed. Or Whitney, either. The

three snapshots, which had been cropped to fit in the wallet, were all of the same girl—a slightly gangly teenager who looked about eighteen in the photos, with blond hair, dark eyes, and a toothy, carefree smile.

Frizzy, dark blond hair, actually.

Just like Whitney's.

And like the girl in the photos she and Lucy had found in the news stories on the Internet.

"What's wrong?" Ty said, glancing up from the Palm Pilot.

"I think I know what the connection is," Maggie said, holding up the clearest snapshot. "This is the same girl Lucy and I read about this morning. The one who committed suicide. At least, I'm pretty sure it is."

"But who is she?" Ty asked, taking the photos to look at the back. Nothing was written on them.

"No clue." Maggie sighed and started piling the other things back into Whitney's purse. "But she looks an awful lot like Whitney, too. Whitney, who, as far as we know, doesn't have children."

"Could be a niece, or a cousin. Could be a surprise younger sister. You don't know how old this picture is, after all."

"True," Maggie said, then froze. Through the open door, she heard Lucy say in a falsely bright voice, "But you don't want to miss dinner!"

Whitney. Or Tony. It didn't matter—either way they were screwed.

"This is why we needed an escape plan," she hissed as Ty threw the PDA and the wallet in the purse.

"I have Tylenol," Lucy called—desperately, it sounded like, since Maggie could hear faint footsteps coming up the stairs already.

"Come on," Ty whispered, throwing the covers back over Whitney's purse and dragging her toward the closet.

They scrambled inside together, nearly getting stuck in the

door, just as Whitney walked in. Maggie dropped to the floor beside Ty, heart pounding. She was not cut out for this. No one was supposed to be cut out for this except hardened criminals. It would serve them right if Whitney flung open the closet door and . . .

She was gone. Already? Ty was peeking around the closet door. He heaved a sigh and slumped against the wall. "That was close."

"She's gone?" Maggie whispered incredulously.

"It doesn't take long to get a Tylenol," Ty said, getting to his feet. "Come on. If dinner is ready, we better get down there."

"Can I tell you how weird it is to keep eating with a strange group of people when you know one of them has committed murder?" Maggie asked, letting Ty pull her off the floor. "And *recently*—not in the distant past, before years of incarceration and rehabilitation, but a few days ago. If I hadn't seen Drew's body up close, I'd be tempted to think we were all part of some bizarre sociology experiment."

"Or a new reality show," Ty said with a crooked grin.

Maggie groaned as Ty peered into the hall to make sure the coast was clear. She shut the door behind her and grabbed his hand before he started downstairs. "What do we do about the pictures?"

"I don't think there's anything we can do, except steer the conversation in the right direction," he said, shrugging. "No matter who the girl is, and whether she was Whitney's reason for wanting Drew dead, we know Whitney didn't kill him, because she was expecting Bobby to do it. But Bobby didn't kill him."

"What about Tony?" It was too much to imagine that Whitney wanted Drew murdered, but hadn't had any hand in the actual deed.

"I don't know if we can figure that out, either." He looped his arm around her shoulders. "We have no way of knowing where anyone was after we went to bed, and we don't know what he was hit with. Besides, I can't see Tony going to so much effort, can you?"

"Not really," she agreed, relaxing in the circle of his arm as they walked down the stairs. Tony's natural speed seemed to be set on slow, and the way he lumbered around, she could hardly imagine him climbing up to the balcony in the guest-house. He didn't seem too fond of these stairs, either.

Still it didn't mean anything. If you really wanted someone dead, you found a way to make it happen. Someone here had, at any rate.

They found the others still in the drawing room, minus Vivian and Stella. The atmosphere was tense and quiet de-spite the Vivaldi playing softly in the background and the clink of ice in glasses. Someone was trying to make it seem like just another leisurely social night at the Redmonds', and instead it felt grotesque. Paige was curled on one end of the largest sofa with Ethan hovering nearby, and Shelby had cor-nered Connor with some story that naturally required her to flip her hair over her shoulders, which made her sheer blouse shift over a noticeably lacy bra. Nell was nowhere in sight.

Maggie followed Tyler to the console table where drinks had been set out and let him pour her a glass of white merlot, watching as Lake sat down next to Paige. She leaned in and said something Maggie couldn't hear, and Paige's eyes filled with tears.

"It's too much," she whispered to Lake. "Everyone's been very understanding but . . ."

Someone here killed my fiancé. She didn't need to say the words out loud, of course. Yet her mother was insisting that she remain a hostess to the very end. Grotesque wasn't even the right word.

"Why don't you go lie down?" Lake said, laying a hand on Paige's arm as she blinked away tears. "I'll tell your mother something. It doesn't matter, really. You don't need to do this."

Paige nodded, and didn't argue as Ethan took her arm and

led her out of the room. Lake met Maggie's gaze and gave her a thin smile. It was a small gesture, but it meant something. Maggie smiled back at her.

Lucy excused herself from the sofa where she had been sitting with Marty and Sybil and made her way over to Maggie and Tyler. "Vivian and Stella are putting the finishing touches on dinner. Chicken cordon bleu, or so I've been told. If I worked off stress with cooking like she does, I'd weigh about a thousand pounds by now." She glanced around cautiously and added in a lower voice, "Sorry about before."

"We managed." Ty's mouth quirked into a grin. "I think Maggie's had some B&E experience."

She shot him a dirty look and led Lucy toward the terrace doors, where she told her about the photos she'd found in Whitney's wallet.

"What does it mean?" Lucy whispered, using her cocktail straw to stir her Sea Breeze.

"No idea," Ty said quietly, resting his hand on Maggie's back. "But it's something to keep in mind."

Lucy had opened her mouth to respond when everyone froze as Bobby bellowed at Tony from the other end of the room, "I don't need to take it easy. I'm fine!"

His definition of fine was pretty loose. He looked awful, as if he hadn't showered for days, his hair greasy and flat, his shirt untucked. He was barefoot, Maggie noticed, and looked as though he was wearing the same jeans as yesterday.

Bogart flapped away from his perch on Whitney's shoulder, landing on the mantel and screeching, "I'm fine, I'm fine!" Shelby scurried away, sloshing her drink all over the carpet.

Whitney grabbed Bobby's arm, and he dropped the highball glass he'd been trying to refill. It shattered on the hardwood floor, where the light from a Tiffany lamp sparkled on the jagged shards.

"Look what you made me do," he slurred. "Look!"

"It's nothing," Tony said, shaking his head and twisting

Bobby away from the wreckage. He looked like an angry walrus, his beard twitching as he growled, "Get a grip, man. You need to go upstairs and sleep it off."

"Nothing," Bobby parroted, stumbling away from him, wincing as his foot sank onto a piece of glass. Blood bloomed from his heel, bright red, and he crumpled to the floor, groaning.

"Oh, God, Bobby, what's wrong with you?" Lake grabbed a handful of cocktail napkins from the bar and knelt beside him, trying to staunch the blood.

"He's been on a liquid diet since Friday night," Connor muttered. "That's what's wrong with him." He put down his own glass with a frown.

Sybil was twittering to Marty on the sofa, and Shelby had screwed up her forehead in contempt. Whitney was trying to corner Bogart, who was still screeching, although he'd switched to, "Nothing! Nothing!" his gray wings flapping and the tip of his red tail flared in outrage.

"Can you try to stall Vivian?" Ty said to Lucy quietly.

"This is not a scene she needs to see," Maggie agreed, wondering where a dustpan might be. Lucy had told her Paige used a cleaning service twice a week instead of live-in help, but she assumed the essential supplies were around somewhere. The glass needed to be cleaned up before anyone else bled on the rug or punctured an artery. Or decided a weapon was necessary.

"I'll do my best," Lucy said with a sigh, heading for the kitchen.

"Calm down and let me see it," Lake was saying to Bobby, who shrugged off her hands with a grunt.

"Will you get *off?*" He sounded like a three-year-old on the verge of a tantrum. Wobbling to his feet, he limped to a chair and pressed the bloody napkins to his heel. "Fuckin' A, this hurts. But it doesn't matter. I deserve it. I should hurt. Someone should slice me open head to toe. Would be better. Should have been me anyway."

Tyler stopped on his way out to find a broom and glanced over his shoulder at Maggie, his brow furrowed in concern. She put down her wineglass carefully. What the hell was Bobby talking about?

It was the million-dollar question, judging from everyone else's expressions. Marty and Sybil looked vaguely appalled, Shelby was curious, and Connor was disgusted.

Whitney, on the other hand, was clearly terrified. She'd gone several shades paler than her usual bloodless white. Lake was stunned, and dropped suddenly from her crouch onto the floor.

Tony was simply furious, his cheeks red above his grizzly beard. "Bobby . . ." he started, and flinched when Bobby flailed a hand at him, choking back what seemed to be a sob.

"Just shut up, okay?" he managed, sniffling violently. "You don't know . . . you don't even *know* what she . . ." He stopped, staring at Whitney, who had managed to corral Bogart and had the bird tucked into the crook of her arm.

"Stop it," she said, staring at Bobby, her jaw clenched. Bogart wriggled, pecking at her arm with his hooked black beak.

"Why?" His laugh was a hollow, angry bark. "It doesn't matter anymore. Drew is dead. *Dead.* Just like Rachel."

Rachel? The girl in the photos? Maggie met Tyler's gaze, deep blue and utterly still as his mind worked out what was going on, and he walked back to her, sliding his arm around her waist. Protecting her, she thought with a vague flare of fondness. Even from a drunken photographer's ravings.

"Shut *up*," Whitney hissed, letting go of Bogart abruptly. The parrot flapped wildly in midair, settling on the coffee table with an injured squawk.

"Who the hell is Rachel?" Tony bellowed, glancing at Whitney with a confused scowl.

"Bobby, this is not the time—" Whitney began, but he cut her off with a sharp grunt of laughter.

"It's exactly the time," he said, his shoulders shaking. He

was truly hysterical, veering between laughter and tears like an out-of-control car. His dark eyes were bleary from alcohol and sleeplessness, and more than a little crazed. "Rachel is the reason for everything, isn't she? Poor Rachel." He sounded sincere enough in his pity, at least. "She couldn't handle it . . . and we couldn't handle her . . ."

"*Who* is Rachel?" Tony barked for the second time, and Sybil jumped, shrinking against Marty.

"Don't you know?" Bobby shook his head and wiped the wet track of a tear across his cheek. "He doesn't *know*?"

"Bobby, you're drunk and you're upset and no one needs to listen to you ranting," Whitney said. Her tone had mellowed, and she'd smoothed her expression into motherly concern, but Maggie could see the wheels turning in her eyes. *Nice try,* she thought, as Bobby wrenched his arm away from the hand Whitney had rested on it.

"Doesn't know what?" Tony asked, stalking toward Whitney. The color had drained from his face.

Maggie braced herself, stretching out her hand to take Ty's. The room was crackling with the tension, and any minute the storm was going to hit, hard and fast. Her stomach had already twisted into a painful knot.

But Lake spoke up before Whitney or Bobby could. Her eyes were huge in the soft light, a doe's mournful, frozen stare. "She's been dead for years now, Bobby. Can't you just let it be? It doesn't have anything to do with what happened to Drew." She looked down at her lap, where her hands were clutching the patterned cotton of her skirt.

"Oh, but it does." Bobby stood up, forgetting the wound on his heel. The bloody napkins fluttered to the carpet. "It's why I'm here. It's why . . ." He broke off, shaking, and Whitney grabbed him again, her face as hard as her grip on his forearm.

"Just stop now, do you hear me?"

"Stop what?" Bobby cried. "Stop feeling guilty that she's dead? How can I when you won't let me? It's not my fault, and it wasn't Drew's, either! So he couldn't love her the way she needed to be—he was as fucked up as she was! And I couldn't kill him, and now he's dead anyway!"

Shelby gasped, and Connor stood up so suddenly, he knocked a delicate green china vase off the end table beside him. It rolled across the carpet and onto the hardwood.

"What do you mean, *you* couldn't kill him?"

Sybil was twittering again, a low, constant warble too soft for Maggie to make out, but Marty shushed her with a wave of his hand.

Lake was on her feet, too, her thin face white, the skin stretched tight over her cheekbones. "What are you talking about, Bobby?"

"He's out of his mind," Whitney hissed, letting go of him and backing away. Bogart squawked and flapped onto her shoulder, parroting, "What are you talking about? What are you talking about?"

"I'm talking about how she"—he pointed a shaking finger at Whitney—"wanted me to kill my best friend. Told me I had to. Said she would . . ." He trailed off, exhausted, his voice breaking on the last word as he sank to the carpet.

"She *what?*"

Maggie gulped. The sensation of hair standing up on the back of her neck was distinctly uncomfortable. But Tony's voice was terrifying, solid ice. Frozen around knives. And a whip.

Whitney was still backing up, with that ridiculous bird clinging to her red silk shirt. She bumped into an end table, and the lamp on its top quivered, the beads on the shade tinkling in the heavy silence.

"She couldn't have . . ." Connor left the sentence unfinished, turning to stare at Whitney in disbelief.

Lake shook her head, a single tear rolling down one cheek. "Yes, she could. She blackmailed me into coming. Why not murder, too?"

"Oh, my God," Shelby breathed. Her blue eyes were wide. "You people are fucking crazy."

Tony ignored the others, stepping around Bobby, who was still shuddering on the carpet, and stalked toward his wife. "I'm going to ask you once more, Whitney. Who is Rachel?"

Her mouth twisted into an ugly grimace, and when she looked up at him, her eyes burned with fury and a hundred other things Maggie could only guess at. Humiliation, frustration, grief, vengeance. "She was my daughter."

Chapter Nineteen

There was nothing like ugly melodrama to cast a pall over an evening, Tyler thought, kicking off his shoes and rolling up the hem of his pants. Swallowing the last of his beer and setting down the empty bottle, he sat on the edge of the pool and dangled his feet in the cool water. He could taste the salt in the moist breeze off the ocean, and the stars overhead were fuzzy in the dark sky. It smelled like rain.

"I'm going in," Shelby said suddenly, getting up out of the lounge chair where she'd been pouting for the last half hour. The flickering citronella candle on the patio table threw its glow across her face, catching the thrust of her lower lip.

"Good night," Lake said, looking up absently.

Shelby paused, her gaze fixed on Connor, who was staring out at the ocean in the distance. He glanced sideways at her and said, "Good night."

Not the response she was looking for, judging by the tight set of her jaw. She released a frustrated breath and padded across the grass to the house without another word.

Ty wasn't sure what she'd been expecting—a wild free-for-all in the pool, after what had happened earlier? It was all most of them could do just to sit here thinking, waiting until it seemed late enough to justify going upstairs to bed.

Ethan had reappeared just as Whitney had blurted out the truth about Rachel, Nell at his side, her severe black linen blouse emphasizing her sharp, angular features. In that moment of frozen, horrified silence, he'd heard Lucy's voice from the kitchen, distracting Vivian with some nonsense about carbohydrates, and then the room had exploded into chaos.

Bobby's voice was a nearly unintelligible moan beneath Tony's angry shouts, and Bogart had taken offense to the whole situation, shrieking, "She's my daughter, she's my daughter!" in a voice eerily similar to Whitney's.

He shuddered now, thinking about it. Connor had wrestled Bobby off the floor and toward the staircase, but Tony and Whitney had beat them to it, Tony shouting and the bird circling and parroting him until Whitney reached their bedroom and slammed the door shut.

There was no keeping Vivian or Stella in the kitchen by then, but Lucy had made soothing noises and steered both women into the dining room with Sybil, Marty, and Shelby, while Tyler and Maggie cleaned up the broken glass and spilled liquor. Lake hadn't moved off the sofa until Lucy came back to get her, and Nell had simply stood under the graceful arch that divided the drawing room, her arms wrapped around her middle, her expression as cool and inscrutable as usual. Ethan had paced back and forth, muttering, until Lucy snapped at him.

Dinner was a nightmare, one of those surreal *Alice in Wonderland* moments, with Vivian attempting to make small talk and pass the salad as if nothing had happened. Only Nell had joined her, and Ty had listened in disbelief as the two of them discussed a charity luncheon planned for July as if the filthy roots of murder, blackmail, and revenge hadn't just been exposed in the other room.

It was unbelievable that after all that, they still didn't know who had actually killed Drew.

No one had objected when Stella insisted on cleaning up after the meal, and Marty, Sybil, Ethan, and Nell had all excused themselves immediately, heading upstairs in pairs.

Tony had disappeared into the billiard room when he'd come downstairs. No one had bothered to call him for dinner, and Tyler knew Whitney was going to be a no-show. Connor said Bobby had passed out almost as soon as he'd dumped him on his bed.

That left the rest of them staring at each other blankly, so Ty had grabbed Maggie's hand and led her outside. One more minute in the sterile, unmoving air inside the house and he was going to go a little crazy, too.

But for the last hour, no one had said much of anything, except when Lucy offered to go inside to get drinks. Even Maggie had been uncharacteristically quiet, curled into a lounge chair beside him, nursing a glass of wine and staring at the gently rippling water in the pool. Someone had turned on the pool light, and the water glowed green-blue.

"I really loathe her," Lake said suddenly. She shrugged, her thin shoulders bare and pale in the meager light.

"Can't say as I blame you," Lucy muttered, thrusting out her bottom lip and mimicking Shelby's pout.

"Don't worry," Connor said, lighting a cigarette and blowing the first long stream of smoke toward the ocean. "She's only a few years and a few more bad career decisions away from making Cinemax After Dark movies."

"That's not nice," Maggie said, but her voice was mild, and she was trying not very successfully to bite back a smile. Ty laughed, and trailed his fingers through the water.

"The thing is, now I understand why Whitney wanted her invited," Lucy said with a frown. She wriggled in her chair, resting her feet on the seat and wrapping her arms around her legs. "Paige was planning the party, of course, but I distinctly remember that she told me Whitney wanted Shelby to come. To make trouble, I guess. In case murder wasn't enough."

"But Bobby didn't kill Drew," Lake said softly, and for a moment it seemed as though the elephant on the patio had raised his trunk and roared at them.

Lucy stared at her, her eyes wide. "Right. I keep forgetting. It's so bizarre to think that more than one person wanted him dead."

"And I don't think Tony carried out the dirty work for her," Connor added. "He was blown away in there."

"Did you know Rachel?" Maggie asked Lake.

She nodded slowly, her gaze far away. "But I didn't know that she was Whitney's daughter. I don't think Drew knew that, either."

Tyler was willing to bet Bobby hadn't known until Whitney decided to enlist him in her plan to kill Drew. If she'd never even told her husband about a child she'd obviously given up for adoption long ago, it didn't seem like the sort of information she would pass around at a cocktail party. He just wished he knew exactly what had happened, and how Whitney had been able to keep tabs on a daughter she didn't publicly claim as her own.

"What did Whitney have on Bobby?" he asked suddenly, trying to sort through the various pieces of the puzzle.

Lake sighed and reached for the glass of wine Lucy had poured for her earlier. She'd left it untouched till now. "I'm guessing it had to do with that whole period. He and Drew were using really heavily, and I'm pretty sure Bobby was dealing on the side. It wouldn't surprise me if he was Rachel's main supplier, either. They did the same drugs—coke, Ecstasy, even crack sometimes. And once in a while they took pain pills—Percocet, OxyContin, whatever they could get their hands on."

Drugs for heavyweights, or professional addicts. Definitely not the kind of stuff someone who just smoked an occasional illicit joint ever touched.

"He got away with it, you know?" Lake went on, her head tilted to one side as she stared into the past. "No real arrests, and as far as I know, no trouble with payments. And then Rachel died, and he and Drew both got clean. From what I've heard, Bobby wants to get into acting, too—the photography was just something that happened, a way to pay the rent, but when he first went out to L.A., he wanted to act."

"So Whitney could be threatening to expose him, maybe even get the police involved," Maggie mused aloud. Then she caught Tyler's eye, and he remembered what Lake had said about blackmail.

The breeze picked up, ruffling the sail-cloth umbrella over the table, and somewhere out on the water, a boat's light arced. Lake continued before anyone could ask. "That's what Whitney threatened to do to me, more or less. She dangled a part that I wanted, too, but she made it pretty clear that if I didn't show up here, she was going to the press with stories about my drug use. Drew and I were in a relationship back then, before Rachel came along, and even after we broke up—after I got clean—I tried to keep an eye on him. I loved him. Paige knew that, although I don't think Drew ever told her how heavily I used at the time."

Lake didn't sound angry, just tired. And maybe a bit relieved at the same time—carrying around a secret like that had to be exhausting, Tyler thought. The public didn't know, not yet, but at least he and the others hadn't judged her. She didn't question why Maggie had thought to ask if she'd known Rachel. Maybe she didn't care.

"I'm sorry," Maggie said with a gentle smile. Lake nodded, and in the candlelight Ty could see tears shining in her eyes.

"She wasn't blackmailing me," Connor said with a dry laugh. "I feel a little left out."

Lake shook her head, a sudden grin lighting her face, and elbowed him playfully. "You're lucky."

"I don't know if I'd call it that," Connor said, standing up and stretching, rolling his head lazily on his neck. "At least not the way you mean. I just feel so fucking sorry for Drew and Paige, and so goddamned stupid that I ever begrudged him anything. You've gotta have balls of steel to work in this industry, present company excepted, of course, and I'm beginning to think I may not be cut out for it."

"But think of the loyal members of the Connor Wheaton fan clubs," Lucy teased, resting her chin on her knees. "I can hear the sobs of betrayal now."

Lake snickered, and Connor made a face at them both. "Sure, sure, joke about it," he said, pretending to be wounded. "A guy tries to be honest, and what does he get? A smart-mouthed female making fun of him. It never fails."

"Poor Connor," Lucy said, standing up and hooking her arm through his. He turned to her with a genuine smile, tugging her closer, and she blew a stray curl out of her eyes.

The hair flip would be next, Tyler thought. Or maybe the flirty head tilt. Not that she needed to do either. Connor was clearly already interested.

Maggie caught his eye again, her brow creased in concern, and he shook his head, mouthing, *Leave them alone.* In another moment they were gone, holding hands as they walked across the lawn, their shoulders bumping together comfortably.

"Well, I certainly put a damper on the party, huh?" Lake said. She swirled the wine in her glass with a guilty laugh.

"Hardly," Ty told her, splashing his foot through the water idly. "I'm sorry you had to go through all that, but I'm certainly glad that you're okay now."

She gave him a grateful smile. "Me, too." She stood up, gathering her glass as well as Connor's. "But I'm also exhausted. I think I'm going to go to bed."

"I bet you're dying to get home, huh?" Maggie said.

"What's home?" Lake laughed, the glasses clinking together in one hand as she reached for the light sweater she'd draped over the back of her chair. "I've seen my apartment in L.A. maybe five weeks out of the last fifty between filming and press tours. Anyway, I want to stick around, if Paige will have me. I want to help her through this." She'd started toward the grass before she turned around, her expression curious. "If I were you two, though, I would have left the minute you got the go-ahead from the police. Why did you stay?"

Maggie opened her mouth and then shut it again, staring down at her lap, so Ty offered, "It's complicated."

Lake nodded. "When isn't it?"

When she was gone, Ty stood up, shaking water off his feet. Complicated didn't really sum it up, though. At least not for him. And getting inside Maggie's head was a lot more difficult than he'd bargained on.

"Why did you stay?" he asked Maggie quietly.

When she looked up at him, the haze of moonlight and the reflected orange glow of the candle gleamed in her hair. The flickering candlelight was caught in her dark eyes as they shifted over his face, but instead of answering, she swallowed hard and said, "Why did you?"

Maybe if he tried to tell her, he could figure it out along the way, he thought, reaching down to pull his shirt free of his pants. And the things he hadn't told Maggie weren't anywhere near as painful as what Lake had shared. "I never told you the whole story about buying the hotel," he said simply, tossing his shirt on the cement. He reached for his belt buckle and watched as her eyes widened.

"Ty, what are you . . . ?"

"There was more to it than boredom," he continued, ignoring her as he unbuckled his belt and slid it free of the loops. "A lot more. Earlier that year, I almost died."

He heard the breath catch in her throat, and she sat up. If he touched her now, he thought, he'd feel her heart racing.

"See these?" He traced the faded scar on his chest, then the one on his forehead. "It was a car accident. One minute I was on Lake Shore Drive; the next I was underneath my car. The next thing I remember was waking up in the hospital, where the nurses made a point of telling me that I'd been technically dead for at least a minute and I was lucky to be alive."

"Ty, oh my God," Maggie murmured, standing up and

walking toward him. When she took his hand, hers was cool and soft—all her energy was focused in the look of stunned horror on her face and the wild pulse in her throat.

"It's . . ." He stopped with a brief laugh. "It was a long time ago. But it made me think. About my life, about what I was doing with it. Which, at that point, was studying for the bar and working in the law library to pay my rent. There was nothing but cases and standards and torts and evidence and contracts. That and trying to stay awake in the library while I was working. No one works when they're studying for the bar, but I didn't want to move back home, and I didn't want to give up my apartment. Every waking moment was the law." He paused and looked out at the ocean. Waves shushed against the sand, and the breeze rustled in the sea grass. Maggie was silent, her hand still in his.

"And when my father told me what had happened in that accident, and how close I came to really being dead, I had to think about what the rest of my life was going to look like," he went on. "I hadn't seen my dad for weeks; I hadn't even watched TV. I couldn't remember the last time I'd eaten more than a cheeseburger from the cafeteria, or a bowl of cereal. And it didn't look like anything was going to change even if I passed the damn bar. I still had to find a good job and concentrate on whatever my area of law was going to be, and all I could see was more hours bent over a desk with a cold cup of coffee and a candy bar. The idea that my life could have ended that way was a wake-up call."

Maggie made a soft noise of understanding and squeezed his hand tighter, but after he squeezed back, he let go and unzipped his pants. Maggie frowned, confused, and he couldn't help smiling.

"I postponed the bar, and my father convinced me to take a trip, get some fresh air, some sun. You know the rest, I guess." He let his pants drop and then skinned off his briefs. "And while I was there I decided I wasn't going to let my life slip by. I wanted to enjoy it, not just get through it. So I bought a hotel. And I hired staff who could take care of it for me, once I could afford them, so I could take advantage of my freedom."

She was staring at him, but he had to tilt her chin up before she was staring at his face. "That's why I didn't say no to spending three days in that hotel room with you. And it's why I stayed here even when I could have left—because I can make choices. I chose to stay so I could spend more time with you. And now I'm choosing to get in this pool. Are you going to join me?"

She frowned again, those delicate eyebrows pinched together over her wide, dark eyes. She was adorable when she frowned, even if she wouldn't have believed it.

But she was more adorable when she wasn't.

"Ty . . ." She glanced up at the house doubtfully, and he sighed.

"No one's watching," he said, turning around to get into the water. The air had felt cool on his naked skin, but it was nothing compared to the shock of the water. He shivered, sliding in to his waist and turning around to look at her.

She was standing on the cement apron, moonlight in her hair and the breeze ruffling her sheer skirt around her knees, and for a minute he considered climbing out and asking if she would at least consider making out in the grass with him.

"Come in," he said. "Keep me warm. You haven't been in the pool yet, and we've been here since Friday."

"It's dark," she pointed out.

"No chance of sunburn."

"It's cold."

"It's good for the circulation."

"What if someone comes outside?"

"It's dark, remember?"

"Not with the pool light on."

He groaned. "You're killing me here, Maggie."

She bit her bottom lip, and for a second he could taste the

plump, soft flesh on his tongue. She had the most kissable mouth he'd ever known.

"Maggie," he said. "Come on in. The water's fine."

And she reached behind her to unzip her skirt.

That's my girl.

He pushed off the side with his legs, skimming backward in the water, watching as she lifted her shirt over her head. Her silky bra and panties shimmered in the moonlight, a dusky blue against her skin.

Need kicked low in his belly when she wriggled out of the bra, then stepped out of the panties. She was so goddamned beautiful with her hair swinging against her cheek as she leaned down to test the water with one toe.

"It's cold," she said doubtfully.

"You'll get used to it."

She sighed, and then suddenly jumped in with a splash, coming up sputtering and gasping. "It's *freezing.*"

"Come here."

She was shivering as she waded through the water toward him, and he gathered her close, sliding his hands over her body under the water. She was slick and smooth, and as he fitted her against his waist, wrapping her legs around him, the water buoyed them both.

"I'm so sorry about what happened to you," she murmured into the hollow between his neck and his shoulder. Her lips were wet and cool on his skin. "I can't imagine what that must have been like."

He'd glossed over it, but he remembered more of the accident than he wanted to. The sudden, violent screech of metal on metal, the smoke and the acrid smell of burning rubber and scorched leather, the confusion as he tried to orient himself, only to realize he was underneath the car, pinned into his seat, with the hot, wet sting of blood dripping into his eyes.

But as horrible as it had been, what was worse was realizing that his life had almost ended. That he hadn't done half of the things he wanted to, and wouldn't have a chance to try if he took the bar and became a lawyer. Not for a long time, anyway.

"It worked out in the end," he said, smoothing her wet hair back. "I changed my life for the better."

"And you don't miss the law at all?"

"I thought I could do some good and make some money as a lawyer," he told her, pushing off the side of the pool and walking toward the center, cradling her against him. "But I've been able to do that with the hotel, too. So no, I don't miss it. I especially don't miss having to wear a suit every day." He felt her smile against his chest.

"But you still drive like a maniac."

"Only when I'm eluding pursuers."

She smacked his shoulder playfully. "That's no excuse. But if you were so broke, how did you buy the hotel?"

"Investors, remember?" He glided them through the water. If they didn't keep moving, they probably *would* freeze. "I had some friends with money in Chicago, some money I'd earmarked for post-law-school expenses, and clean credit. It was a stretch, but I managed. Don't you ever think about opening your own design firm?"

He tilted his head back to look at her, sure he saw a flash of envy in her eyes before she closed them and laid her head against his shoulder. Her hair felt like wet silk against his skin.

"No," she said. "I mean, not anytime soon, at least. I'm strangely fond of eating. And paying my rent on time gives me a thrill."

He repressed a sigh as he ran his hands down her back and over her ass. It wasn't his business if she didn't want to take the risk of striking out on her own, although given everything he knew about her, he didn't doubt for a second that she'd have all of New York lined up at her door, begging her to redesign their living rooms.

It wasn't what he really wanted to know, anyway.

"You never told me why you stayed," he murmured, turning his head so his lips brushed her damp cheek.

She stiffened—even her hand tensed where it rested on his back. "I told you, I didn't feel right leaving Lucy alone here."

Bullshit. Or maybe not entirely bullshit, but certainly not the whole truth, either. She wouldn't even admit to wanting the extra few days with him, and he'd poured out his whole frigging life story.

"But I feel guilty for being here without doing anything to help," she went on, apparently oblivious to his slow burn. Any minute now, he was going to start steaming up the water, and not the way he'd planned when he'd pictured them skinny-dipping. "Or at least anything really useful. There has to be something we've overlooked."

She pulled away, untangling her legs and gliding backward in a graceful float. Her breasts bobbed just above the water, gleaming wet in the moonlight, and he stamped down the urge to wade after her for a nice, leisurely taste.

He tried to stamp it down, at least. With his lips fastened around her rigid nipple, failure tasted pretty good.

She released a shuddering breath as he slid a hand underneath her, supporting her weight, still kissing her breasts. She was cool and wet and faintly tart, which he supposed was the chlorine.

"We should go inside now," she murmured.

He wasn't about to object. Even if he'd never pictured himself in the position of wanting more from a woman than she wanted from him—and what Maggie wanted was clearly sex, no strings attached, and very little conversation, either. So little conversation she wouldn't even admit that she'd stayed partly to be with him.

Not that he wanted anything more than those few little words from her. He didn't want a commitment or anything like that. He was pretty sure, anyway.

There was one good way to put a stop to that irritating train of thought, at least. He helped her out of the pool, determined to convince her that they didn't need to go inside at all.

Chapter Twenty

Solving a murder really wasn't the easiest way to take your mind off a man, Maggie thought the next morning, staring at the abandoned guesthouse over her third cup of coffee. Especially when everything she knew about detective work came from novels and TV shows, where the sleuths in question were naturally talented, brilliant, and usually disproportionately good looking. She'd never watched *Columbo*.

She rolled her neck carefully, wincing when it pinched— she'd woken up curled into the warmth of Ty's chest with her head at a weird angle. So much for resisting him. She'd wound up in his room last night, which of course meant in his bed. Again. Despite her best intentions.

And that was *after* the lounge chair by the pool, which had proven to be a lot sturdier than she would have guessed. She still had strap marks on her butt, though.

"More coffee?" Ty asked, leaning an elbow on the table and propping his head in his hand. In the sunlight, his hair was nearly blue-black.

"I'm good," she said, wrapping her hand around her mug. She was on caffeine overload already, and trying to decide how to get through the day without completely caving in and just staying in bed with Ty had made her jittery already.

They'd come downstairs sometime after nine to find Vivian baking blueberry muffins with ruthless energy. Stella was standing by, her usual disapproving frown fixed firmly in place along with her glasses. Most of the others had been gathered at the table with coffee and the newspapers, but Whitney, Tony, and Bobby were noticeably absent. Nell and Shelby were, too, although that wasn't a surprise—Nell was clearly sick of the lot of them, and Shelby was probably planning on getting through most of the day by sleeping.

It was an idea she should have given some thought to, Maggie mused now, sipping the cold coffee and trying to avoid Ty's gaze. The problem would have been unearthing a bed Ty couldn't find.

Still, even giving in and curling up with him would probably be more productive than sitting out here on the terrace staring at the horizon line. It would definitely be more enjoyable than trying to pry information out of the other guests.

Marty was clearly so appalled by last night's display, he and Sybil had returned to their room as soon as they'd made a polite show of sampling Vivian's muffins. Ethan was close to taking up Sybil's job of chief twitterer—Maggie had caught him mumbling into his coffee twice. Lake and Connor looked too exhausted to approach, and she couldn't imagine either of them with a reasonable motive anymore.

Paige hadn't made an appearance, either, and nothing short of a fire was going to make Maggie knock on her door, or Whitney's.

But here she was, with no plausible excuse for leaving, since she'd told Ty she'd stayed for Lucy's sake. And Lucy wasn't going home anytime soon. Plus, she hadn't been lying when she'd told him she felt guilty about not helping get to the bottom of Drew's murder—the man was dead, and she'd hung around just to satisfy her own rebel hormones. The least she could do when Ty wasn't making her incoherent was try to figure out who had gone homicidal.

"You know, if you furrow your brow like that for too long, it'll stick that way," Ty said, examining the empty inside of his cup. "What are you thinking about?"

"That we need to *do* something," she said, setting down her own mug and leaning forward. "Detective Vaughan hasn't come back since yesterday morning—I think he's hoping we'll just starve to death in here and he won't have to bother charging anyone."

"I doubt that," Ty said dryly, arching an eyebrow. "They probably can't rule out the idea that someone got onto the grounds and broke into the guesthouse, which means questioning neighbors and canvassing the neighborhood. I guess."

His last words sounded doubtful, and she didn't blame him. Between the lust, the ambition, the envy, and the resentment, there were more than enough motives to choose from among the guests. No one had ever mentioned Drew receiving crazy hate mail from antifans, either, and while that didn't mean he hadn't gotten some in the past, she figured Paige would have mentioned specific or recent threats.

"Are the faithful still gathered at the gates?" she asked idly, still staring at the yellow tape festooning the guesthouse. It was a gray, cool morning—the sun seemed to have given up for the time being, and the air was heavy with the smell of rain. The crime scene tape was a neon slash of color against the dull white façade of the little house.

"Oh, yeah," Ty said with a derisive laugh. "Camera crews, reporters, mourners—they're all still there. Some of them look like they're setting up camp. I swear I saw one girl with a tent."

It was fascinating how murder could make anything less surprising, Maggie thought. She didn't doubt that Drew sightings and stories of him faking his death would turn up a few weeks from now.

But sitting here thinking about that wasn't getting anything accomplished. She sat up straight and looked at Ty. "I'm going to check out the guesthouse again. There has to be some kind of clue the police missed."

Startled, Ty opened his mouth to speak, but nothing came out.

She gave him an impatient frown. "Are you coming or not?"

He blinked. "Uh, yeah, I'm coming."

She glanced at the main house's graceful lines as she got up from her chair, wishing she knew exactly where everyone was. She had no idea if Paige would care that she planned to poke around in the private quarters she'd shared with Drew, but given the way everything else had gone down this weekend, it was a good bet that someone would protest if she and Ty were noticed.

He followed close behind her as she crossed the lawn. She wished he didn't smell so good. It was bad enough that he was so near she could vaguely sense the warmth of his body, clad this morning in comfortably worn khakis and a loose blue oxford with the sleeves rolled up. He looked like a walking Abercrombie & Fitch ad, all casual, careless sex appeal.

"This is pretty," he murmured, fingering the collar of her sleeveless blouse.

She fought down a glow of satisfaction. It was a pretty shirt, white linen embroidered with black silk in a funky swirl pattern, and it was one of her few never-fail pieces of clothing, the kind that she fell back on when nothing else felt right because it always looked good on her.

Plus, she got to wear her sheer cream bra underneath it.

Stop it. None of that mattered right now. If she had any sense—and if it wasn't, of course, at home in her closet—she'd be wearing her stained orange Mets sweatshirt, because that had always made her look like a demented jack-o'-lantern even when it was brand-new. The point was to concentrate on figuring out who the murderer was, not how to make Ty want her. He was doing that well enough on his own anyway.

"Thank you," she said finally, wriggling to shake off his fingers, which were wandering down her back now. "And behave yourself."

"Yes, ma'am," he grumbled, but he was still close enough for her to feel his heavy sigh against her neck.

"Let's go around the back," she said, stepping around an azalea bush and hopefully out of groping range. Both doors were most likely locked, but at least behind the guesthouse they'd be out of sight while they were peeking.

"You're all business this morning," he said as they rounded the corner, suddenly snaking out a hand to tickle her.

She choked back a shriek of surprise and lunged sideways into the carefully pruned bushes alongside the back porch, giggling in spite of herself. Then the heel of her sandal struck something hard, and she stepped back.

"What is it?" Ty said, squinting down as the sun emerged from behind the low bank of clouds over the ocean. In the silence, the drone of a motorboat on the water was a faint buzz.

She crouched down and pushed aside a branch thick with hot pink azaleas, revealing a heavy, bell-shaped cognac glass.

"Don't touch it," Ty warned when she reached for the glass. "If it has anything to do with Drew's murder, it will have fingerprints on it."

"Who's all business now?" she asked him, but she smiled. He was right, too—if it was evidence, they needed to leave it alone and let the police handle it.

"I wonder whose it was," she said aloud, thinking back over the past few evenings.

"Well, it wasn't Drew's unless he came out here to drink without Paige noticing," Ty said, crouching beside her. "But the police didn't mention anything about a blood/alcohol level."

"Why would they?" Maggie argued. "Vaughan was furious that Detective Szabo told us there was head trauma."

"True." He stood up and paced away, hands jammed in his pockets and his shirttails flapping gently in the breeze. The sun had disappeared again. "That's a cognac glass, isn't it?"

"Yup." She angled her head to look at it more closely, trying to picture what everyone had been drinking. She remembered the empty beer bottles piling up around Bobby Friday evening, not that it really mattered. She thought Tony had been drinking scotch from a highball glass, and everyone else had been drinking wine—except for Nell.

She'd had a bottle of Armagnac with her in the conservatory on Sunday night, when Maggie and Tyler had discovered her noodling around on the piano. And she'd been drinking the same thing at Friday night's dinner—Maggie could picture her getting up at least twice to refill that heavy snifter from the bottle on the sideboard during the meal.

When she looked up, Tyler was already staring at her, his face set in a frustrated scowl. "It doesn't prove anything," he said. "Even if her fingerprints are all over that glass. She wandered outside before the screening—she might have left the glass out here then."

"Way out here?" This time Maggie lifted an eyebrow. "Behind the guesthouse?"

"I'm not saying it's logical," Ty argued, "just that it's possible. And it still doesn't prove anything. Plus, why would she want to murder Drew?"

"I don't know," Maggie said, getting up and pushing hair out of her eyes. The breeze was picking up, and now it felt faintly wet. The sky was pewter. It was going to pour any minute.

"Let's go in," Ty said, taking her hand. "We can talk upstairs as easily as we can out here. And stay dry while we do."

Only if he meant upstairs in the attic, Maggie thought mutinously. Or the hall closet. No way was she going into either of their bedrooms with him. With nothing to do but toss around theories on the most likely murder suspect, and very few suspects left to choose from, they were going to wind up bored and restless. On the kind of rainy afternoon when being in bed was the most attractive option anyway.

No way. She had to preserve at least a shred of self-control here. Even if all that meant was waiting till nightfall before tearing his clothes off again.

If she'd expected peace and quiet inside, she'd been wrong. She followed Ty through the French doors on the terrace into the family room and was greeted with the chaos of raised voices.

"Who would do this?" Vivian shrilled, her wild-eyed gaze fixed on Stella, who blanched behind her glasses, her mouth pressed into a tight line.

"Do what?" Tyler said, letting go of Maggie's hand as they approached the group gathered around the table, which was still strewn with the remains of breakfast.

Paige was sitting at the table's head, pale and silent, her cheeks wet with tears. Lucy was seated next to her, one arm draped around the other woman's shoulders. She looked up at Maggie and shook her head wordlessly, glancing at the framed photos strewn on the table.

Connor and Lake hovered nearby, both of them frowning and apparently at a loss, and Ethan was practically sputtering with rage.

"What on earth . . . ?" Maggie murmured, and stepped closer to the table, peeking around Marty to find that each of the frames had been shattered. And what had been pictures of Drew and Paige together were now photos of Drew alone— Paige's face had been ripped from each one roughly, obviously without the luxury of scissors, leaving a frayed edge where Paige had once held Drew's hand or stood in the circle of his arm.

"Uh-oh," Ty murmured into her ear. She glanced over her shoulder to find him right beside her, scowling again, his eyes dark with concern.

"That's an understatement," she whispered back.

Vivian was still ranting at her assistant, who was trying unsuccessfully to settle the older woman in a chair with a cup of tea.

"I don't need tea, Stella, for heaven's sake!" she hissed,

waving at the mug in irritation. "I need some answers, and so does my daughter! I don't know what kind of people Drew was involved with, but this is just . . . too much!"

Talk about your understatements, Maggie thought wryly. Murder was distasteful and inconvenient, but decimating the family photos was apparently a crime for which no punishment would be too great. Vivian looked rattled, and all of a sudden much older than usual—her hair was mussed, and her melon-colored blouse was untucked. And Maggie wasn't even sure if she realized that this new wrinkle meant Paige might be in danger, assuming the photo murderer was the same person who killed Drew.

Maggie motioned to Lucy, who patted Paige's arm awkwardly and got up, following Maggie over to the bay window.

"What the hell happened?" Maggie asked, moving over to let Ty sit down next to her.

"I don't know." Lucy shrugged in amazement. "After you two went outside, I went upstairs to make some phone calls, um, with Connor"—she blushed—"and the next thing we knew, Vivian was shouting and Paige was crying, and then Stella was trying to calm them both down. I guess Vivian found one of the photos in the upstairs hall and went looking for others, only to find them all equally trashed. And equally Paige-less."

"This is not good, in a serious way," Ty said, shaking his head. "Whoever did this is psychotically angry at Paige, and whoever did this *has* to be one of us this time around."

Maggie nodded, watching as Lake sat down beside Paige and held her hand. Connor was brushing up pieces of loose glass that had shaken free of the frames when they were tossed on the table, as pale and worried as the rest of them. Every once in a while, he glanced back at Lucy, and his eyes warmed in pleasure when she smiled at him. Where was everyone else, Maggie wondered.

Lucy said Shelby was still upstairs—she'd poked her head

out of her room during the earlier melee, but had shut herself back inside almost immediately, still in a very brief, very sheer nightie that had made Stella blush.

"It doesn't mean anything," Ty pointed out. "She could have destroyed the photos last night—I didn't notice the one in the hall this morning, did you?"

Lucy shook her head, her unruly curls bouncing.

"I didn't either," Maggie said, frowning. "Not that I was looking."

"She has good reason to resent Paige," Lucy pointed out.

"Not anymore," Maggie argued. "Drew's dead. Why take out her frustration on Paige, especially if it's not going to get her anywhere. She's too lazy."

"I'll give you that," Lucy agreed, glancing over her shoulder as Vivian's voice rose again. Stella looked ready to quit on the spot, her cheeks flaming with embarrassment and her hands clenched into white-knuckled fists at her sides.

Connor and Lake weren't likely suspects, even if Maggie had nothing to go on but instinct, and Bobby was most likely still asleep. Tony hadn't been seen since the night before, but he had absolutely no motive to make more trouble after Whitney's little show.

Whitney, on the other hand . . .

Just then, Nell and Sybil wandered into the room, Sybil passing a magazine back to Nell. "What's going on?" Sybil asked, blinking in dismay.

"Never mind," Marty said, crossing the room and taking her arm. "Let's go upstairs for a while, honey."

"I just came from there!" she protested, but she didn't argue when he steered her out of the room.

Nell peered at the table in mild curiosity, her smooth eyebrows drawn together in a frown. "How awful," she murmured. "I remember that picture," she said to Paige, pointing at one of the larger frames. "You had it taken at that vineyard in Montauk."

Paige didn't reply, and Nell paused, as if searching for

something to say. After a moment, she simply crossed the room and curled into one of the sofas, reaching for the TV's remote control.

The sound of the Fox News anchor's voice broke the uneasy silence with a report on a baseball brawl, and Ty glanced at it. Maggie could practically see his ears perk up. She elbowed him, and he turned back to her with a sheepish grin.

"Just wanted to be sure it wasn't the Cubs," he said.

"Has anyone called Vaughan?" Maggie asked Lucy, who nodded.

"Stella did right away, after she assured Mrs. Redmond it was essential. Viv didn't want any more 'trouble,' although judging from her reaction, she's not too concerned about making a scene herself."

"Well, they should be here any time, then," Ty said. "I guess we'll just have to wait. They can get fingerprints off the frames, even if they have to fingerprint all of us to get a match."

It sounded reasonable, but after almost an hour, Maggie was restless. Nell insisted on flipping channels, switching from the news to cooking shows to soap operas without any recognizable logic behind it, and Ethan grunted under his breath each time she did. Connor had fallen asleep on the opposite sofa and was snoring, Lucy seated on the floor beside him, her head resting against his arm, and Lake was pacing around the kitchen island, poking through the refrigerator every few minutes. Paige had never left the table, but she'd drawn her feet up onto the seat and was hugging her knees to her chest like a wounded child.

When the phone rang, startling them all, Stella rushed to answer it. She murmured low into the receiver, nodding and glancing around the room, and hung up a moment later.

"They won't be here for a bit," she said crisply, addressing the room at large, back to her usual stiff disapproval. "Something else has come up, but that . . . Detective Vaughan said, and I quote, to 'sit tight.'" Maggie could have sworn she'd left out the "awful" she'd been tempted to insert before the detective's name.

"That's it," she murmured to Ty, who had sprawled in one of the club chairs a few feet away when the window seat in the bay got too uncomfortable. She had to get out of this room and do something. Waiting here to reel off the latest developments—Whitney and Bobby's plot, aborted though it may have been, the cognac glass in the bushes, and the ruined photographs—was only going to make her crazy. "Let's take a walk."

Chapter Twenty-one

Not impulsive, his ass, Ty thought as Maggie led the way down the damp lawn. When she got an idea in her head, she damn well did fly by the seat of her pants.

It was a good thing her pants were usually so well fitting, though. Watching her bottom sway gracefully in the black shorts she'd put on that morning, he had to admit he didn't hate walking behind her.

It had rained only briefly, but the sky was just as foreboding as it had been two hours ago, leaden with clouds that were still misting the grass so softly, the air simply felt wet. Not the time he would have chosen for a nature hike, of course, but he couldn't deny he'd wanted out of that room as much as Maggie obviously had. The tension was vicious, brittle and crackling like a loose wire.

"Any particular destination in mind?" he asked, stepping over a soggy pile of grass clippings near the tennis courts. The gardener would be in for it next if Vivian caught sight of that.

"How about the beach?" she replied. "In Tahiti."

"How about the beach in Key West?" he asked lightly, and regretted it when she didn't even give him one of her patented scathing glances. He was pretty sure her back stiffened, too.

Okay, so no joking around. Well, that sucked, to be blunt about it. He wasn't serious, not completely anyway, but he was beginning to wonder what the hell was wrong with him. She'd gone into his arms willingly enough last night, by the pool and in bed, but otherwise she was buttoned up like a winter coat.

And the trouble was, he couldn't figure out what he wanted from her, other than a little reassurance he wasn't just a convenient lay for the duration. And that he had been more than a convenient lay five years ago.

Convenient wasn't the right word for this weekend, he thought, still following as she headed toward the boardwalk that would take them over the dunes and down to the beach. Her first reaction to seeing him again had been more along the lines of, "Oh my God, run and hide!"

And given everything he knew about her—which still wasn't anywhere near as much as he wanted to know, he realized with an uncomfortable jolt—she wasn't even the casual sex type. Everyone, men and women alike, had their moments, but on the whole, Maggie was way too careful, despite her infrequent flashes of spontaneity, to sleep around just for the hell of it.

That was good, he guessed. Did it matter, if he was never going to see her again? And why did he need to know so intensely if he was going to see her again when he was always the one to walk away first, satisfied with a friendly fling and nothing more?

Sex was one of the best ways he knew to shut his brain off for a while, but he didn't think Maggie was going to be up for it in the damp sand, and anyway, hadn't he realized that his brain refused to shut off when he was with her, naked or not? For the first time with a woman, it kicked into a higher gear, or at least a more analytical one, processing every sigh and every groan, every gentle smile, every time she curled against him afterward, warm and sated, just for the pleasure of staying in contact with his body.

He grunted aloud, and Maggie glanced over her shoulder

in question. *Think earned run averages,* he told himself. *The condition of your stock portfolio. Anything but this.*

"You okay?" she asked, and he forced his eyes up to her face, taking in the wide, deep brown eyes and that flirty little mole and the soft curve of her mouth. It was far better than the rear view, and the rear view was pretty damn awesome.

"Uh-huh." He nodded, jamming his hands in his pockets. He felt like a ten-year-old caught with a dirty magazine.

She looked at him for a moment longer, her brow furrowing again, but then she turned away, stepping up onto the worn, silvered planks of the boardwalk.

He caught himself looking at her feet, admiring the red polish on each toe, visible in her flimsy little sandals, and noticed as her second foot followed the first that a dark bulk rested in the sand against the wood. Crouching, he blew away a thin frosting of sand and realized it was an empty bottle of Armagnac.

Perfect for hitting someone in the head, he guessed.

"Maggie!"

She turned around again, frowning, her hands on her hips, and then hurried toward him when she realized what he was doing.

"Oh, God," she whispered, gazing down at the bottle. He turned it gently with a loose stick he'd found behind him at the edge of the dune, and there on the heavy base was a sticky patch furred with sand, but sporting a few unmistakable strands of hair. Short, dark brown hair, also sticky, with what looked like blood.

"What do we do?" she asked him, her eyes wide. "Leave it and bring the cops down here, or take it back to the house?"

"I don't know," he admitted, his mind racing back over the last few days. Just because Nell had been drinking the cognac didn't mean she was the killer—anyone could have used the empty bottle to hit Drew, unless fingerprints proved otherwise.

"It's Nell's," Maggie said, echoing his thoughts in a somber voice. "She was the only one drinking this stuff. Which is hard enough to believe in the first place. She's been chugging it like a wine cooler all weekend."

"But it doesn't mean she killed him," he pointed out, standing up but still staring at the bottle. "And why would she have killed him anyway? She's Paige's friend, for one, and second, she's not exactly doing the happy dance that Ethan has elected himself Paige's main source of comfort."

"I know." Maggie bit her bottom lip as she puzzled it out, staring out at the water. "It doesn't make sense, but circumstantially, at least, it looks like Nell did it. Which is just so creepy, I can't even process it. She's been the only one who's kept her cool the whole time, except for that night at the piano."

He thought back, trying to remember what Nell had said that evening. Most of it had been wiped out by Maggie's subsequent seduction, of course, but he seemed to recall Nell's bitterness over Ethan's job—or was it over the fact that he was ignoring his job to care for Paige? God, he was such a guy. He could remember his blow job in graphic detail, but no one was going to question him about that.

"Do you think she ruined those photos, too?" Maggie asked him, stepping closer as a breeze rolled off the water, stiff and salty.

"It makes sense that whoever killed Drew destroyed them, yeah, but I still can't figure out why Nell would do either one. It seems too . . . I don't know, *messy* for her, don't you think?"

"Oh, yeah," Maggie agreed. "In the right circumstances, she's definitely a hire-a-hitman type." He stared at her, and she shrugged carelessly. "I'm just saying. And what I really can't figure out is the connection, twisted as it may be, between her and Paige and Ethan and Drew. Something's there that we're missing. Right now, I just wish Vaughan would get here so he could handle it."

"Well, when he does show up, we've got plenty to tell him." He glanced around the sand and spotted a scrap of paper, which he grabbed and used to pick up the round black bottle, holding it by the neck.

"It's a good cognac," Maggie observed, but she was keeping her distance, her voice too studiedly casual. The blood-stain was freaking her out. "XO, too. Nell has expensive taste."

"This surprises you?" he said, wrapping his free arm around her waist as they headed back to the house.

She didn't protest, and he breathed in the scent of her hair, clean and sexy and comfortingly normal, just as the rain started to come down again.

Tyler paused on the terrace, his face twisting in concentration, and Maggie stopped beside him, wondering what was wrong. She was getting wet. But when she strained her ears, she heard what had made him pause, and she was startled to realize that blood actually could run cold. Hers was, at least, icy and way too fast.

It was Nell's voice, just as icy, through the open French door to the drawing room.

Icy or not, it sounded crazy. And when Maggie took hold of Ty's shirt and followed him closer, where they would have a view into the room, it was definitely crazy. Because Nell was pointing a gun at Paige and Ethan, who were huddled together in front of the fireplace. Nell's back was to them, slim and erect in a pale blue silk blouse. Her dark hair bobbed wildly against her shoulders as she spoke.

". . . always known," she was saying, "always. It was so clear, even all those years ago. And this week has just proved that nothing's changed."

"Jesus Christ," Ty whispered, and whirled around to face her. "Take this. And stay *down*." He thrust the cognac bottle at her, and she took it in confusion.

"What do you mean . . . ?" As he settled into a crouch, his

plan dawned on her, and she hissed, "Oh, no, you don't! Tyler Brody, don't even think about it! She's got a gun! A *gun!*"

"Maggie, relax," Ty whispered, turning those bright blue eyes on her as if they would convince her he hadn't lost his mind, too.

Oh, no. Impulsive was one thing. Rash was another. She set down the bottle and grabbed his shirt again. "Please, Ty, let the police handle it. They should be here any minute! I mean, they should have been here by now already, but still, they're coming, they will, and they know how to deal with—"

He put a hand over her mouth, shushing her. "I know, I know, it's stupid. But if she shoots Paige or Ethan, I couldn't live with myself. At least I have a chance to surprise her."

"And if she shoots you instead?" Maggie argued, her heart banging against her ribs painfully. She brushed wet hair out of her eyes. The rain was coming down hard now, splattering the terrace in fat droplets. "Then you don't have to worry about living with yourself, do you, because you'll be *dead!*"

She wriggled away when he tried to grab her arm, determined to take another look. It was then that she noticed the blond and brown heads of Lake and Connor just visible behind the farthest sofa, and what looked like Vivian's champagne-colored twist off to the side. Maggie's heart skipped in panic. Where was Lucy? And Stella, and the others?

"What I couldn't believe was that Paige didn't want you, Ethan," Nell was saying, and her voice trembled on her husband's name. The gun swerved dangerously at the same time, as Nell's arm relaxed, making a swooping arc off to her right and toward the floor. "I mean, to have someone like you in love with her and not feel . . ." She swallowed hard and shook her head. "It didn't make sense. But then Ethan wanted me, and I was so happy. So happy. You don't even know. He was everything I wanted—and he had such a wonderful future in front of him, one he was inviting me to share."

Tyler edged closer, listening, and Maggie let herself lean against him as Nell continued.

"But it never stopped, no matter what I did. Every chance he has to brush against you, he takes." She swung the pistol at Paige again, where it quivered in Nell's outrage. "Every chance he has to invite you to a party, he does. He probably sees your face when I make love to him." She choked on that, emotion clogging her throat, and her arm shook wildly. "But no more. I can't take it anymore."

"But . . . but why did you kill Drew?" Paige whispered, tears streaming down her cheeks. The top of her thin pink T-shirt was wet with them.

"Because I thought it was the one thing that would drive Ethan away." Nell's laugh was a bark of disbelief. "I thought Drew himself would be enough—the scandal, the drugs, the drinking. Ethan's nothing if not terribly proper about that sort of thing. I can just imagine what his mother must think of all this. Her precious little boy, stained by the filth of Hollywood."

Ethan grimaced, his thin face bloodless beneath his glasses. As Maggie watched, his Adam's apple bobbed up and down as he swallowed. In panic or in anger? It didn't matter. Either way, while Nell was swinging that gun around the room, he was stuck right where he was, and pissing her off would be a bad idea.

"But that didn't work," Nell went on, walking forward, the pistol bobbing awkwardly. Paige flinched, but when she realized she'd moved closer to Ethan, she stepped back, her shoulder blade hitting the mantel with a dull thud.

"So I thought that maybe the scandal of a murder would stain Paige," Nell said, "finally make her distasteful to him. The rumors, the doubts, the drug-addicted brother—I thought all of it would be too much for him to take. But I guess I was wrong. Again." She stopped to draw breath, and although Maggie couldn't see her face, she was sure Nell was crying, too. Her shoulders were trembling.

"Lake and Connor and Vivian are in there, too," Maggie whispered, shrinking away from the door. "I don't know where anyone else is. Oh, God."

"Move over," Ty said grimly. "Someone has to put a stop to this. And I'd rather it wasn't you."

Maggie swallowed hard, a sudden vision of him lying in a pool of blood on the floor swimming into focus, and she grabbed his hand.

What the hell had happened while they were outside? Nell had to know the police were on the way—she'd been right there in the room when Stella got off the phone with them.

Of course, they still hadn't arrived, she realized, squeezing Tyler's hand. Nell still had time to get her revenge, even if it meant twenty-to-life in the women's penitentiary reading out-of-date magazines.

Finally, she glanced up at him, trying to read his thoughts in his eyes. She saw frustration, anger, and a little bit of fear, which was probably a good thing. Fear would at least make him careful.

"Be careful," she whispered anyway.

"I will." He grabbed her by the back of the neck, hauling her close for a hard kiss, just like in the movies. *This had better have a happy ending,* she thought wildly, letting go of his hand as he crawled toward the door.

She could hear Nell raving again as she crept behind him. There was no way she wasn't watching, just in case she had to yell out for him to duck.

"I don't even care what the tabloids would print," Nell was saying. For a confession, she seemed happy to go all out. "It wasn't the idea of a divorce and how ugly they would make it—the people who read those papers are stupid and trashy, the same stupid, trashy people lined up outside with their dollar-store teddy bears and their ridiculous homemade cards. It wouldn't matter what they thought about me getting a divorce, or even what my friends and my mother's friends would say." She hiccuped as if in punctuation, and Maggie watched as Tyler crawled closer over the soft antique carpet. The bottoms of his shoes were covered with wet blades of grass.

"The thing is, you see," Nell said, gulping back a sob, "I love Ethan. I don't *want* to divorce him. No one believes it— they all call me an ice queen, a standard-issue society bitch who wants nothing more than another Tiffany box and another trip to Paris, but I would give up all of that if he would look at me, just once, the way he looks at you!"

The gun swung back at Paige, whose chest heaved with a shuddering, frightened inhalation of air.

Nell laughed then, but the sound was hollow, crazy. "I don't have anything else, you know. I went to Vassar the way I was supposed to, and I got my degree in English literature, and I worked the requisite year in publishing, but I never cared about any of that. I wanted to be married to Ethan, and I wanted to have his children. Well, we're married, for what it's been worth, but the children haven't come. They won't, either, not when he never wants to fuck me."

Maggie's hands clenched as Tyler raised himself into a crouch two feet behind Nell. The tone of her voice had gotten shriller and more hysterical with every word, and Ethan was openly crying now, too. He tilted his head, and a single teardrop rolled down his nose, landing with a silent splat on his shirt.

Oh, God, Maggie thought, realizing with a vague flash of awareness that it was pouring. Rain was sliding down her neck and into her shirt, and her hair was plastered to her head. *Oh, please, please won't someone stop her, someone who's not Tyler. . . .*

"It's over," Nell said then, and her voice had a frozen finality to it, as if some part of her had died, too.

Which was when she raised her arm, shaking with the effort, and Tyler lunged at her, grunting.

But what Maggie saw in that moment was that Nell was turning the gun on herself, not at Paige or Ethan. Her arm was bending up, the pistol slowly aiming for her temple. She wanted it to be over, not for them, but for her.

Tyler's tackle hit the back of her thighs, and she stumbled forward, the motion throwing her arm back. The gun went off with an explosive crack, whizzing through the room and striking the heavy gilt frame of a painting on the wall to her left with a hiss. She groaned, falling forward, the gun clattering free onto the strip of hardwood between the two gorgeous carpets, Tyler landing on top of her in a weird pile of limbs.

Paige crumpled against Ethan as Maggie scrambled into the room, snatching the gun off the floor, watching her hand shake as she did. The room smelled acrid and sharp, and a thin serpent of smoke still hung in the air.

The others jumped up from behind the couch just as footsteps pounded down the hall into the room—Lucy skidded inside first, stopping with a hand to her mouth as she caught sight of Tyler and Nell tangled on the floor. Stella was right behind her, with Tony, Marty, and Sybil bringing up the rear.

Then everyone was talking at once, helping Ethan and Paige onto one of the sofas, shouting back and forth for water and cold cloths, Stella on her knees beside Vivian, who was still gasping, sweat beaded on her temples.

Maggie laid the gun carefully on the table by the window and knelt beside Tyler, who was still holding on to Nell.

"Tyler, it's over," she murmured, reaching out to touch his shoulder tentatively. What if the bullet had grazed him? What if he was really hurt? Oh, God, what if he didn't answer her?

Her heart felt like a frantic little jackrabbit, and she gulped, waiting. Then Tyler turned his head and looked at her, a wry, amazed grin on his face.

"Maybe this hero business isn't for everybody," he said.

She laughed out loud, aware that a tear had slid down her cheek, dripping off the end of her chin. "Maybe not," she said, "but you did great. I mean, it was a completely insane thing to do, but you did it with, um, flair."

"Is that what they call tackling the suspect these days?" he said, letting go of Nell's middle. She gave an incoherent moan, and they both looked down to see that the hair on the back of her head had been singed. Beneath it, her scalp was dark and sticky with blood.

"She got hit," Maggie said, standing up. Her legs weren't entirely happy about it, trembling with adrenaline and relief, but she stayed upright as she said, "Someone call an ambulance."

"Who needs an ambulance?" a surly voice demanded from the doorway.

Maggie turned with the others to see Detective Vaughan standing beside Detective Szabo, scowling as she blinked in surprise.

"How did you get in?" Tyler asked, getting to his feet slowly and brushing off the knees of his pants.

"Mrs. Redmond gave me the gate code in case of emergency," he snapped, his gaze landing on Nell's crumpled form. "What the hell happened here?"

"An emergency," Maggie told him wearily. "And you're just a little bit late."

Chapter Twenty-two

"Well, I did promise you it wouldn't be boring," Lucy said to Maggie two hours later, sorting clothes into clean and dirty piles on her unmade bed. She tossed a paperback, a nail file, and a CD into a tote bag.

"No, you didn't," Maggie said dryly, looking up from where she was lying on the bed. She hadn't completely recovered yet. She'd never taken a Valium in her life, but she wouldn't have refused one today. It was good to know she wasn't cut out for police work in case she ever had to change careers. "You said I wouldn't regret coming. Clearly, you were wrong."

"Oh, come on," Lucy protested, tossing a T-shirt that smelled like beer at Maggie's head. "There were movie stars and free food and a pool. And intrigue, yeah, and murder, not to mention a few minor nervous breakdowns, but there was also Tyler. You don't regret that, do you?"

"Did you secretly sneak away to a keg party sometime this weekend?" Maggie asked, sniffing the shirt and wrinkling her nose. "Or did you and Connor decide to relive your college years and play quarters last night?"

"Stop avoiding the question." Lucy snatched it back and threw it on what Maggie hoped was the "dirty" pile.

She sighed and rolled over onto her side, taking the opportunity to ignore Lucy for a moment longer when she went into the bathroom. Several things clattered into the sink, and she heard Lucy's muffled, "Shit."

She couldn't think about Ty yet. The day had been eventful enough already without emotional angst on top of it.

Nell had been taken away in the ambulance, with Vaughan and Szabo shepherding Whitney and Bobby to the police station, muttering about charges of "conspiracy to commit murder." Tony had packed Bogart and his and Whitney's belongings into his rented Mercedes and followed them, with strained good-byes and apologies to Paige and Vivian. Maggie wondered if Nell would finally reveal exactly how she had gotten Drew up to that balcony, and how she'd managed to push him off it.

Vivian had been packed off to bed for the rest of the day *with* a Valium, thanks to Stella, who had probably palmed one for herself. She still seemed stunned by the situation she'd walked into Sunday afternoon, but then she wasn't exactly drawing combat pay.

Shelby had been wakened from her daylong nap by the sound of the gun firing, and was actually peeved that she had missed "all the excitement." Maggie had stifled the urge to slap her just in time, settling for dropping a piece of carpet fuzz she'd brushed off Ty's pants into Shelby's water glass.

Marty and Sybil had already left for a hotel in town, claiming that Paige and Vivian needed peace and quiet, which wasn't far from the truth, even if both of them were wearing the expression of wrongly accused inmates at a psychiatric hospital. Marty had promised to be in touch about services and Drew's will, but he'd done so calling back over his shoulder, since Sybil was leading the way out the front door and pulling Marty by the sleeve of his sport coat.

Lake had taken Paige upstairs, and Ethan had curled up on a sofa in the family room under a chenille throw, a cup of hot tea ignored on the coffee table beside him. He'd turned on the TV and had been watching a movie when everyone wandered away, and Maggie thought he was probably afraid to be alone, either with his thoughts or in the room he'd shared with Nell. At least the TV would provide human voices.

"Come on, fess up," Lucy said, coming back into the room with a handful of shampoo, gel, and makeup, which she dumped unceremoniously on the bed. "Seeing Tyler again was a good thing, wasn't it?"

Maggie sighed and sat up, hugging her knees to her chest. "No, I don't regret it," she said slowly. "Except for the part of me that does."

Lucy raised her eyebrows, a pair of electric blue panties stretched between her hands.

"It's complicated," Maggie said weakly.

"I'll say." But she didn't press it, and Maggie was thankful for that.

It was too complicated to explain to Lucy when she wasn't sure she understood how she felt herself. At least not entirely.

Seeing Tyler again had been wonderful. And frightening. And liberating, in a strange way. And inconvenient. And wonderful, again. But Maggie didn't know how to make those feelings fit into one course of action. She didn't want to say good-bye to him, and she couldn't wait to say good-bye to him. It didn't make sense, and she was too tired to work it out. She wanted to sleep for about ten years, right here on Lucy's paisley-patterned bedspread, and not think about anything more stressful than the most comfortable position.

Someone knocked lightly, and then the door opened. Connor poked his head into the room, grinning, and paused when he saw Maggie.

"Sorry, didn't mean to interrupt," he said, his dimple deepening when Lucy twirled another pair of panties around one finger before tossing it onto the bed.

"No, no, I was just leaving," Maggie said, swinging her legs over the side of the bed and feeling around on the carpet for her sandals. "I have packing to do myself."

As she closed the door behind her, she glanced over her shoulder to see Lucy walking into Connor's arms. A moment later, she heard Lucy's delighted squeal as he toppled her onto the bed.

That was nice, she thought. They were nice together. But she wasn't sure what "they" meant in this case. The beginning of a serious relationship? A fling? Friends with benefits? It wasn't her business, of course, although Lucy would spill all eventually, but she wondered why it was so easy for her friend to jump into something like that, head first, when she was still dipping a toe into the water every time she went for a swim, testing the depth and the temperature and the pH balance, for God's sake.

And all her usual habits were failing her. The crisis had passed, justice was about to be served, and she was free to go, which normally would have meant getting out a pad and a pen for a packing list, double-checking the bathroom and the closet and the bureau drawers for any stray items, checking her purse for money and whatever she'd need for traveling . . . God, it was all so boring and predictable and neurotic, she could scream.

But it wasn't the only reason she didn't want to pack, she thought as she wandered downstairs. She didn't know what to do, for maybe the first time in her life. She didn't even know what she *wanted* to do, which was a definite milestone. In the Keys five years ago, she'd wanted to run away from everything and stay with Tyler in that hotel room until they starved to death or finally found a sexual position they didn't like, so she'd immediately gone home.

Maybe she needed therapy.

In this case, she wanted to see her apartment, and pet her struggling little peace lily and curl up on her very own sofa, but she also wanted to forget all that and kick down the door to Ty's room and make love to him again. Several times.

And she wanted to walk on a beach with him without stumbling into a murder weapon, and she wanted to see what he'd done with the Moonstone, and she wanted to meet his father. Introducing him to her family, on the other hand, wasn't as high on the list of priorities. But she couldn't do any of that with her job and her life in New York to consider.

The thing was, she also wanted to finish her latest design projects and see if she would be promoted by the new year. The plans she had for the Goldsmiths' kitchen renovation alone were going to knock her boss on his ass, not to mention the Goldsmiths. And she had promised herself to join the book club Lauren in accounting had been talking about. But she couldn't do those things if she disappeared to the Keys with Ty.

Ty. Who was everything she wanted, and everything she didn't. Well, everything she wanted and everything she was scared of, anyway. He was the anti-her, Mr. Impulse. He'd organized his life so he never had to make a plan, so he could take off whenever he wanted and do whatever he wanted. Without worrying! Without constant back-and-forth arguing with himself.

And probably without a thought for anyone but himself. What would happen if tomorrow or next week he decided he didn't want to be with her anymore?

It didn't work. Nothing fit together the way it should to qualify as a plan. And for the first time, she was tempted to forget all of it, throw away her Filofax and her to-do lists, and ask Paige if she could move in here and just adore the antiques for a while.

She ran a finger over the Chippendale in the hallway and peeked into the empty ballroom as she passed by. But that was a bad idea, because the memory of Ty standing there Friday afternoon flashed through her head so graphically, she could have sworn he was standing there, as beautiful and desirable and infuriating as ever.

And then he turned around, just like he had that day that felt like months ago now, and her heart stuttered in her chest. Because he was standing there, and then he was crossing the room to meet her in the hall.

* * *

"Hey, stranger." Ty gave her his most neutral smile. There was going to be no begging. Not even any persuading. Nothing but the truth, as simple and as blunt as he could make it, and Maggie's reaction to it, good or bad. "I thought you'd snuck out in the back of a patrol car there for a while."

"I think Detective Vaughan is sick of the sight of me," she said, her cheeks flushed with color. "I was upstairs with Lucy."

"Heading to the kitchen?" he asked, carefully remembering not to touch her, even though the instinct to pull her against him as they walked was going off like an alarm in his head.

She tilted her head up to him, her eyes wary. "Yeah. I just wanted something to drink. And maybe to eat. Apparently watching a murderer confess to her crime gives me an appetite."

"Well, attacking the murderer made me kind of nauseous, so I think I'll just watch," he said lightly.

Ethan was still on the sofa, but when Ty checked, he was asleep, his mouth slightly open. His glasses had slid down his nose, and the fringe on the edge of the throw tucked beneath his chin fluttered with every exhaled breath. Reaching for the remote, Ty turned off the TV.

"I don't know whether to feel sorry for him or slap him," Maggie murmured as she took a bottle of spring water out of the fridge. Her hand was trembling a little bit. With nerves? With leftover adrenaline? He wished he could look inside her head for just one minute and make a map of everything she was feeling.

"Slap him why?" he said instead, pulling up a stool at the counter. She was foraging in the cabinet and came out with an ancient-looking bag of pretzels.

"Because he was so incredibly thick. I mean, an emotional moron from the word go. He had no idea how he was hurting his wife? He had no clue how much she loved him?" She shook her head as she opened the bag, wincing when the cellophane crackled. She lowered her voice, examining a broken piece of pretzel as she spoke. "I'll grant you that Nell is not the most effusive person on earth, today excepted, but he had to have some clue how she felt about him, didn't he?"

"Sometimes it's not that easy," he answered, studying the countertop instead of looking at her.

She paused in mid-chew, and he finally looked up to find her staring at him, the bottle of water in one hand and a second pretzel in the other. She didn't flinch when he looked her right in the eye, but she didn't say anything either. She was strangely frozen, her cheeks pale again, her hair hanging loose against them, brushing the gentle angles of her jaw.

Time to go for it, then, he thought, taking a deep breath. He wasn't exactly sure what he wanted, or even what he was asking her, but he was going to do it anyway.

"I made some calls when everyone was gone," he told her first, resting his elbows on the counter. "Returned some calls, actually. My managers had left messages this morning which I hadn't picked up yet, and then they left more when Fox News broke the story about the shooting. I have some business I need to take care of right now, so I'm leaving. Now, I mean. This afternoon."

She swallowed—he saw her slender throat flex in surprise, and her eyes mirrored the emotion, widening suddenly.

But when she opened her mouth, she sounded calm. What was the word? Unruffled. That was it. As if he'd just told her he was going upstairs to take a shower.

Maybe she'd just swallowed her pretzel wrong.

"Is everything okay?" she asked. She set down the water bottle and wiped her damp palm on a tea towel that was lying on the counter.

"Yeah, no emergency," he said, trying not to growl in frustration. "Just something that needs handling as soon as possible. I waited on it and . . . Well, I shouldn't have." *Way to be concise,* he thought. *Way to be blunt and honest.*

"How are you . . . ?" She stopped and bit her lip, and for a moment he thought he would hear something honest from her.

"I already called a cab, and I'm taking the train back to the city," he said when she didn't continue. And when she still didn't reply, he took the plunge. "I'll miss you, Maggie. I'd like to see you again. I'd like to see you tonight, in my hotel room. And then . . ."

Now it was his turn to stop. Was he really going to say the day after that? And then the next day? What *was* he asking her here?

"I . . . I told Lucy I'd drive back with her tomorrow," she said finally, but her voice was hardly more than a wisp of sound, and he thought he saw the faint gleam of tears in her eyes.

Well, that was something, he guessed. Not much. Not even definitely anything, come to think of it, unless she reached for a tissue and started sobbing, which would be horrible anyway. Christ, he didn't want to make her cry. He just wanted to make her say that she'd enjoyed being with him. That she might be with him again. That it wasn't over in the permanent, official sense.

And as he watched her biting her lip again, fiddling nervously with the water bottle on the counter, he realized the one thing he'd forgotten in all of this. He couldn't *make* her say anything. Well, maybe he could, but it would mean less than shit. It would mean nothing if it didn't come from her need to tell him.

So that was it, then. He was leaving, and she was staying, and apparently they weren't even going to discuss the future, whatever that might be, because she was coming around the counter. She kissed him, on the cheek of all things. Her hand rested on his arm for a moment longer than was necessary, but he heard her mumbled, "Good-bye, Ty."

And then she was gone. Again.

Chapter Twenty-three

"You are crazy," Lucy said the next day at noon, when they had said good-bye to Paige and Vivian and the others. Lake had promised to e-mail, and Connor was meeting Lucy in New York in a few days. Paige was going to call about Drew's service and wanted to keep in touch, which Maggie was happy about.

It was all very civilized and surprisingly enjoyable, after everything that had happened. Yesterday afternoon with Tyler, on the other hand, had been the first, but not the second.

Definitely not the second.

She hadn't even cried, which surprised her. Maybe she'd been too shocked, too overwhelmed. She'd taken a shower for what felt like three hours, first hot and then cool, washing her hair and shaving her legs and grooming everything she could think of, until she realized she was staying in the tub because she didn't know what to do when she got out. And then realizing she was as sleek and smooth and moisturized as if she'd prepared for a nude photo shoot, which was absurd. What was more absurd was that as lovely as her silky calves felt to her, Tyler wasn't around to enjoy them. That was when she'd curled up under the covers and slept until this morning.

Lucy glanced at her from the driver's seat as she waited for the gate to open, then grimaced at the crowd still gathered outside. The assorted mob chanted and shoved their signs up against the closed windows, but Lucy laid on the horn, and the majority of them backed off in a hurry. One reporter yelled something rude, but Lucy just turned up the radio. She had the air-conditioning blasting since the sun had come out this morning with a vengeance, making up for yesterday's rain, and it was already close to eighty outside.

"I'm sorry," Lucy said suddenly. "I take it back. You're not crazy, Mags. You're . . . just you. And if letting Ty go is what you want, then I'm behind you. A hundred percent. A hundred and fifty, in fact. Really. I mean it."

She looked so miserable and confused, Maggie had to smile. Actually, she looked miserable and confused and glowing with all the sparkly warmth of a new romance. Which was an interesting expression to pull off.

"Don't worry," Maggie told her as they headed for the highway. "I'm okay. I just want to close my eyes and relax and try to remember what my apartment looks like."

Lucy nodded, but she reached over to squeeze Maggie's hand briefly before slipping her Norah Jones CD into the stereo.

Maggie was in the mood for something heavy and pounding, with a lot of bass and mostly unintelligible lyrics, because music like that never made her want to cry, which this CD unfortunately did, but she didn't protest. She laid her head back on the seat and slipped her sunglasses on before closing her eyes, but she knew right away it wasn't going to work. She kept seeing Ty's face—damp and wicked in the tub that night, and in the moonlight on the terrace, grinning across the table at her in the restaurant, cooking her pasta in the huge kitchen, his brow furrowed in concentration. And the truth hit her with an alarming jolt. She wasn't just used to that face; she was in love with it.

There. She'd said it, right here on the Sunrise Highway. Or at least thought it, which was all that mattered for the moment. There was no use denying it. And yet she'd let Ty go thinking she didn't care, or didn't care enough. She'd let him go, period.

It was ridiculous and kind of troubling that the people she'd met this weekend had provided an example, but as Lucy hummed along to the music, Maggie realized that if Paige could risk her quiet routine and her financial safety to the PR machines of Hollywood for the man she loved, Maggie had no excuse for letting Ty go. Even Nell had been willing to sacrifice everything for Ethan, although Maggie certainly didn't approve of her methods.

Suddenly it didn't matter that she didn't have a plan. Or that the only plan she had was simply telling him how she felt. She had to do it. And the minute she decided, she felt that soaring, anchorless freedom again, the kind she felt with him, and she knew that no matter what happened, taking the leap was the important thing. If she needed a parachute, she'd find one.

"Take me to JFK," she said suddenly, sitting up, and startling Lucy, who hit the horn accidentally.

Her voice sounded funny in her ears—sharp and decisive and not one to argue with. It was the way she sounded at work, or when the waiter had brought her the wrong entrée. It was the voice she used when she knew exactly what she was doing.

At nine-thirty that night, a cab dropped Maggie off at the Moonstone, on the corner of Simonton and Caroline Streets. She handed the driver the last of her cash and waited while he hauled her luggage out of the trunk.

It was dark, but the air was sultry and salty, and the moon was bright. What Maggie remembered as a rundown covered porch at the entrance had been set back to allow for a U-shaped drive, sheltered by a graceful new arching roof.

"Thank you, ma'am," the driver said, tipping his fishing cap at her, and she nodded. This was it.

She could hardly believe she was here. She was jittery with nerves all of a sudden, although she'd slept off the adrenaline rush of her decision, and her jog through the airport, on the plane. She'd spent half of next month's rent on a last-minute ticket, and now she was standing here staring at the doors to the lobby like a fool.

Taking a deep breath, and wishing she wasn't one huge wrinkle, she went inside, breathing in the cool air-conditioning and the faint scents of lime and coconut.

"I'm . . . looking for the owner, Tyler Brody," she told the girl at the desk, whose smile was a glaring white flash of teeth in her tanned face.

"He's out of town, ma'am," the girl said mildly, but her interest had sharpened the moment Maggie said Ty's name. "He's not expected back until tomorrow night."

"Tomorrow . . . night?" It had never occurred to her that Ty's business might be somewhere other than here. Damn it. She was on thin ice at work already, and to wait another day . . .

But she had to. She was here, and she was going to wait even if it took till next week.

Of course, the girl behind the desk was waiting for her to say something coherent, so she managed a smile and said, "I don't, um, have a reservation, but if it's available, could I have room 14, please?"

"It is!" The girl grinned and reached under the desk, coming up with a card key. "How long will you be staying?"

"Until tomorrow. Night. No, wait, make that the next day." She was blushing furiously, but at least the girl behind the desk was polite enough to pretend not to notice while Maggie filled in the paperwork and handed over her abused credit card.

While she waited for the bellboy, she glanced around the lobby, which produced an immediate pang of envy. It was beautiful, old-world Key West with dark wood and vintage tropical prints, all rich greens and the sunset shades of gold and peach and raspberry. Palms and creamy yellow hibiscus flowers peeked out from between what looked like authentic mid-century rattan side tables.

She could have designed the lobby for him. She would have designed it very much like this, too, with maybe a bit more cream and a few lighter greens mixed in. But she hadn't, because the first time she'd met him, she ran away.

"This way, miss," the bellboy murmured, and she dragged her attention back to the present, following him although she knew exactly where her room was. Up the wide, curving stairs and down the hall, and then inside with the brand-new card key.

She handed the bellboy a dollar she found wedged into the bottom of her purse and hoped Ty had thought to install an ATM machine somewhere. As the door closed behind him, she closed her eyes, too, wanting to see the room as it had been once more, before she saw what Ty's decorator had done to it.

Lime green shag, that horrible striped bedspread . . . screw it, what she wanted was the memory of Ty in this room with her. No, what she wanted was Ty actually *in* this room with her, right now, and that wasn't going to happen. So she opened her eyes, sighing with pleasure when she took in the sunset yellow walls against more of that rich, dark mahogany and the simple, soft carpet on the floor. The room had a romantic British West Indies feel, and as she inspected the bedside table she was sure that the pieces were authentic instead of reproduction.

So Ty was successful. The lobby had proved that, actually, not that it was a big surprise, but to renovate the hotel like this, with the attention to detail and the list of amenities the bellboy had handed her, no wonder it was a hot spot in the Keys. A little glow of pride flickered inside her, and she caught herself grinning in the oval mirror over the bureau. She should have known. Ty would be a success if he decided to breed llamas. In Detroit.

Taking another deep breath, she collapsed on the bed, and then seconds later she was up again, unpacking, stripping off her wrinkled, sweaty clothes and pulling her favorite sleep T-shirt over her head. She would sleep, and she would wait for him, and everything would be fine. She hoped.

But the minute she turned the light out, her mind started racing. Turning on the light again, she pulled a notepad and a pen from her purse and sat cross-legged on the bed, thinking and scribbling notes. And smiling.

At least with room service, she could charge a meal to her bill, she mused the next morning as she surveyed the mess she'd made of her breakfast. The remains of orange juice, coffee, an omelet, toast, and strawberries littered the tray. Maybe spontaneity made her hungry. It certainly hadn't prepared her to have change for the soda machine in the service room down the hall.

She looked out the window, squinting into the hazy sunshine beyond the palm tree out in the courtyard. She could take a walk and explore some of the shops—not that her credit card needed to see the light of day anytime soon—especially if Ty wasn't going to be around until this evening.

She swallowed back a lump of panic when she realized she was assuming he'd want to see her when he arrived. That he'd walk in, she'd sweep him off his feet, and all would be well, when the truth was he might have given up on her. He might be too angry to care, too pissed off to listen. It might be a disaster of enormous proportions.

Stop it. It was only noon, and if she kept this up, she'd be a complete wreck by the time he did arrive. She needed to get out, get some fresh air, clear her head. And possibly have some kind of tropical drink to calm herself down. It couldn't hurt.

She picked up her bag and slid her feet into her sandals, then opened the door—only to find Tyler on the other side of it, hand poised to knock.

And he didn't look mad at all.

Her heart swelled dangerously, and suddenly she felt like one huge jangling nerve. If he didn't hug her soon, she was going to start jumping up and down just to work off the excess nervous energy.

"Hi," he said, that familiar naughty-boy grin on his face. "Going out?"

"Not anymore."

"Good." He nudged her backward and shut the door behind him, somehow pulling her into his arms all at the same time. "I can't believe you're here."

"I can't believe *you're* here," she murmured against his shoulder. She felt as if she hadn't seen him in years, and his hard, solid body against her was a relief. An intoxicating, tempting one, but a relief nonetheless. "They said you weren't expected until tonight, even though I never thought you'd be anywhere *but* here, which was probably stupid, but . . . where *were* you?"

He pushed her away just far enough to look into her eyes, and she melted a little bit at the sight of his, dark blue and warm and looking at her as if he'd never seen anything he liked more. "In New York. Waiting for you."

"You weren't." She laughed, the absurdity of it hitting her.

"I was. I did have a meeting, because I've been thinking about buying a hotel there, too—that was the business I had to handle when I left—but then I decided to wait around, see if I could convince you to talk a little bit about . . . us."

"Really?" She couldn't help it—all the tears she hadn't shed yesterday welled up, threatening to spill out in a happy, messy stream. "And here I was waiting for you. But how did you find . . . I don't know, my apartment? My phone number?"

"I picked up a few sneaky habits over the weekend," he said with a grin, steering her toward the bed and sitting her down. "I looked in your wallet. But I also made Lucy give me her cell number in case of emergency, which was a very good thing. She told me you'd flown down yesterday afternoon, and I took the first flight I could get this morning."

"I had to come," she said, letting him lay her back on the bed and putting her arms around him when he leaned over her. "I had to tell you . . . I was so stupid. I . . . I never should have let you leave like that, and I should have told you . . . I mean, I should have realized what you mean to me days ago."

"I know what you mean to me," he said softly, dropping gentle kisses on her cheeks and nose between words. "I don't think I was ready to believe it, either, but I love you, Maggie Harding. And I want to spend every day with you. Every day that you'll give me. I've been living so long with the idea that I shouldn't tie myself down, that I should take advantage of every possibility that's offered, I never realized the thing I was missing was loving someone, every day, through good and bad, forever. You, to be precise. If you'll let me."

She swallowed hard, afraid that the tears would spill over if she spoke, and nodded her head instead, pulling him close. Finally she managed, "I love you, too, Ty. So much. I've never felt the way you make me feel. Like I can do anything."

"Maybe you could start with taking that shirt off," he teased, and she laughed.

"You first," she said, wriggling to one side to give him room on the bed. "God, I was so worried you'd be fed up with me, that I was too late."

"I was ready to be when I left," he said honestly, tugging his shirt over his head. "But it didn't last. I sat through that meeting thinking of your face, and of all the things I wished I'd said, and I just couldn't walk away."

"I'm so glad," she breathed when her own shirt was disposed of, and Ty was unhooking her bra expertly. Then his hands were on her, hot and hard and so perfect, she groaned.

"So you did miss me," he murmured, laying her back on the bed again and tugging off her shorts and panties.

"Oh, yeah," she managed when he'd fastened his mouth

on her breast, his tongue hot and wet. This wasn't going to last long. She wanted him inside her now.

But suddenly he was sitting up, frowning. "There's more to this than just missing each other, you know," he said. "The truth is, my life is mostly here, even if I buy the place in Manhattan. And your life is there."

"It doesn't have to be," she said, angling up on one elbow and reaching out to trace the silvered scar on his chest. "There are things I could do, things you could do, if we work it out together."

"Like maybe opening your own studio?" he said cautiously, fixing her with a serious look.

"Maybe."

"It would be a risk, you know. Everything is. Even this." He swept one arm wide, taking in the bed and the two of them on it. "Even us."

"I know," she said with a smile, reaching up to pull him down to her again. "But don't worry. I have a plan."

Please turn the page for a sneak peek at
Lori Foster's enchanting new fantasy
STAR QUALITY,
available now from Brava . . .

Stan's gaze lifted and locked with hers. Sensation crackled between them. His awareness of Jenna as a sexual woman ratcheted up another notch. Even without hearing her thoughts, what she wanted from him, with him, was obvious to any red-blooded male. Heat blazed in her eyes and flushed her cheeks. A pulse fluttered in her pale throat. Her lips parted . . .

Amazing. A mom of two, a quiet bookworm, a woman who remained circumspect in every aspect of her life—and she lusted after him with wonton creativity.

Not since the skill had first come to him when he was a kid of twelve, twenty-eight years ago, had Stan so appreciated the strange effect a blue moon had on him. It started with the waxing gibbous, then expanded and increased as the moon became full, and began to abate with the waning gibbous. But at midnight, when the moon was most full, the ability was so clean, so acute, that it used to scare him.

His parents didn't know. The one time he'd tried to tell them they'd freaked out, thinking he was mental or miserable or having some kind of psychosis. He'd retrenched and never mentioned it to them again.

When he was twenty and away at college, he signed up for a course on parapsychology. One classmate who specialized in the effects of the moon gave him an explanation that made sense. At least in part.

According to his friend, wavelengths of light came from a full moon and that affected his inner pathogens. With further studies, Stan had learned that different colors of lights caused varying emotional reaction in people. It made sense that the light of a full moon, twice in the same month, could cause effects.

In him, it heightened his sixth sense to the level that he could hear other people's tedious inner musings.

Now, he could hear, *feel*, Jenna's most private yearnings, and for once he appreciated his gift. Nothing tedious in being wanted sexually. Especially when the level of want bordered on desperate.

She needed a good lay. She needed him.

He wanted to oblige her. Damn, did he want to oblige her.

Casually, Stan moved closer to her until he invaded her space and her alarm thumped louder with every beat of her heart. He left himself wide open to her, relishing each tingle she felt, absorbing each small shiver of excitement—and letting it excite him in return. He no longer cared that he had a near-lethal erection.

Reaching out, he brushed the side of his thumb along her jawline, up and over her downy cheek, tickling the dangling earrings that suddenly seemed damn sexy. "Maybe you need the iced tea," he murmured, his attention dipping to her naked mouth. Jenna never wore lipstick, and he liked the look of her soft full lips, glistening from the glide of her tongue. Oh yeah, he liked that a lot. "You feel . . . warm, Jenna."

Her breaths came fast and uneven. "I've been . . . working."

And fantasizing. About him.

Lazily, Stan continued to touch her. "Me, too. Out in the sun all day. It's so damn humid, I know I'm sweaty." His thumb stroked lower, near the corner of her mouth. "But I didn't have time to change."

Her eyelids got heavy, drooping over her green eyes. Shakily, she lifted a hand and closed it over his wrist—but she didn't push him away. "You look . . . fine." *Downright edible.* She cleared her throat. "No reason to change."

Stan's slow smile alarmed her further. "You don't mind my jeans and clumpy boots?" He used both hands now to cup her face, relishing the velvet texture of her skin. "They're such a contrast to you, all soft and pretty and fresh."

Her eyes widened, dark with confusion and curbed excitement, searching his. He leaned forward, wanting her mouth, needing to know her taste—

The bell over the door chimed.

Jenna jerked away so quickly, she left Stan holding air. Face hot, she ducked to the back of the store and into the storage room, closing the door softly behind her.

Well, hell. He'd probably rushed things, Stan realized.

Hot nights and hotter romance . . .
Here's a first look at
TAKE MY BREATH AWAY
by Tina Donahue,
available now . . .

Beyond the expanse of lush lawn, where tables and chairs had been set up, Thaddeus's Spanish-style villa hugged the hill above the sea. The sprawling compound was crowned with a red-tiled roof. Clusters of scarlet, purple, and yellow bougainvillea clung to the dwelling's startling white walls and fluttered in the persistent breeze to scent the balmy air. Coconut palms and ferns were in abundance though more widely spaced than the thick foliage of the rain forest that lay behind. There, monkeys and other wildlife played and watched. Here, the sounds of the ocean were muted as it licked a beach that looked like powdered sugar beneath the lowering sun.

Okay, Cole thought, *so this* is *nice . . . but still dangerous, given the old guy's niece.* Sort of like a Club Med Hell since there was no escape until his pilot returned tomorrow morning—unless, of course, Cole opted to swim to the next island.

His gaze drifted in that direction. From this vantage point, that island looked like a speck of dirt in an endless sea.

He looked away. Coming here hadn't been such a good idea after all, but Cole reminded himself that he had been in far worse situations. Not the Marines, mind you, but dealing with the suits and creative types in Hollywood. That was enough to give nightmares to a soldier of fortune. So, this couldn't be that bad. He'd meet Ariel, whom he was going to dearly love before this was all over, be polite, listen to what she had to say, then cut out as quickly as he—

Cole's thoughts paused when he heard the unmistakable *whap-whap-whap* of a helicopter in the distance. As he lifted his head and looked in the direction of that noise, Cole wondered if his pilot were returning. Had the guy forgotten something? Would it be possible to actually escape this place before—

"Ah," Thaddeus said, his voice serene and filled with love as it cut into Cole's thoughts, "that must be my dear niece— Ariel."

"Yes, sir," Cole said, steeling himself for the worst as the helicopter finally came into view from behind a cluster of thickly crowned palms, then headed straight for them.

The aircraft, at least, was sexy as hell. A sleek, black Bell 407 that effortlessly cut through the air and brought to mind strains of ominous music—something classical and Wagnerian— with lots of low tones and clashing cymbals. The kind of refrain that might have opened an old Schwarzenegger or Bruce Willis action flick. Music that Cole figured he'd use, along with this scene of a helicopter coming closer, closer, closer as it opened his political–military thriller and gave a hint of what was to come once the insurgents—or in this case, Ariel— landed.

"She's quite good at that, isn't she?" Thaddeus shouted above the noise.

Cole looked at the old guy. Thaddeus was holding onto his panama hat, while his weathered face was raised to that copter as it reached the helipad to the left of this area.

"Good at what?" Cole shouted.

"Why, flying that helicopter, of course!"

She pilots helicopters? Cole thought, then glanced to the side and saw the silhouette of only one body in that bird. *Well, what do you know.* Not only was Ariel piloting the thing, she was landing it pretty damned well, too.

Glancing up from that flawless descent, Cole tried to see details of her, but was out of luck—or maybe in luck. Who knew? The next few minutes were pure torture as the blades of the copter slowly *whap-whap-whapped* to a stop. During this, Ariel leaned down until she was completely out of sight as she fiddled with something inside the cabin.

"Patience," Thaddeus said.

Cole pretended not to hear.

"She'll join us in good time," Thaddeus added.

That's what Cole was afraid of as the door to the copter finally popped open and Ariel stepped outside.

She was immediately surrounded by Thaddeus's housekeeping staff, who had run across the lawn to the helipad. As Ariel came around the copter door and bent at the waist to lower something to the ground, she was again obstructed from view.

Cole wondered if that were a good omen . . . or maybe a bad omen of things to—

His thoughts suddenly stopped as the staff moved aside just as Ariel straightened.

Thaddeus called out, "Please be certain you get those books she's brought to me!"

The staff chorused, "Yes, sir!"

Thaddeus leaned toward Cole. "Ariel's found a simply delightful bookstore that deals in rare volumes."

Cole nodded absently to that.

Thaddeus shouted more directives to his staff, the gist of which escaped Cole. Lowering the bottle of beer from his lips, he pushed up in his chair as his gaze simply prowled over Ariel Leigh.

Patience, Thaddeus had said.

Not a chance, Cole thought. He couldn't explore every part of her quickly enough. She was a tall woman, probably five-ten, with a sleek and well-toned body that was a delicious caramel color from days spent outdoors. As she moved fully into the sun, it intensified the color of her hair. That reddish-gold mane was worn in a thick braid, while delicate tendrils danced over her tawny cheeks with the constant breeze.

Warmth continued to flood through Cole, settling in his groin. *That's Ariel?* Not only was she nothing like what he had feared, she was exquisitely female—the real deal, not the Hollywood version of what femininity should be. From this distance it appeared she wore little, if any, makeup.

She didn't need it. Her charm was natural, her beauty unique and more stunning than anything Cole had seen in Los Angeles where plastic surgery and excess were the norm. Even Ariel's clothing was simple, yet elegant—a white, sleeveless cotton top, white shorts that revealed an amazing expanse of her sleek legs, and white moccasins on her feet.

Cole's body continued to respond as he imagined licking her long, slender toes before he worked his way up those taut calves and creamy thighs to those delicate curls between her legs. Were they auburn, too?

A man could hope. A man should really know.

Of course, to do that, he would definitely have to stay longer than just tonight, possibly several days, which wasn't out of the question if he played dumb about this survival stuff, pretending he knew absolutely nothing about it. That would get her to show him everything she knew for as long as was needed. That would give them time to get to know each other.

Here's a first look at Linda Lael Miller's hilarious
"Batteries Not Required"
from BEACH BLANKET BAD BOYS
coming in June 2005 from Brava!

The last thing I wanted was a man to complicate my life. I came to that conclusion on the commuter flight between Phoenix and Helena, Montana, because my best friend, Lucy, and I had been discussing the topic, online and via our Blackberrys, for days. Maybe the fact that I was bound to encounter Tristan McCullough during my brief sojourn in my home town of Parable had something to do with the decision.

Tristan and I had a history, one of those angst-filled summer romances between high school graduation and college. Sure, it had been over for ten years, but I still felt bruised whenever I thought of him, which was more often than I should have, even with all that time to insulate me from the experience.

My few romantic encounters in between had done nothing to dissuade me from my original opinion.

Resolved: Men lie. They cheat—usually with your roommate, your best friend, or somebody you're going to have to face at the office every day. They forget birthdays, dump you the day of the big date, and leave the toilet seat up.

Who needed it? I had B.O.B., after all. My battery-operated boyfriend.

Just as I was thinking those thoughts, my purse tumbled out of the overhead compartment and hit me on the head. I should have realized that the universe was putting me on notice. Cosmic e-mail. Subject: *Pay attention, Gayle.*

Hastily, avoiding the flight attendant's tolerant glance, which I knew would be disapproving because I'd asked for extra peanuts during the flight and gotten up to use the rest room when the seatbelt sign was on, I shoved the bag under the seat in front of mine. Then I gripped the arms of 4B as the aircraft gave an apocalyptic shudder and nose-dived for the landing strip.

I squeezed my eyes shut.

The plane bumped to the ground, and I would have sworn before a hostile jury that the thing was about to flip from wing-tip to wing-tip before crumpling into a fiery ball.

My stomach surged into my throat, and I pictured smoldering wreckage on the six o'clock news in Phoenix, even heard the voice-over. *"Recently fired paralegal Gayle Hayes, perished today in a plane crash outside the small Montana town of Parable. She was twenty-seven, a hard-won size 6 with $200 worth of highlights in her shoulder-length brown hair, and was accompanied by her long-standing boyfriend, Bob—"*

As if my untimely and tragic death would rate a soundbite. And *as if* I'd brought Bob along on this trip. All I would have needed to complete my humiliation, on top of losing my job and having to make an appearance in Parable, was for some security guard to search my suitcase and wave my vibrator in the air.

But, hey, when you think you're about to die, you need *somebody,* even if he's made of pink plastic and runs on four "C" batteries.

When it became apparent that the Grim Reaper was otherwise occupied, I lifted my lids and took a look around. The flight attendant, who was old enough to have served cocktails on Wright Brothers Air, smiled thinly. Like I said, we hadn't exactly bonded.

Despite my aversion to flying, I sat there wondering if they'd let me go home if I simply refused to get off the plane.

The cabin door whooshed open, and my fellow passengers—half a dozen in all—rose from their seats, gathered their belongings, and clogged the aisle at the front of the airplane. I'd scrutinized them, surreptitiously of course, during the flight, in case I recognized somebody, but none of them were familiar, which was a relief.

Before the Tristan fiasco, I'd been ordinary, studious Gayle Hayes, daughter of Josie Hayes, manager and part owner of the Bucking Bronco Tavern. *After* our dramatic breakup, Tristan was still the golden boy, the insider, but I was Typhoid Mary. He'd grown up in Parable, as had his father and grandfather. His family had land and money, and in ranch country, or anywhere else, that adds up to credibility. I, on the other hand, had blown into town with my recently divorced mother, when I was thirteen, and remained an unknown quantity. I didn't miss the latest stepfather—he was one in a long line—and I loved Mom deeply.

I just didn't want to be like her, that was all. I wanted to go to college, marry one man, and raise a flock of kids. It might not be politically correct to admit it, but I wasn't really interested in a career.

When the Tristan-and-me thing bit the dust, I pulled my savings out of the bank and caught the first bus out of town.

Mom had long since moved on from Parable, but she still had a financial interest in the Bronco, and the other partners wanted to sell. I'm a paralegal, not a lawyer, but my mother saw that as a technicality. She'd hooked up with a new boyfriend—not the kind that requires batteries—and as of that moment, she was somewhere in New Mexico, on the back of a Harley. A week ago, on the same day I was notified that I'd been downsized, she called me from a borrowed cell phone and talked me into representing her at the negotiations.

In a weak moment, I'd agreed. She overnighted me an airline ticket and her power-of-attorney, and wired travel expenses into my checking account, and here I was—back in Parable, Montana, the place I'd sworn I would never think about, let alone visit, again.

"Miss?" The flight attendant's voice jolted me back to the present. From the expression on her face, I would be carried off bodily if I didn't disembark on my own. I unsnapped my seatbelt, hauled my purse out from under 3B, and deplaned with as much dignity as I could summon.

I had forgotten why they call Montana the Big Sky Country. It's like being under a vast, inverted bowl of the purest blue, stretching from horizon to horizon.

The airport at Helena was small, and the land around the city is relatively flat, but the trees and mountains were visible in the distance, and I felt a little quiver of nostalgia as I took it all in. Living in Phoenix for the decade since I'd fled, working my way through vocational school and making a life for myself, I'd had plenty of occasion to miss the terrain, but I hadn't consciously allowed myself the indulgence.

I made my way carefully down the steps to the tarmac, and crossed to the entrance, trailing well behind the other passengers. Mom had arranged for a rental car, so all I had to do was pick up my suitcase at the baggage claim, sign the appropriate papers at Avis, and boogie for Parable.

I stopped at a McDonald's on the way through town, since I hadn't had breakfast and twenty-six peanuts don't count as nourishment. Frankly, I would have preferred a stiff drink, but you can't get arrested for driving under the influence of French fries and a Big Mac.

I switched on the radio, in a futile effort to keep memories of Tristan at bay, and the first thing I heard was *our song*.

I switched it off again.

My cell phone rang, inside my purse, and I fumbled for it. It was Lucy.

"Where are you?" she demanded.

I pushed the speaker button on the phone, so I could finish

my fries and still keep one hand on the wheel. "In the trunk of a car," I answered. "I've been kidnapped by the mob. Think I should kick out one of the tail lights and wave my hand through the hole?"

Lucy hesitated. "Smart-ass," she said. "Where are you really?"

I sighed. Lucy is my best friend, and I love her, but she's the mistress of rhetorical questions. We met at school in Phoenix, but now she's a clerk in an actuary's office, in Santa Barbara. I guess they pay her to second guess everything. "On my way to Parable. You know, that place we've been talking about via Blackberry?"

"Oh," said Lucy.

I folded another fry into my mouth, gum-stick style. "Do you have some reason for calling?" I prompted. I didn't mean to sound impatient, but I probably did. My brain kept racing ahead to Parable, wondering how long it would take to get my business done and leave.

Lucy perked right up. "Yes," she said. "The law firm across the hall from our offices is hiring paralegals. You can get an application online."

I softened. It wasn't Lucy's fault, after all, that I had to go back to Parable and maybe come face to face with Tristan. I was jobless, and she was trying to help. "Thanks, Luce," I said. "I'll look into it when I have access to a computer. Right now, I'm in a rental car."

"I'll forward the application," she replied.

"Thanks," I repeated. The familiar road was winding higher and higher into the timber country. I rolled the window partway down, to take in the green smell of pine and fir trees.

"I wish I could be there to lend moral support," Lucy said.

"Me, too," I sighed. She didn't know about the Tristan debacle. Yes, she was my closest friend, but the subject was too painful to broach, even with her. Only my mother knew, and she probably thought I was over it.

Lucy's voice brightened. "Maybe you'll meet a cowboy."

I felt the word "cowboy" like a punch to the solar plexus. Tristan was a cowboy. And he'd gotten on his metaphorical horse and trampled my heart to a pulp. "Maybe," I said, to throw her a bone.

"Boss alert," Lucy whispered, apparently picking up an authority figure on the radar. "I'd better get back to my charts."

"Good idea," I said, relieved, and disconnected. I tossed the phone back into my purse.

I passed a couple of ranches, and a gas station with bears and fish and horses on display in the parking lot, the kind carved out of a tree stump with a chain saw. Yep, I was getting close to Parable.

I braced myself. Two more bends in the road.

On the first bend, I braked within two feet of a loaded cattle truck, jackknifed in the middle of the highway. I had already suspected that fate wasn't on my side. I knew it for a fact when Tristan McCullough stormed around one end of the semitrailer, ready for a fight.

My heart surged up into my sinuses and got stuck there.

The decade since I'd seen him last had hardened his frame and chiseled his features, at least his mouth and lower jaw. I couldn't see the upper part of his face because of the shadow cast by the brim of his beat-up cowboy hat.

What does Tristan look like? Take Brad Pitt and multiply by a factor of ten, and you've got a rough idea.